ISBN 978-0-483-79102-2
PIBN 10203973

This book is a reproduction of an important historical work. Forgotten Books uses
state-of-the-art technology to digitally reconstruct the work, preserving the original format
whilst repairing imperfections present in the aged copy. In rare cases, an imperfection in
the original, such as a blemish or missing page, may be replicated in our edition. We do,
however, repair the vast majority of imperfections successfully; any imperfections that
remain are intentionally left to preserve the state of such historical works.

STEPS UPWARD.

BY

MRS. FRANCES DANA GAGE.

AUTHOR OF "ELSIE MAGOON," "GERTIE'S SACRIFICE," ETC.

PHILADELPHIA:

J. B. LIPPINCOTT & CO.

1871.

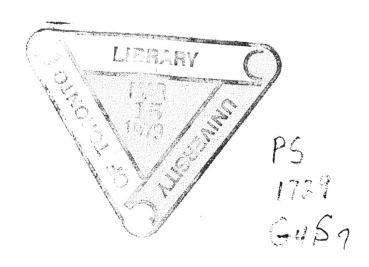

PS
1739
G4S7

CONTENTS.

CONTENTS.

PREFACE.

STEPS UPWARD was originally written for and published in the columns of the TEMPERANCE PATRIOT. As its publication progressed, its increasing interest created a demand for the paper so unexpected, and unprepared for, that many could not be supplied. Believing that this story, the last and best effort of its talented authoress, might be made the means of accomplishing great good in the cause of Temperance, strengthening the weak, encouraging the faltering, and exalting the lowly, and urgently counseled thereto by many friends of the cause, the Publisher has consented to send it forth in this form on its errand of mercy and love. No one who marks the steady and determined perseverance of the heroine, and sees her taking those little but sure Steps Upward, undismayed by trials and obstacles that would have discouraged many another, until she attains the goal for which she set out, can fail to be cheered and encouraged in their labors, and nerved to new efforts, and sacrifices if need be, for the uplifting of their fellow men. That the weak, the struggling, the doubting, in this great battle with appetite and temptation, may be encouraged and strengthened by the perusal of this book, to continually take new Steps Upward, is the one sincere wish of the Publisher.

STEPS UPWARD.

CHAPTER I.

PREFATORY.

READER, whoever you may be, a word with you. Don't begin this story of mine with any anticipations of intense interest; of being so overwhelmed with its details that you will weep or laugh very often; nor expect to be shocked into nervous tremors over horrible tragedies or unheard-of coincidences. I pledge myself neither to disturb your sleep, nor so to tax your sensibilities that you need forget life's nearest duties, in your deep pity over the beings that no longer require your care or tears. I shall have no startling *denouement;* only a straightforward story of common lives; lives full of pleasant and painful duties, of successes and failures, lives made more difficult, mayhap, because you and I, or our ancestors, have not these many years past been doing all our duty. Lives that with half the labor and pain might have been serene and beautiful if society dealt fairly and justly with her members, and judged each one according to his or her own worth. If there be ought in such a tale to interest a passing hour, then read on, and glean, if possible, wisdom, hope or courage from the examples I have given.

Diana Dinmont, who is to be our heroine, was the daughter of Heckel Dinmont, a poor day-laborer, whose ancestors came a long time ago from over the big waters, and claimed their descent from the fearless Huguenots of the sixteenth century. Those ancestors had come to America with a hope of religious freedom, and the leaders of the clan were doubtless men of great courage and breadth of thought. But there were among them, probably, those of a lower grade, "the hewers of wood and the drawers of water" for their more noble and enterprising brethren. Be this as it may, the retrogression had been swift and sure; and though Heckel Dinmont regularly boasted of the staunch "Huguenot blood" that ran in his veins, no one could have suspected so wonderful an ingredient in his nature from anything in his life or character.

Heck, as he was called, was honest and generous; one who always worked well for his neighbors. Two centuries and a half of transition from the old world of France to the new world west of the Alleghanies, had not rubbed out from soul and brain this much of the faith of his fathers. But beyond these, alas for the record! Heck worked well for his neighbors, but had no power to put his force and energy into active operation for himself or his family. Like a huge piece of machinery, he needed something outside of himself to fire up and set the wheel in motion. This was, perhaps, hereditary subservience, or the last remnant of the vassalage condition of the olden time.

He was a finely.formed, athletic man, full of fun and good humor, and overflowing always (outside of his own cabin) with love for his fellow men. Call on him for a day's work, and tell him there was need, and no one worked with more will and speed. Send him word that your wife was out of wood, and he would astonish you with his alacrity and strength. But when your wood-pile was in order, his own wife's bread might sour by the week, or she might go searching among the fence corners to find bits of bark or broken fragments to cook it with, till her back broke! Just get up a raising, build a bridge, launch a boat, prepare a platform for a Fourth of July oration, build tents for a camp-meeting, or send out to post bills for a political meeting, and not in fifty miles around was there a more honest, determined and reliable worker than Heck.

He made gardens in the Spring, helped harvest in Summer, and butcher in Autumn, husked corn in Winter, and did odd jobs at all times. He ate good meals three times a day, found plenty of listeners to his long, queer stories, and enjoyed himself hugely so long as he could do it in other people's houses.

Of course, he seldom had a realizing sense of the misery of his own domicil, to which he rarely brought any part of his earnings, better than a few pounds of fat pork, a bag of corn, or a jug of whisky. The balance was spent at the Smithy at Oxbow, where men of his class congregated nightly to smoke and drink in the little bar-room, and Heck paid his full share of the bills.

His house, if the tumble-down building could be called by such a dignified name, was full of poor man's blessings, of whom Diana was the eldest. His wife, Mary, who might have been a lineal descendant of " Good Old Queen Bess," so bright was her hair and so blue were her eyes, had become somewhat of a scold; either because she did not know any better, or because it was the only way in which she could move things, Heck, in particular, out of the way. He would sit in the chimney corner and smoke his pipe for a week at a time if no one wanted him in the neighborhood, and the weather was too bad to fish or hunt.

Mrs. Dinmont had no knowledge of her parentage. Her first recollections were of being a bound girl, in a hard, unloving household. They told her she had been taken from the poorhouse, and exacted of the frail, beautiful, blue-eyed, golden-haired child, tasks that well nigh wore out her life ere she reached her maidenhood. Out of this kitchen, from pure love and pity, Heck, when a young man, had taken her, promising to love, cherish and protect this orphaned waif of oppression " till death should them part." Mary Dinmont was a good wife. She knew how to work, and worked hard and steadily; and had Heckel Dinmont performed his part of life's labor as earnestly and industriously for the good of his own household as did his wife, the world would have gone well with him.

I have said she worked hard. How could she avoid it? The mother of eight children, ere the eldest was twelve, three of whom sickened and passed away after years of care. She had loved Dinmont with a deep, abiding love and faith when she married him. He was all she had to love, and her longing, trusting, craving nature, bore with his shiftless, careless ways, in deep and terrible suffering of body and mind, before she grew into that much abused and long tried creature, a scold.

Would not you scold, fair reader, if your husband helped raise for others nice houses, while your own was falling over your head? if he mended other roofs while the rain flooded your floor in torrents? if he put 'up other garden fences and left yours to seduce every cow or pig to make free with the cabbage patch and potato hills which you had cultivated while he slept off the effects of a half drunken carousal?

Some are born scolds. Not so our humble housewife of Rocky Glen. Never was there a more joyful, hopeful nature, never a more loving and willing heart, never a more free, gushing soul. The dawning of day, the glory of the rising sun, the wild chorus of birds in the forest around her, filled and thrilled her with an ecstasy of delight, that made her for a moment forget all the sadness of her life, and clasp her hands in mute worship of the beautiful.

Circumstances, cold, bare facts, long since buried beneath the fragments of other cold, bare facts, as one layer of autumn leaves buries another, had buried her early life history in darkness, leaving not one trace visible of father or mother, kith or kin, and had cast a cloud over her life. The foundling hospital of New York, had received her from a policeman on a cold winter morning. He had found her rolled in a blanket and laid upon his beat. All beyond was mystery. A lady had chosen her for her beauty, and taken her west. This lady died and she was again a waif upon the troubled waters. The husband became a drunkard and the child was bound to a family that wished a nurse, a drudge for their growing children.

The farmer, so he called himself, owned an unproductive and badly managed bit of land in a sparsely settled region, remote from schools and churches. Thriftless, and addicted to those habits that make such homes a frightful caricature of what home should be, he thought little and cared less for the orphaned child.

His wife, feeble, petulant under her privations, knowing that there was wrong somewhere, and that somebody ought to be punished for it, vented her

spleen and ill temper on the one that never dared
retaliate either by word or act; and by blows, oft
repeated, and violence terrible to a child's sensitive
nature, made the little life entrusted to her charge
as blank and sterile as the life of a slave. She never
did a chore of work that Mary could do; and thus
from the call at day dawn, " Get up, Mary, hurry,
build the fire, put on the kettle, bring in the water,
wash the potatoes, set the table, hurry, you lazy
huzzy, you don't earn your salt," until the sun sank
to his rest, the busy, active, willing little feet pattered
to and fro, dodging the hands that would have boxed
her ears, or skipping out of the way of the tongs, or
poker, or pot hook, if thrown at her, not always
escaping, but always bearing the pain and indignation as best she could, in patient silence.

. The nearer to the brute the human nature can be
brought, the more submissive and forgetful it can be
made. The dog that shows evidence of reasoning
and affection that almost make us feel that he is half
human, will bear the harshest treatment, the heaviest
blows and curses, and yet lick the hand that inflicts
the first, and gambol joyfully if but a kind word
falls from the lips that uttered the last. May not
the human be brought down and the brute elevated
until they almost stand on a level?

Mary knew nothing better than her present lot,
and thought not of rebellion. She was glad of
enough to eat; joyful if she could get the baby to
herself under the shade of the big oak on the bank

of the stream near by; delighted if while hunting the cow she could find violets in the spring, lilies in summer, and golden rod in autumn; grieved and angry when Mrs. Bent snatched them from her loving hands and threw them into the kitchen fire to wither and burn, because she had stayed too long or was looking too bright and happy.

We will not tarry by the way with this child of nature, deformed by ignorance, selfishness and tyranny. This one family was all she knew. This one low type was all she had to follow. Her clothing could only be called rags; her beautiful hair scarce knew a comb, and hung in tangled masses around her head until in its exuberance of growth it became too long, and then it was docked off in the most unsightly locks. She had nothing, really, to love but the house dog, the cow and the baby; but with even these she could not be wholly depraved and lost. This little love kept her womanly.

No wonder, then, that Heckel Dinmont, a boy of eighteen, tall and symmetrical, with jet black eyes and hair, rosy lips and cheeks, health and strength, a jolly spirit and a kindly heart, should have claimed, at once, the outgushing love of this guileless child of oppression, or that this love should have opened to her soul new revelations of herself. Heck worked for " Old Bent " a year. Meantime this love went on artlessly and purely. Heck, who had traveled all the way from Maine since he was fifteen, with no incumbrance but his stick and his little bundle tied in a red cotton handkerchief, stopping by the way to help folks, and earn a penny to take him a little farther, had never stayed a month in one spot until he found Mary. He loved her and stayed near her. Of course, in his long journey he had learned many things. One was that Mary needed to have her hair combed out and smoothed on her pretty head. This he kindly did for her one Sunday morning when the old folks had gone miles away to a meeting, leaving the young ones to care for the baby and "see to things." The older children ran off to the woods to hunt nuts, and the young lovers had a long happy time. The golden hair was straightened out and made to curl beautifully around Heck's long forefinger, while he told her, as well as he knew how, how sweet she was, and that if she would be his wife he would go to town next week and get a license, and Squire Hide would marry them, and they would leave old Bent and the cruel, scolding old woman, and go to seek their fortunes. She should be his wife, and he would work all for her, and she should have a new calico gown and a pretty handkerchief, and be mistress in a house all by herself. Mary, who thought Heck the wisest and best of all possible beings, could only lay her brown, sunburnt cheek against his and give her entire consent to any thing if he would not go and leave her behind. The smoothed hair, the clear, bright face, mantled with happy smiles, the bird-like song of the girl, and her cheerful step told to her oppressors, on their return, a tale that neither was slow to comprehend.

"Jist what I reckoned on," said my lady after Mary had gone to milk and Heck was out feeding. "They've been and fell in love with each other; he's goin' next week and then it'll be no good I'll get out o' her."

"Wall, I reckoned on it tu. It's on'y natur; we'd as good let 'em go. Tom is big enough to help some, and Jerusha orter to be sot agoin'. She's twelve now, nigh about."

"Jonas Bent, I don't think there was ever sich another old fool as you born."

"Wall, mebbe not, but I guess it come mighty nigh ontu it when you turned up; but what hev I done neow?"

"Talkin' o' givin' up that gal jest as she's old nuff ter be o' some use. It'll be tew year come corn plantin' 'fore her time's out. And our Jerusha bein' sot to work! I tell you, Bent, *that* child shall be brung up 'spectable."

"H'ity t'ity, woman, hold yer yop neow. I hain't been off ter preachin' all day ter come home here an' git inter a mess about nothin', arter promisin' Elder Harris that I'd try an' git religi'n, an' jine 'fore next monthly, an' you a snivelin' an' a promisin' ter live a better life. Don't go fur to makin' me mad, now. Let's hev some supper, I'm tarnal hungry;" and Bent, who knew how to hold his position as head of

the house, walked out and left his helpmeet to sput-
ter and mutter to her heart's content.

The next day Heck asked leave to take Mary out
of the house and was flatly refused.

"Then pay me my wages and let me go," said .
Heck.

"That will I," said the old farmer, who had
already resolved to rid himself of his help. Twenty
dollars was all that was left of his year's wages.
This was paid over ungraciously, and the young
man was gruffly told to take himself out of the way
and not be "a foolin' 'round that gal, or he'd suffer
for it."

The next morning when the sharp voice sounded
over the house, "Mary, you lazy thing, it's after sun
up, what are you about?" there was no response;
and never more did the sound of Mary's voice gladden the ears of Mrs. Bent.

CHAPTER II.

TEACHER AND SCHOLARS.

We will not drag the reader over all the rough paths that our friends were compelled to travel before they found a place of rest. Heckel Dinmont loved Mary too well to deceive or beguile her. Stealing out at evening and traveling with swift feet, supporting her tottering steps, almost carrying his frightened bird over brooks and up steep hills, cheering her with words of hope and love through the long, weary night, they reached, just as day dawned, the village for which they had been aiming. As soon as a frugal breakfast had been eaten they sought out the proper authorities and were legally made man and wife. Hurrying from the office of the justice, they embarked on a steamer and were soon beyond the reach of pursuers.

With a stroke of the pen we will blot out of your sight the years, and pick up our narrative again, with our heroine, Diana Dinmont, just entering her fourteenth year. Born of the deep, earnest love that these two desolate ones felt for each other, she had inherited the best each had to give. Her father's

aptness, and that versatility which was almost
genius, united with her mother's patient, persevering
energy, made a combination so desirable that at
thirteen years of age she had attracted the attention
of the wife of the rich man of the county, and had
been taken into service as nurse for the youngest
scion of the lordly house; working for her board and
clothes, the cast off garments of the household, the
leavings of their luxurious table; and robbing the
pigs of pails of milk and butter-milk which she was
allowed to carry home at night on the promise of
an early return to baby in the morning.

Judge Hancock owned a large tract of land upon
which stood the cabin that Heck had called his
home for many years, and where he seemed likely to
stay for the rest of his life. After his marriage, his
inability to plan for himself and disposition for
rambling seemed to increase; in a word, he was
thriftless. He loved Mary and Mary loved him.
Her scolding and worrying tried his temper all the
more because he did love her and deserved every
reproach; while his sad ways, made all the more
unbearable by his proximity to the Judge's great
distillery, in and around which he found many of
the jobs that kept him from home, filled Mary's
heart with bitterness that gave vent too often in
upbraiding, making things worse instead of better.
We have hinted that poverty and want bore rule in
the cabin home. To relieve this, the mother, weary
and overborne, consented that Diana should " work

out," and she had been one year in service at the commencement of our story.

Physically, mentally, spiritually, had Diana gleaned the best from both her parents. Her hair was soft, wavy, and a beautiful brown, half way between the raven and gold; her complexion fair, almost blonde, with the rich tint that reminds one of the fresh blown rose of spring; but her eyes, those great, quiet, brown eyes, looking out with steady subduing light from under her long, drooping eyelashes, had from her babyhood claimed attention from every passer-by.

Diana was as yet undeveloped in body and mind; not over medium height, disposed to be angular and thin, shy in her manners and very quiet, yet alert and agile as a young gazelle. She was soon found to be an invaluable help in the bustling aristocratic family at the white house on the hill. She was happy, too, for, like her mother, her love of the beautiful was very great, and found ample food in the adornments of the mansion: the pictures, the statuary, the mantel ornaments, the conservatory and garden, and even in the well-set table glittering with its array of polished silver, painted china and neatly dressed dishes.

"Mother," said the brown-eyed girl one evening, after she had seen the children enjoy the remnants of the rich repast that she had brought home in her basket, "Mother, Nettie Hancock knows how to read, and she reads me such pretty stories out of such pretty books. Why did you never learn to read? and why don't you and father let me learn?"

"Hush! child, we're too poor. How could I learn when no one ever teached me when I was young? and how can I learn now with all these children? Mind your work, child, and don't be thinking about them things. It's no use."

"Mother, it is use. We must help ourselves. Nettie Hancock can't sweep as I can, she can't get Jessie to sleep, she can't sing half so pretty. Old Ruth says I can do everything about the house better than she can, and I know I can. Why, then, can't I learn to read? We are just of an age, born the very same day. Why can't I?"

"'Cause you can't. 'Taint for folks like us to know anything;" and the mother, moved to her very heart's depths, set down the dish from which she was eating and went out into the moonlight to sob away, unobserved, the emotion that the child had awakened in her sore, despairing heart. Die followed after a few moments and found her leaning against a tree, and going noiselessly to her side, put her arm around her and pressed her lips to the weary brow.

"Mother, we can and we will. Come in, now, and rest; the dew is falling heavy. I am growing big and strong, and Judge Hancock said to-day that when I had been with them a year or two he would pay me wages. Only think of that, mother," and the dutiful child drew her mother in doors and enlivened her by her merry plays and gambols with the rest of the children.

The next morning she went back to her tasks with a fixed purpose. She would ask Nettie Hancock to teach her the alphabet. And before nightfall she had found her time, while they played with Jessie in the garden.

"Teach you to read? Indeed, I will. You shall be my sister. See, we are just of a height, and you can wear my clothes; and that man that came to-day, to see papa, called you Miss Hancock; wasn't it funny? and you are ever, *ever* so much prettier than Olivia. Papa said so."

Away she ran for her books, and while the sweet baby slept in her carriage, rocked back and forth by her young nurse, Nettie patiently pointed out the A, B, C.

"Six letters at a time, Die, that was all Miss Jones would let me take."

"Why, Nettie, I know the names of every one now, just as you sing them, and the tune, too, but I don't know which is which."

"There, now, I'm schoolma'am, and you musn't talk. A, B, C. Look at them and say them after me."

"A, B, C."

"Now shut the book and count twenty."

"I can't. I never learned to count."

"Oh, Die! as old as me and can't count. How many fingers have you?"

"Ten, I've heard you say, but I don't know how to count them. Oh, Nettie, I'm such a stupid. But teach me and I will, yes, I *will* learn. I want to cry now, but I won't, for then I should not say my lesson. Please count my fingers;" and while the sweet lips quivered and the great brown eyes swam in tears, the steady voice followed the child teacher in the one, two, three, and so on to twenty.

"Now open the book and show me B."

"There," said Die, in a voice that said "I know it and I will always know it." "That is A, and that is C;" and the new beginner astonished her teacher by pointing out the whole six.

"Die Dinmont, you cheated me. You knew them before. It took me a week."

"But I had the lesson half learned, you know, in the names. I did not know a letter."

"Now can you count right, too?"

"I'll try." But this was a harder task. She missed many numbers. The lesson was repeated again and again, and before baby had waked from her soft, sweet slumber, Die Dinmont, the neglected, uncultured child of poverty, ignorance and hardship, was the rich possessor of a treasure that would tell upon all her future life. She knew one-half her alphabet and could count her fingers twice over before night. Happy child! The earth was all aglow to her. Never had the sun shone so bright; the fields been so green. The very ground beneath

2

her seemed velvet to her feet, and her whole frame pulsated with joy.

"Nettie," said Die, as they drew the carriage up the garden path, "are the papers that Ruth kindles her fires with, and burns to scorch the hairs off the chickens made with just such letters as these in your book?"

"Just *presactly*. My father says that twenty-six letters make all the books and papers in the world."

"Oh, my!" exclaimed Die, with a bound of delight. "Ruth said yesterday she'd rather have one basketful of pine knot splinters, such as Tom goes a fishing with nights, than all the old papers in the world. Tom knows where the pine knots are, and he shall bring me some, and then Ruth will give me the papers. Oh! oh! oh! won't I learn?"

"Why, mercy sake, Die, you may have all the old books in the closet. We don't want them. Mother said keep them for poor children. There's all of Livy's, and Em's, and Wash's, and mine; 'cause you know we all have new books to begin with every time."

That night Die carried her pail of milk as usual, but her basket held more than bread and meat. Nettie had half filled it with old spelling books and primers.

"Mother, oh, mother dear, see what I've got. I told you I could learn. Nettie teached me, and I have books, and I know thirteen letters and can count twenty."

"Are you crazy, child?" answered the mother, angrily. "Set down your basket and help me get the supper. We're hungry if you ain't, and don't go for to setting the young ones wild over your books and nonsense. They ain't made for poor folks."

Die said not another word. She put the porringers on the bare table, filled them with skimmed milk, dipped the mush from the pot into a wooden bowl, and set each one's portion in its place. Then slipping to her basket she brought out a plate with a good slice of beef, white bread and butter, a piece of pie and a doughnut.

"There, mother, that's not half my dinner that good old Ruth gave me. I had all I wanted and she said I might bring the rest to you. Now, mother, eat it all, you are so tired."

The mother did eat, saving her piece of pie for him who might come. For down deep in her neglected heart she knew, and knew well, though she had never heard the words of Mrs. Browning, that

> "Those never *loved*
> Who dream that they loved once."

While she was eating this palatable and grateful meal, Die was busy about the fire, and seemed to be mysteriously hiding behind a chair, with an old garment thrown upon it, something that was occupying her special attention.

"What are you at there, Die?" called out the mother; in answer to which the child produced a new tin tea-pot, with the fragrant beverage steaming and ready to be drank, a cup and saucer and an iron spoon.

"Now, what on airth!"

"Mother, Judge Hancock said if I would water and feed his pet pony while he was gone, and not forget her once, he would bring me something nice, and asked me what I would have. I told him a pound of tea for you; and when he came last night he said the pony never looked so nice, for I have curried her every day; and he went down town and bought me the tea, and a pound of sugar, and this bright tea-pot, and two spoons, and two cups and saucers, one for you and one for father, and here is your first cup."

"Oh, Die!" sobbed out the glad heart, and then the tea was drank, while the little ones looked at their own faces in the bright pot, and thought nothing was ever half so pretty, nor anybody in all the world half so good as sister Die. Egbert, six years old, slipped behind his mother and whispered, "Don't scold Die any more, ma."

"Now," said Die, "we've washed all the dishes and swept the hearth, mayn't I teach school?"

"Yes, if you're a mind," was the quiet answer, and again the six letters of the alphabet were called out, and the weary mother, refreshed and made happy, forgot her toil, and at the age of twenty-nine began a new lesson in life, repeating with the rest her A, B, C.

By and by, as the silver rim of the new moon sank below the horizon, Heckel Dinmont came staggering home, too drunk to be sober, not drunk enough to be a madman.

"Don't scold," whispered Tom.

"Give him a cup of good, hot tea," whispered Die, setting the new tea-pot upon the coals in the corner.

"Father's cute," said Tom, "let's have him join our school. Oh, won't it be jolly if we can all say the letters! By jingo! won't I keep up with you, Die! Bet my pile on that."

"Stand in your places," said Die, with authority. "Say your lesson, A, B, C, D, E, F."

"Hurrah! what the d—l you up to?" roared Heck as he staggered into the door. "Teachin' school, by G—! Hurrah for our side! Who's mistress?"

"Why, Heckel Dinmont! ain't you—"

"Don't, mother, please."

"Where'd ye git yer books?"

"Nettie Hancock give 'em to Die," sung out Egbert, "and I know one letter now."

"Father, here's a piece of pie and a cup of good hot tea."

"Where'n the d—l 'd they come from?"

"Why, father, I earned them."

"You earned them?"

"Yes, I did, and you must drink to my health and then stand up in my class and learn your letters like a good boy."

"Ha! ha! ha! aint that jolly? Nary 'nother old rip in these diggins haint got sich young 'uns, ha! ha! ha!" and down went the hot, strong tea, killing the fumes of the whisky and partially restoring to his senses the half besotted man.

Soon the very uniqueness of the proceeding aroused his attention, starting into activity all that love of excitement which made him such a vagrant, and up he sprang, to the head of the row, vowing in no polite terms, he'd be "the best boy in school."

"Then you must not say bad words."

"Musn't, hey?"

"No; that's against the rules."

"Well, then, bring on yer letters."

Die placed the book before him.

"That's A."

"A, is it? Wall, that's just like the first letter of old Adam's sign, where I used to get my grog. Wall, that's right; now let me see where's the next letter of the sign; and running his eye down the column he put his finger on D.

"Hurrah!" shouted he, "taint so d—d—ask your pardon, missus, didn't mean to say nothin' bad;" and drawing down the corners of his mouth and looking scared out of his eyes, he burst out into a pretended cry.

Off went the whole troop into a shout of laughter.

"Ain't this jolly?" said the bewildered man, " to come home to a cup of tea, a house full of fun, and a laugh equal to old Frobishes' bar-room, instead of a scold—"

" Don't father !"

" Let's see how many can tell a letter without showing," said Die.

" There's A, and there's D," said Heck.

" And that's C, and that's E," said Tom.

" And that's B," said Egbert.

Every one had learned something. The evening had been cheerfully spent, and all went to bed in a more hopeful and peaceful frame of mind than for years before. There was a step upward. Seven human souls were made better, because they were made happier by a calm and useful effort, that left no sting when the pleasure had passed away. Seven human souls—father, mother, and five children. True, the younger ones had learned no letters, but the stray beams of light that had penetrated the dark surroundings of their little lives were brightening, for all the future, the sombre shadows that blighted their souls.

Die went back to her chores and the baby early on the morrow, coaxing her father to go with her and see if the Judge would not give him the job of clearing out the garden, and fixing up the grape trellis which was falling down from the accumulated weight of vines growing luxuriantly in the sunshine. Heck readily got the job, and at Die's suggestion, took his pay at night in substantials for his home and family.

The school was again improvised, and the father and mother as ready to join in its half sport, half earnestness, as the rest. It was a new sensation, and as such was sufficient to hold them in sympathy; and as every letter was a new thought, every number a new acquisition, the interest seemed to increase rather than diminish. Die gained daily and took home at night, with a miser's care, all she had gathered; and though no one quite kept up with her in this singular race, she was pleased and gratified. One week gave her the alphabet, all her own, forever. Then, with intuition which outran the wise ones of the time, she said to Nettie:

"Show me the words that make the names of things. If I see how they look after the letters are put together, I will remember."

"Well," answered Nettie, "that word is tree; it takes a *t*, and an *r* and two *ee*'s to make it, and there it stands."

"I will always know it now and how to call it," said Die.

"*Pronounce* it," said Nettie.

"*Pronounce* it," said Die, repeating the exact tone, "I will remember that, too."

And there, under the blossoming lilacs, in the quiet garden, the two children unconsciously began that system of word-teaching which has since come over to us from foreign lands, as the culmination of the wisdom of the most learned for centuries.

Die found another source of improvement and

delight. **Mrs.** Hancock was a weak, nervous woman, and as Emma and Nettie had a music teacher at home, and were required to practice certain hours each day, to the great annoyance of their mother, the nursery, a fine, large, airy room, situated at some distance from the apartments of the invalid, was turned into a music room. Jessie was now nearly three years old, a puny little thing, but very sweet-tempered, and under Die's quiet manipulations, seldom troublesome; so it was decided to transform the nursery into a music room for the children, which would not prevent its being used by Die and the baby at all seasonable hours. Jessie loved her room, and her playthings and doll-houses occupied the corners. She loved the tinkling of the piano, too, and begging Die to carry her there at the first sound of the music, she would sit and nurse her doll in profound silence through a lesson of an hour's length.

Olivia Hancock, the eldest daughter, whose education had been completed at a Catholic school in Baltimore, had taught Die to crochet and embroider beautifully. Not that the haughty, selfish girl cared at all for her improvement, but she realized that the child would be a ready help to her more idle hands; and, besides, why should she not be doing something while she sat by Jessie's cradle or watched her in her play? "Di-an," as she called her, "must be kept busy." She needed but little teaching. The intuitive brain, with needle-work, as with the alpha-

2*

bet, took in at a glance or hint what would have
required line upon line and lesson upon lesson for a
duller head. And sitting in the music room by
Jessie, her fingers busy with some such work, Die
was learning the exact lesson that was being taught
to Nettie and Emma, and when the teacher was gone
and Nettie said :

" Oh dear ! what did she tell me ? I can't remember ; "Die knew, and touched the right key, to the
wonder and delight of the two sisters.

" Oh, Die ! you're such a genius," exclaimed
Emma, " do help us !"

And Die did help, and in helping them helped
herself. Her love of music, her exactness of time,
her retentive memory were all brought out. They
called upon her to play their exercises, to sing their
songs, to help them along at every step, and the
cabin maiden soon outstripped her companions.
Not a word of the teacher was forgotten, not a tone
or motion but was perfectly imitated. The
neglected child was fast becoming educated in many
ways. Every day helped to develop her womanhood. The tall, angular frame was covered with
soft, firm flesh, rounding out into beautiful curves
and outlines, while the enthusiasm of her nature
brought into play by her manifold duties and
employments, every one of which was an enjoyment
to her, gave a glow and a freshness to her cheek and
lip, an elasticity to her step and a grace to her
whole being. Two years had wrought a marvelous
change.

Five of the inmates of that once desolate and poverty stricken home could read. Tom supplied without failure the pine kindlings for Ruth, and Ruth saved all the old books, papers and hand-bills, that used to go into the stove, for Die, declaring that—

" Mas'r Tom's kindlin's was heaps de best."

When Die entered her fifteenth year she could read her Bible and other books, could sing sweetly, play quite difficult music upon the piano, and could rival a French nun in embroidery.

These were " steps upward."

CHAPTER III.

THE HANCOCKS.

JUDGE HANCOCK seemed to be one of the few men who were born into this world with silver spoons in their mouths.

He was the only remaining son of the rich John Hancock, who claimed the illustrious John of the Declaration of Independence as his grandfather's cousin. It was hard to tell which he thought most of, his wealth, or the "blue blood," as he called it, that flowed profusely through his veins. Certain it is that he owned countless acres among the Pennsylvania hills and vales—rich in ores and fertile with all the good gifts of that fertile soil—adding wealth to wealth as the days and months sped by.

One possession for which his estates were famous was a huge distillery, which added immensely to his bank stock, while it diffused misery and ruin, in untold quantity and unadulterated quality, among the lowly inhabitants that did his bidding for ten miles around.

On a beautiful high ground overlooking a broad valley, and giving a grand view of the windings of the Alleghany far above and below, stood the sightly old mansion. It was built of the limestone from the surrounding hills, and had been bleached to almost marble whiteness by the rains and sunshines, the dews and winds of a hundred years. It stood, like some old baronial castle, half way up the hilltop, with a dark background of mountain, covered with lofty pines, stretching a mile away. It was but two stories high, it is true, but it was well spread out; ample in length and breadth, and had been so bewinged and battlemented, so ornamented with turrets and observatories, so added to by balconies and bow windows, and so surrounded by cottages, out-buildings, farm-houses, fancy stables and magnificent barns, that it impressed the passing traveler as he wound his way along the picturesque stream below, as being the beginning and end of some ambitious village that had begun well, grown to its present age and size in prosperity, and paused of its own accord to await the demands of a coming generation.

It might have seemed young and snobbish but for its winding avenues of stately trees, that had been overlooking its well-kept lawns and meadows, and shading its thoroughbred horses and cattle for almost three score years and ten.

This grand old home on the hill was called " The Lodge." One mile below was the distillery, with all its necessary appurtenances of storehouses, granaries, tenement houses, workshops, cabins, stables,

wagon sheds and hog pens. For years it had poured
out, with steady persistency, its stream of fire.

In a sudden curve of the hills half way between
the distillery and the "Lodge," lay a quiet glen, as
perfect in shape as if it had been fashioned by a
skillful workman. On three sides of this glen the
hills rose abruptly, the surface partially covered to
the very apex with broken rock, and shaded by
forest trees, that asserted their right to every inch of
soil that escaped the pressure of the trap. Gnarled,
bent and struggling for the light, they had many of
them stretched upward into sunny altitudes. Down
below on the north, where sunshine never came,
their roots were warmed and nourished by crops of
luxuriant ferns, while the east and west gave birth
to innumerable masses of wintergreen, trailing
arbutus, violets, wakerobins, and their neighbors and
friends of the wildwood. A few acres of level land
lay within the snug embrace of these hills, and the
southern sunshine at midday filled the beautiful
valley with light and warmth. From among the
rocks, many feet above the level of the valley, burst
a clear spring, which went leaping and dancing in
crystal brightness to the plain below, where it had
worn for itself a pretty basin, whence in joyful over-
flow it wound its way in irregular meanderings to
the banks of the Alleghany, and there pitched in
headlong, foaming haste over the rocky banks and
was lost in the majestic stream. At the front or
south of this glen, only a few rods from the water-

fall, stood the home of Heckel Dinmont, unseen
until you passed either point of the hill, and then
bursting upon your vision like a beautiful picture
richly framed; enchanting to an artist's eye for its
tumble-down ruin of a house, its leaping spring, its
little lake covered with noisy ducks and geese, and
the jolly urchins, that usually were seen rollicking
with a house dog about the door, or swinging on the
hanging branches of a huge grape vine, which
smothered with its foliage an old oak upon the verge
of the Alleghany.

This old house was probably the shelter of the
Hancocks in the long ago, when the "Lodge" on
the hill was in embryo. No living man about
Oxbow remembered when it was *not* there, with its
half stone and half wood, low, one story and gables.
But time nor tide had quite annihilated it; though
every timber had been removed, the old cracked
stone walls refused to fall. And here Heckel Dinmont, by virtue of patching, propping and mending,
had managed to make a home for Mary and her
children for a dozen years.

Tradition said the great grandfather of the present
Judge had lived many years in this sheltered nook,
but had left it for the grandfather to begin and finish
the stately edifice called the "Lodge," and to the
father to add and ornament, while he lived a jovial
life with the lordly scions of the first families,
making the old house of his father ring with mirth
and music for many a year. The "blue blood" of

his noble ancestry grew more blue at the end of his
Roman nose as he became more and more the patron
of his own distillery, after he had gained the summit
of a man's natural life. The first lady of the
" Lodge " gave him four stalwart sons, bore his rollicking and roistering till they were men, and then,
as if motherly love could bear no more, she faded
and died, and rested from her toil. The eldest sons
knew no restraint, and not one survived the riotous
dissipation of his youth. And when the father laid
down *his* life's burden at fifty, one son only, the Judge
of our story, was left to inherit the princely estate.
The son of a second wife, more delicate of constitution than his brothers, with a taste more cultured by
his gentler mother, he desired and received an
education at Yale, and spent several years on the
Continent; thus escaping the terrible fate which
seemed to hang over his father's household. At the
age of thirty he returned to find himself sole heir
to all this wealth and power, his good mother having
died during one of his absences at Newport. While
sowing his wild oats upon the sandy beach, he found
little Emily Adams, whose bank stock was said to
be over a million. He liked her lily face and soft
confiding ways, and like a kitten she had crept and
purred around him until he took her to his heart and
mingled the two great fortunes into one.

She had married for pure love. He had married
a fortune and a wife ; she was fond and devoted, he
always kind and courteous. Child·after child came

into the family circle, to be sighed over and petted by the mother, and allowed by the father to spend all the money she desired.

Olivia, the eldest, was a tall, angular girl of imperious nature, fashionable, showy and hollow-hearted, drawing all young men within her reach that she could, and spurning all that dared approach too near. Those that she would have accepted went by on the other side; the fortune hunters she was too wise not to understand.

One sister and one brother had died, and six years had passed before a baby made glad the mansion of the Hancocks. The father was John Hancock. Why should not this young scion of a noble house be called George Washington? No one knew why, and George Washington he was christened in due form. Emma, the third daughter, took her place; a pretty blonde, happy in herself, her mother and brother, and caring little for the rest of the world. Nettie and Jessie completed the list, and have already been introduced to our readers.

At the time of which we write, Wash was nineteen—a student of Yale, like his father—had spent his last summer's vacation among his mother's relatives in Maine, and had not been home for over two years.

Of course, he was talked of and praised by all the household. His picture, painted in oil, hung in the parlor; his photographs were scattered all about the house; even old Ruth, who nursed him from the

first day of his life and loved him better than anything else on the "airth," as she often averred,
carried a copy in her bosom, and took it out and
looked at it every day as a lover would look at the
image of his betrothed. A bright, joyous boy's face
—a face made up of good open-heartedness, a generous impulse and sensuous feeling.

No wonder that Die had been touched with those
praises; that looking daily into the deep, gray eyes,
that mirrored forth so much truth and nobleness, her
heart should have been touched. A mere child she
was in years, yet a woman in the experiences taught
by hardship and poverty; a girl more than a child,
yet a very baby in those mysteries which young girls
learn in the common associations of life. She had
been too busy with her own lot to think beoynd it.
Invaluable she had grown in the house of the Hancocks, learning all there was to learn, from Olivia's
hard set tasks in fancy work to Ruth's marvelous
recipes for concocting cakes, puddings and pies, to
roasts and fricassees.

Gloriously had the work progressed at home;
they not only could read, but were beginning to
think; with thinking came consciousness of wrong
somewhere. No great advance had been made, but
little steps upward gave to their eyes visions of the
far beyond, which created longings that grew first
into spasmodic action, then to more persistent effort.
Surroundings were not so wretched; Heck had
shingled his own house and rebuilt his own chim-

ney. Tom was working for a farmer, who helped
him to bread and meat for the little ones; but best
of all Heck did not drink so many drams, and
brought home more of his wages.

Never was a purer, sweeter friendship than was
growing into maturity between the two girls born
the same day. Nettie was a thoughtful girl of her
years, not a bit pretty, as her sisters said. Her form
was not symmetrical or her motions graceful, but
she was good and loved Die, and Die loved her; the
company of the latter in the kitchen or nursery,
where they could laugh and talk without reserve,
was far better to her than that of her brilliant sisters
in the parlor. Poor Mrs. Hancock, born and bred
to nothing, went through her life duties on compul-
sion, bearing her lot of motherhood, aye, and wife-
hood, as a kind of martyrdom to be endured by
women; not accepted as God's highest, holiest, most
soul satisfying inheritance. All her life long her
soul's cry was for love, but love came not, because
there was no basis upon which it could rest. A
little energy, a little earnestness, a little self-denial,
once might have won it, but the day had gone by, the
die had been cast; she had married for love, and had
her girlhood been rightly taught, and her husband
been reared to look upon woman as a friend, helpmeet and companion, instead of a plaything, a beautiful statuette to adorn his princely mansion and
amuse his leisure, things might have been different.
But they were not different. He went and came.

looked well to his leisure, kept an eye to his political and judicial standing, but cared little for the moaning, complaining woman, whom he had engrossed body and soul.

And she had no language with which to awaken the long sleeping emotion of the man's heart. He, Judge Hancock, talk of love? He bend to kiss the frail, fading flower? He did not need her love, yet there were times, could he have known how much he was to her, when he might have unbent, and taken a little warmth into his cold heart; but he did not know, and could not comprehend her need or the yearnings of her soul. The world is full of such couples, and must be until the whole social, moral, and intellectual atmosphere of life, is vibrated with the thunderbolts of reform, and men and women are taught to feel through all their years, that love and duty must go hand in hand from the marriage altar to the grave, to make life good, and true, and beautiful, and that only thus can the soul be satisfied.

Mrs. Hancock took no notice of the intimacy that was growing between the two children, the poor man's child and the rich man's heir. Matters had gone on happily and smoothly many months, the two children never enjoying any sport like their own low, earnest talks alone. Neither knew or thought of the meaning of the word *love*, other than their love of each other. One bright July morning Die was scouring knives, to help Ruth along with the labors of the day; she had been talking merrily

of "brother Wash " to Ruth, and 'Sarah, the housekeeper, and telling them of Nettie's plans for boat
riding, and flower hunting, and wood pic-nics, when
he should come home.

" God help the chile," said Ruth to Sarah, but loud
enough to be heard by the "chile " herself, " I does
believe she's dead in love with Mas'r Wash 'fore he
gets here; running on as if *he'd* keer for *her*, his
mammy's nuss and scrub gal. Oh, go 'long. Dese
white folks mighty big fools."

Scarcely had Ruth's voice ceased echoing through
her dominion when Nettie came flying in, her very
soul beaming out of her grey eyes. She caught Die
about the neck and whirled her around like a top.
Die held a long, sharp carving knife in her left hand
and her scouring cloth in the other. Instantly the
clean, white apron was soiled, and there is no knowing what might have befallen eye and cheek if the
thoughtful knife scourer had not lifted the formida-
ble weapon above her head, exclaiming in terror:

" Why, Nettie Hancock! what ever is the matter
with you? Are you gone stark mad? Look at your
clean apron now."

" Who cares for aprons! Oh, Die, brother Wash
is coming, and they have kept it from you and me
all this time. I just heard Olivia telling Emma in
the hall. And old Ruth, you ugly old thing, you
knew it, too, and never told us. You stupid Die!
why don't you lay down that knife, and shout and
be glad?" and Nettie whirled a waltz of exuberant

glee around the ample kitchen, only pausing to again demand of Die, who stood pale as a statue, " Why aren't you glad ?"

"He is not my brother."

" O, sure enough, you never saw him.   O, Die, he is handsome, and *so* good, and *so* funny; we'll have grand times when you get acquainted."

"Maybe," said Die, showing more coldness than ever had met Nettie before.   The two seemed to have changed natures.

The calm Nettie was quivering with excitement, and the outgushing, sympathetic Die seemed wholly indifferent.

" Well, let me do my work, or I shall have Ruth about my ears.   If your brother is coming, and other company, all the more need for me to be busy. They are nothing to me, I am nobody, working in other folks' kitchens."

"Don't talk nonsense now, when I'm so happy. You know you're my sister, and I love you best of anything in this whole house—"

" No, you do not, and it's no use saying it ; so go clean yourself up again, and let me polish my knives.   *I* don't care for your brother Wash."

"Oh, Die, you are cruel," exclaimed the sister, and she sped out of the kitchen, sadly disappointed and hurt.

The knife scouring went on, but something had taken all the sunshine out of the world, all the brightness from the work.   The heart of the maiden was swelling to bursting with a sensation painful and incomprehensible, the repressed tears burst forth and fell in fast droppings upon the vigorous young hand.

Die strove to hide from the keen eyes of the old cook her unaccountable emotion. The words "fell in love with him" had struck like a heavy blow upon her heart, her song was hushed, and her mirth and jest failed for once to cheer her companions in toil.

Ruth, one of the shrewdest of her race, read the whole mystery at a glance into the troubled face; and full of mischief, little comprehending the deep, sensitive nature of the girl, she seized the first moment after her turkey was fairly imprisoned in the oven to slip near Die and whisper her ear, "All de gals gits in love, honey—needn't cry."

Die straightened herself with the dignity of a queen, "Ruth, never speak to me such words or thoughts again while you live," her face glowed, her brown eyes flashed lightning, and Ruth stood appalled.

"Laws, chile," said the old cook, apologetically, "Old Ruth didn't mean nothin'—never will again—didn't think you'd be mad—laws, now, dry up your eyes, for missus 'll be calling ye to take Jessie out—and if ye goes in thar with yer red eyes and swelled up cheeks, she'll be askin' what's the matter? then what will yer say? She'll know there's been a muss."

Die knew Ruth was right, and with a strong will stifled her sensation, and finished her task, washed her face in cold water, and answered the bell from the sitting room.

" Why, mercy on us, girl, what is the matter with your face and eyes?   Olivia, look here, Die's face is all blazing red and her eyes are terribly inflamed. Hasn't she got the sore eyes that are going about? I would not have Jessie and Nettie take them for the world; do come and look."

" Mother, how can you be so inconsiderate.   I wouldn't for the world look at them; that is the way they are taken; send her right out of the room, don't let us run any risks, for Heaven's sake.   Oh, it unnerves me to think of it."

" Miss Olivia, please, my eyes are not a bit sore."

" Not sore? what do you mean, you untruthful thing? don't look this way.   Mary, take her away!"

" Indeed, then, mem, I'll be doin' that same, for it's a sad thing, them sore eyes.   I had them, meself, once, and stone blind I was for six long weeks, and every soul in the house took 'em just lookin' into my face, and a sorry time we had of it, 'cepting old Capt. McEron and his woman, they never got 'em; and 'twas a mercy there was no one else, or I couldn't have done all the waitin', and cookin', and washin', and ironin', and runnin', and fetchin', only for there was just us three, I never could have got through it, and me so blind."

"Mary!" shrieked Olivia, "stop your prating, and take that girl out of the room."

Die was sobbing again, fearfully, and Mrs. Hancock, in terror, ordered her to stop or she would be worse, and before Mary, the chambermaid, had finished her story, Die was out of the room.

Poor child! what a whirl of misfortunes had overtaken her. She had fairly fallen in love from hearsay with Nettie's bold, bright brother, and had never dreamed how silly it was, until Ruth flashed the whole horrid truth into her mind by that simple sentence of five syllables, "missus' scrub and nuss gal." Stung to the quick, she had offended her dearest friend by her pretended indifference, had cried her eyes red, and been dismissed on a false pretense, not even allowed to explain or deny; so she went sobbing into the garden, and worried with excitement, yet conscious of no wrong, she threw herself on a bench beneath a cool grape vine arbor, and sobbed as if her heart would break. Summer winds were sighing through the trees, and the soft murmer of the bee-house close by, lulled her into quiet. "I have done no wrong," she said over and over again to herself. "Nettie will forgive me, and my eyes will not be red to-morrow, and I will not, nó I will not be silly; I *am* a scrub and a nurse girl, and it is honest and right to be so. I will cry no more." So thinking, she mastered herself, and fell at last asleep.

CHAPTER IV.

'SQUIRE PAXTON AND MRS. FROBISH.

A MAGNIFICENT spur of the Alleghany hills that bordered the river, came down precipitately to within half a mile of the bank, and then sloped gradually and beautifully into a wide-spread, rounding, swelling interval of land, as if it had been in the ancient of days, waves of the sea transformed by powers divine into rich alluvial for the use of man. These waves pushed their way to the very edge of the stream, curving it into the shape of an ox bow, from which the town took its name.

On this well-selected plat of *terra firma* the sagacious ancestors of the Judge had set the distillery so near the shore as to make the river not only a drain for all their waste, but an easy means of transportation up and down for the needs of the great establishment. This distillery drained the country of its rich grain harvest, and sent away in untold quantities the poison extracted therefrom, to the royal market of Pittsburgh, whose ravening maw was never filled; thence it floated down the Ohio, carrying with it through all the towns and villages located on La Belle Reviere its vitiating power, its degradation and death. The mills necessary to this great growing establishment were turned by the force of the current with little expense to the owner; and all the breadstuffs used throughout the surrounding country were made at the Hancock mills. This brought to the town large numbers of people, and demanded mechanics, tradesmen, lawyers, doctors, ministers, churches, schools, and taverns; so the town, from the force of circumstances, grew with the growth of the country, and became the seat of justice for the county.

First and foremost among the inhabitants was the superintendent or overseer of the works, who was a man of some science and much natural shrewdness, to which long experience had added skill and ability. A short set man, rather rotund than otherwise. At fifty—at which age we introduce him to our readers —his dark brown hair was well frosted, and his whiskers almost white, heavy and long, concealed a good part of his large, jolly-looking face. His eyes were dark and clear, and on the whole he was not a bad-looking nor a bad man. If a current of events had floated his easy nature into some little quiet eddy of home joy and home affection, where he could have made all the threads of life hold out comfortably and happily through the year, leaving a surplus in his money-box at the end, he would never have thought of the distillery at Oxbow as a means of lengthening out those ends. But circumstances did not so drift him. His father had had charge of the

still before him, and, though this epitaph might have
been written with truth upon his tombstone, "Died
of his trade;" and though his son's eyes had been
wide open, and noted the daily progress of that disease which was destroying the parent—though Peter
Rand knew, as no other man knew, that his parent
distilled the "old Alleghany," which distilled *his*
own heart's blood into disease and death, yet he held
not back his hands from the diabolical work. Oh,
strange fatality! or, rather, strange infatuation!
which leads father and son, from generation to generation, to follow the same path, to guide their barge
upon the same waters, and to strand themselves and
all their life hopes upon the same rocks.

But so it is; so too, governments professedly
established for the best interests of the common-
wealth, sitting in grave council by months and
years, discussing with patient care and wisdom, the
well being, health and happiness of the people;
spending time, talent and treasure without stint;
enacting laws to regulate physical, moral, educa-
tional and even spiritual welfare; laws to restrain
the progress of sin and wickedness and to punish
crime, have yet, through all the ages of the past, left
unrestrained the deepest and direst cause of the
transgressions of mankind.

At the foot of the hill and near the granary,
where all the farmers deposited their stores, stood
what was called the tavern, with its high swinging
sign of a big broad horned head, thrust into an old

fashioned oxbow; not emblematical so much of their town as of the fate of every man or nearly every man that entered in at those doors; almost surely his neck went into the yoke from which few ever escaped ungalled. Of Simon Frobish, we shall only say that he was exactly suited to his place, and his wife, too, was a model for a whisky tavern land-lady.

It was a large three story frame house, divided off above and below into the smallest possible rooms that could by any amount of stretching be made to accommodate two persons; tolerably kept and fur-nished, though the walls and floors were painted in profuse variegation, by the continual flow of tobacco juice and the not infrequent deposits of the over-loaded stomachs of the half inebriated customers of the Oxbow. Altogether it was the very ideal of a whisky tavern in that part attached to the bar room.

Listen to Mrs. Frobish: "Here, you Molly, did yon see to number twelve where that old Kempt slept last night?"

"No, I did't; the old boss didn't get him out 'til noon, and then I had dinner to get."

"You lazy huzzy! go this minute and put it in some kind of order;—needn't be too particular, they're nothing but hogs any way; such men. Lord bless my soul, there is 'Squire Paxton of the hill with his wife and gals. Hurry Patsy, git that bread in the oven while I run and pretend I'm *awful* glad to see 'em. Humph!"

"Jule aint doin nothin'; call her; I'm cleanin' the dishes."

"You Jule, come and see to this bread; it's all running over now. Hang that girl. she's put too much stillhouse emptyin's in it; it'll be as sour as swill."

"Where's the dish towel, Mrs. Frobish. Can't find it no place."

"Well, take that dirty table cloth; plague take the girl! can't you think for yourself?"

"That's just what you jawed me for doing yesterday."

"Shut your mouth, you saucy jade."

(Aside) I'll not shut my mouth for her."

"Jule! send Tom to kill two of them chickens, and don't you wait for 'em to flop; dress them instanter; that Mrs. Paxton is one of the nicest housekeepers on the hill, and I'll get 'em on a good dinner. Paxton likes good dinners, and then I'll coax him into the bar. My! but wont the old woman be mad; I'll get twenty-five dollars out of his old stuffed wallet before bed time. Fly round girls, and you shall every one have a ribbon for your hair next Sunday. *I'll* fix 'em; he, he, he."

The latter part of this speech was said in a low familiar tone, to the maids in the kitchen, and had its desired effect, for they were all poor and degraded enough to be made proud by this wonderful landlady's confidential whispers.

We will meet Mrs. Frobish at the front door; **in**

a jiffy her kitchen garments have been laid aside ; a clean dress, a white apron, a jaunty cap with red ribbons have transformed the dowdy manager of the kitchen into a smirking facetious hostess, as with the blandest of smiles she meets the coming travelers.

"How do you do, Mrs. Paxton ; now isn't it queer that you, of all the world, should come in upon us to-day."

"Why not we as well as anybody else," asked Mrs. Paxton, a little coldly.

"I'm sure I don't know, but it's strange. I told Julia, my cook—she is a capital cook, too ; makes such beautiful bread and muffins ;—but as I was saying, I told Julia to have some spring chickens killed and dressed, for I knew by my feelings some friend that I thought all the world of was coming, and you are the very one I'm always gladdest to see ; pull your things right off."

"No, we can't stop now, it looks like rain, though 'twas clear when we started . We'll leave our things and go down to the store."

"Oh, now ! you'll stay and have dinner. Girls, you are well I hope. How beautiful you're looking —blooming as my blush roses."

"No, Mrs. Frobish, we've got to get back before dark, and we'll have to be spry. We brought lunch in the wagon, and have not a bit of need for more ; come girls," and away went the good lady and her daughters.

Pretty soon, Paxton came in from the stables where his team was snugly waiting for their oats, (the barns were well kept if the house was not), and was met by the gracious woman at the bar room door."

"Good morning, 'Squire, pleasant morning."

"Beautiful weather for harvest."

"Didn't expect you could be got to town this week, for love nor money."

"Oh, the women folks wanted some traps; there's going to be a harvest home, or somethin'; gals must have fuss and feathers you know."

"Why, how tired you look, do come in and take something. Its a long ride from Brookville down here, especially when one's worked out, in hot weather." Suiting the action to the word, a capital strong dose was presented, and though the 'Squire hemmed and hawed and pretended, he at last took the glass and drank it to the dregs.

"Frobish out of town?"

"No, he's run round to the superintendent's; will be back presently. I'll hurry on a good dinner, and your folks will have a cup of tea when they come back."

"We brought lunch along."

"Oh! fie on a cold lunch, when a man's tired as you are; the girls are hurrying for dear life to get you some spring chickens."

"Well, may be we'll stop a bit; just as my woman says."

" Oh, they'll do just as you say."

" Well, my horses are cooled off by this time, and I'll go and see Tom give the oats. I allers tend to my own feeding, think as much of my critters as I do of myself."

" That's what every humane man should do, 'Squire."

After the 'Squire went out, the landlady mixed a stronger and sweeter dose, with which to stay his step when he returned, which he did in five minutes after.

" Found all right, 'Squire ?" asked the landlady, with the blandest tone and the most insinuating smile.

" All O. K. Mrs. F."

" Just take another sup, poor man, you look so done up."

" Well, I don't care if I do. Fact is, I am about used up with the haying and wheat harvest."

" Splendid crops this year ?"

" Never were beat ; thank you, Mrs. Frobish, that's capital—most too stout," and the 'Squire smacked his lips and sat down.

The first dose was working, and the second was not slow to help it ; the wily bar tender knew the strength and weakness of all the doughty drinkers in the vicinity, and mixed her potion accordingly.

Leaving the liquor to do its work she slipped into the back part of the house to give orders, in the highest glee, to her handmaidens.

3*

"I've got him," she exclaimed, triumphantly—
"he's good for a week's spree; two drams down,
and he'll be howling for more in ten minutes. Got
them chickens, Jule?"

"No, ma'am, Tom couldn't catch 'em.'

"Glad on't, old Mrs. Starch won't stay a minute
after she finds what a fix he's in; she and the girls
will take the horses and drive home, and won't
there be a time of it, he, he, he. I do love to come
it round such stuck up folks."

"Landlady," shouted the 'Squire, "give us another
sup. Where are you gone to?"

"Hillo! coming, coming, 'Squire."

"Give us another, lan'lady; one more, 'fore the
old woman comes; she'll blow me up, she will," and
the farmer, already beginning to maudle and speak
his words incoherently, staggered towards the
kitchen."

"Don't be impatient, 'Squire, I was just giving
the girls orders about your dinner." Chuckling at
her success, which had been gained easier than she
had hoped, Mrs. Frobish replenished the glass which
was at once emptied, and her diabolical work was
done.

Wheeling the bar room lounge into a shady corner,
the 'Squire was urged to lie down and rest a little,
before the folks got back."

"A ten minute's nap will make you all right."

"I'm—I—I'm all right now. Give us another taste,

I've got money, I'll pay, old Paxton allers pays. Whoop, hurrah!"

" Here is your grog, so don't make a *noise.*"

Down went the fourth dram, and down went the poor victim on the lounge to rise no more that day. Was not Mrs. Frobish a landlady? And was not this her trade? Poor victim! Why do we call him thus? Did not this sagacious farmer put himself voluntarily into the way of temptation? Was it the first time this wily woman had lured him to this fall? Shall all the blame be laid upon her? She was only doing well her licensed work. If there were no drinkers in the community there would be no bars. If public opinion among " the good and true," as they are called, was right, there would be no whisky taverns to entice the weak and wavering.

Public opinion was *not* right, and Esquire Paxtons were found among all the hills and on all the mountain sides; they dwelt in the valleys, and gave of their wealth to enrich such men and women as the landlord and landlady at Oxbow.

An hour after, when mother and daughters returned ready to take their way homeward, they met the cunning woman at the door, ready to condole with and comfort their grieved hearts. " He persuaded Tom to give him a taste, and before I knew it—dear Mrs. Paxton, don't take on so. I'm sure I never was so sorry, to think it happened here."

" We must go," said the poor weeping wife and

mother; " oh, girls, what did we come for ? he said he would not. Order the horses, Mrs. Frobish, we must go home and see to the work hands and the cows; we'll send for him in the morning."

" Stay and have a cup of tea."

" No, I could not swallow it, O ! my God."

" Don't give father any more liquor, O ! Mrs. Frobish, don't ; have him go up to bed as soon as he wakes, and we will send early," said the eldest girl.

Mrs. Frobish sympathized and promised. The wife and daughters drove away with sad and weary hearts, hoping, O, how women *will* hope and love. Do our readers need any further introduction to Mrs. Frobish as she was ten years ago ? Cool, calm, witty and conquering was this woman ; good looking, tasteful, pleasant in address and fascinating to most men ; who shall calculate the mischief such a one can do. With a face as bland as cream, she had given her solemn word to give the drunken man no more liquor. With apparent disgust and horror she had said, " Dear Mrs. Paxton, I feel for you in the depths of my soul, and you may be assured I will do all I can to bring your husband back to himself."

Yet on the first symptoms of returning consciousness this man, who never got into such a state except when he came to town, was plied anew with that which had sent his wife and daughters home almost broken hearted. Mrs. Frobish thought she was only doing wifely duty. Frobish had more heart. Not even for the whole contents of the fat wallet would

he have done quite so cruel and vile a thing. When
he came in and was told by his wife that he and
Tom must carry the farmer up to bed, and to put
him into the identical number twelve, all reeking
and foul as it was with the debauch of the last
occupant, he ventured a remonstrance.

" Why, Rena! that room is not a fit place to put
any Christian man into!"

" I hope you don't call that dead log a Christian
man; the place is good enough."

" Rena, wife, this won't do, let us put him in a
decent room at least."

" Yes, and I'd like to know what kind of a room it
would be to-morrow morning—decent, faugh!"

D—n me, wife, if I hadn't rather given ten dollars
out of my own pocket than to have you get Paxton in
this fix."

" Frobish, you're a fool."

" If I am, madam, I'm not a devil."

Mrs. Frobish, finding the atmosphere getting too
warm, and knowing from past encounters that when
" Frob," as she called him in her anger, got his back
up, she had best draw her own down, answered with
a sneer:

" Take him into the bridal chamber, my saint," and
went off, gaily singing—

" When the devil was sick, the devil a monk would be,
When the devil got well, the devil a monk was he."

And with Molly, Patsy and Jule to laugh in con-
cert, she had a jolly glee over her midday work.

Are women all angels, as some would make us believe? Are they all pure and true, gentle, loving, kind and considerate? I fear not.

Had Mrs. Frobish ever been drunk, had she ever seen her husband drunk, possibly she might have had some little charity; she would at least have known weakness and how to pity it; but these experiences had never come to her, and not by one jot or tittle could she abate her scorn for a man frail enough to become her dupe.

"Frobish," she used to say, "if ever you dare to take one drop of that hell broth between your lips, you and I part company."

And the man that could rule half the town with his iron will, dared not meet and match the hardened steel of his wife's fury.

Have we disgusted you, reader, with this hideous portrayal? Do you think the line too sharply drawn? Go to any licensed tavern or hotel and examine it closely—look into its bar, its bed-chambers, its back rooms, its rubbish sheds, and you will tell me that I have not half filled out the sad details; that I have left out the profanity, the obscenity, the vulgarity, the diabolism, till the scene is tame and commonplace.

Oh, that I should have to answer you, "I know that it is even so," and over all this beautiful country, bright with God's promise of health and happiness, there are men and women who are acting exactly the parts of Mr. and Mrs. Frobish.

Not many women, oh! not many women, but men
by the thousands. Mrs. Frobish was not all bad;
she was a mother, and that holy vocation had kept
somewhere in the secret chambers of her soul, a
glowing spark of humanity which the Father above
would have recognized as pure.

Agnes, her daughter, was fifteen, and a pleasant,
good girl, though born and brought up in the
Oxbow. So jealously had this worshipping mother
guarded her only remaining child, that the contaminating influences had not soiled even the hem of her
garments. Mrs. Frobish had had her heart wrung
three times by the sudden going out of little lights
that glowed upon her hearthstone, which might,
had they been left to brighten her way through life,
have made her a better and holier woman.

They were all boys, and never woman hated the
weakness of drunkenness more than she. There
was no principle in *her* hatred—not a bit; she lived
by, and gloried in what she hated, because she had
been taught so to do; but had *her* boys lived, had
they leaned in the slightest toward that bar, she
would have raised herself like a Pythoness to have
destroyed it forever.

"Frobish," she said one day, as she looked down
into the sweet blue eyes of her baby, twinkling up
into her face, "If I thought my child would ever go
staggering out of that bar-room like that boy,"
pointing to a youth of eighteen who was reeling out
of the door, "I would set fire to this whole house

with my own hands, and take my children into the wilderness where they should never see, taste, or smell the cursed stuff that makes drunkards and fools."

"Hoity, toity, Rena, that's pretty talk for a woman that puts the cup to the lips of every other mother's son that she can get hold of."

"I'm not responsible for other mothers' sons; for my own *I am responsible,* and *so help me God they shall never die drunkards.*"

"Amen!" said the keeper of the Oxbow, "and between you and I, Rena, my girl, if every other mother would resolve as you have resolved, we might turn the bar out of doors and keep a decent house in six months."

"Simon Frobish, you never said a truer word since you was born; mothers don't do their duty. There's that Mrs. Owen over the way with her eight children; her husband is going to the bad as fast as his feet can carry him, and she goes to church three nights in a week to pray, while her three boys, Tom Ed and Jerry, come over here to "hear the fun," as they call it, in the bar-room, to hear the swearing and to laugh at the dirty anecdotes, smoke the ends of cigars and drain the tumblers. Little good her praying will do them; but she means well."

"She's a nice, good woman, wife."

"So she is, but she's a precious fool, Frobish, for all her goodness; the Lord wants something besides prayers."

" What would you have her do? Owen is one of the hardest men in town when he's tight."

" That may be, but he'd soon find he had a hard woman to match if I had him to deal with."

" What would you do ?"

" Stay at home from one week to another if it was needed, and I would make my prayers in ears that would hear in that bar-room."

" Pretty muss you'd get into. 'Twouldn't do. If we keep the bar, I hope the women will not take after your notions."

" As sure as you live, Simon, I would follow him as often as he went for his grog. I would stand by his side morn, noon and night. I would say ' William Owen, we twain are one flesh by the marriage contract; as you do, so will I do, as you live, so will I live. You are in danger; it is my duty to warn you; you are wasting your substance; it is my duty to care for it; you are degrading yourself; it is my duty to save you, if possible; you are disgracing us all; it is my duty to see to my own reputation and the reputation of our children, that they are not reproached upon the streets and in the schools as the drunkard's children; when I married you, you was a Christian; it is my duty to save you for the kingdom of God.' That's the way *I'd* do."

" Pity you would not turn temperance lecturer," said Simon, more touched than he cared to be, and yet a little piqued at his own inconsistent mood.

" Simon Frobish, I hate this work, and if my boys

live we must get out of it." She was already beginning to feel the sting of conscience.

"It was my father's business and it's mine; we're
in it, and I don't see how we can get out of it."

"Where there's a will, Simon, there's a way."

"But there ain't a will."

"We must make one, then."

"I can't do anything else; I've been brought up
to it."

Just then a knock at the bar called for Simon, and
the mother's heart, filled to overflowing, poured
itself out in a flood of tears. Straining her babe to her
bosom she vowed again and again he should not be
a drunkard.

The three boys did not live; one by one they
passed away, and as years came and went, the heart
that was so soft to its own became harder to others,
exemplifying the adage that the sweetest fruit makes
the sourest vinegar, the softest iron the hardest steel.

Agnes was her only darling now, and was kept
away at school; the mother choosing rather to
forego the pleasure of her child's company than to
have her live about the tavern. Daily was she
learning lessons of truth and humanity from a
mother's love, and the young girl seeming to inherit
all that was good, true and beautiful in the natures
of her parents, was indeed a girl to love and to be
loved.

CHAPTER V.

THE SUPERINTENDENT'S FAMILY.

OH! dear reader, how tired you are becoming of this tedious detail; have patience; you can't build a good house without first laying a good foundation, nor can a good book be written without gathering together good materials and arranging them in order.

We need only the most common, every day brick and mortar, 'tis true, but there needs to be skill and cleverness in laying them together so they will stand firm and endure a lifetime. Whether your humble servant has that cleverness remains to be seen.

Peter Rand and his wife Helen lived on the hill above the village, and had a tasteful home with plenty of ground around it, upon which he had expended sums of money sufficient to make it very attractive.

Helen Gordon, his wife, who had been in her younger days a teacher of a young ladies' seminary, was accomplished, after the ideas of her time; was elegantly dignified in her manners, exceedingly fastidious in her feminine ideas, and exclusive in her social habits; very strict in her religious observances, and devotional in her daily walk of life. Tired of the drudgery of her school work and knowing but that one way to earn her bread, Helen Gordon accepted the offer of the hand and home of the good looking, pleasant spoken, smooth tempered, rich Peter Rand, and became mistress of his house and purse. Bred in a circle of society far above her husband in intellectual and literary attainments, and quite beyond him in politeness and refinement, she had yielded to his request to become his partner in life, to become what to her tastes and culture would have been utterly repulsive if the whole had not been garnished with silver so dazzlingly.

He was exceedingly proud of his stately, elegant wife, while she was proud of her beautiful home and surroundings; and each felt a measure of esteem for the other which made life quite tolerable. He was too good natured to wrangle and find fault, she too well disciplined to let her disgust at his departures from high life etiquette disturb her serenity. One son was the only fruit of this marriage, and loving this son as Mrs. Frobish did her daughter, with an entire and absorbing affection, she pursued an entirely opposite course in his early training and education.

Mrs. Frobish, uncultured herself, watched her daughter with the most earnest and patient care. There were no indulgences. That which was not good for Agnes, Agnes could never have, and from her baby hours a system of self-denial and self-control was established with her child which laid the foundation of a most serene and attractive character.

On the contrary, Mrs. Rand, forgetting all her life teachings, yielded without an effort to her selfish mother-love, and was never known to crucify this passion in any particular for her child's sake.

Crucify herself and her physical life, she would and did at all times for her darling; but her love, never. Gordon Rand had things all his own way from the beginning; cried, was rocked; cried, was fed; cried, was dosed; cried, was trotted and sung to; was walked, talked and played over, until at six months old he was a nuisance of a baby, and kept on growing more so every day of his life. His mother would not have him crossed, and cheerfully, yes, joyfully and lovingly, gave her whole time and strength to making him happy, vainly supposing that he could be made happy through the indulgence of his whims and fancies. She forgot, in her excessive love to mould

> " The larger plan
> What the child is to man,
> Its counterpart in miniature."

Oh! woeful forgetfulness. As the rankest and most poisonous weeds spring up and thrive in the richest soils, even so with their roots deep set in the purest and most genuine of all nature's impulses, grow the most terrible of all habits, the habits of self-indulgence fed and watered by a mother's love.

"I cannot deny him anything because I love him so," was Mrs. Rand's reply to her husband's oft-repeated remonstrance against these oft-repeated and injurious gratifications.

"Helen, you will ruin our boy."

"Oh, no, Peter, I don't like to cross him now; when he is older, you know—"

"But when he is older, if you keep on indulging him, he will be past all control."

"Never you fear, papa. Will Gordie be good if mama gives him some sugar?" she would ask of her snarling boy, and the sugar was given, while the little gleam of sunshine that brightened the young face as an affirmative, only lasted until the lump was swallowed, followed by a more imperious demand for "two sugars."

On, on, on, through little steps of wrong doing, through continual aggressions of self-indulgence, this bright, beautiful boy went toward manhood; quick of comprehension, sparkling with wit, gushing with sympathy, domineering over others, where he could, impatient of restraint, no wonder this only branch of the family on the hill was always in trouble, and that being always in trouble his loving mother took his part—or that with her dignity and money she bore down all opposition and brought off her darling as conqueror.

Turned from one school, he was sent to another, another and another, until by bribes and hush-money, and his own wit and power, the reckless boy had picked up education enough to give him, at eighteen, an entrance to Yale with George Hancock, the son of his father's employer.

On the same beautiful balmy day of July, and at about the same hour that our tired and grieved heroine, Diana Dinmont, was sobbing herself to sleep with the murmuring honey bees, under the grapevine arbor in the Lodge garden, Mr. and Mrs. Rand might have been found upon the pillared piazza that fronted upon the village of Oxbow, and gave a wide and long lookout over the country above and below.

Mr. Rand sat in his cosy, rustic chair, peering through his gold bowed spectacles at the last *New York Herald*, but one could see at a glance that his gray eyes wandered restlessly towards the line of dusty road which went meandering in and out along the sinuosities of the river like a russet ribbon bordered with green. Mrs. Rand, dressed in a richly embroidered white wrapper, with her black hair coiled in elaborate braids around her finely formed head, and adorned with a head-dress of rich lace, walked uneasily about, picking off a dead leaf here, lifting a stray vine there, drawing out an opening bud that was blushing unseen, into fairer and fuller light, until at last the clock in the parlor struck one, when she turned, flushed and tremulous, to her hus-band :

"My dear, don't you think the stage is late?"

"Not at all—never gets here till one, you know."

"Oh, yes, it passed Frobish's yesterday at half after twelve."

"Well, don't get uneasy; they have got to stop at the Lodge to leave Wash. It will take half an hour to drive up the avenue, unload all his traps and get out to the road again."

"And then Mrs. Frobish expects Agnes to-day," rejoined the mother with a sigh.

"That's so, and ther'll be another stop."

"Oh, dear me, I feel as if I could not wait another minute."

"Fudge! Fudge! my dear woman, sit down here beside me and keep cool, no use in getting nervous."

"I'm not nervous, Mr. Rand, but my only son has been gone nine months, and if you loved him as I do—"

"Don't I, my dear?"

"No you don't, I'm sure, or "—she sprang forward —"don't you see a dust, Mr. Rand?"

"Just by the big sycamore?"

"Yes; it is, yes, I'm sure its the stage."

"Only an old cow, my dear; not one bit *nervous?* ' and the cool superintendent burst into a hearty ha! ha! ha! at his wife's disappointment, which sent the proud Gordon blood rushing indignantly to her temples and tender motherly tears to her eyes. She was about to leave the porch when the really good, well-meaning man put out his arm and intercepted her. Drawing her tenderly towards him, he left a kiss upon her glowing brow, saying at the same time, " There, dear, never mind, I didn't mean to be rude; you want to see the boy more than I, I dare say. Mothers do love more than fathers, I know, but we must take it coolly. There he is, upon my word; we looked clear over the coach coming up the hill and saw only the cow. There, dry your tears;" and with another hasty kiss he rushed to the gate to receive Gordon in his arms.

Gordon loved his mother devotedly and respected his father profoundly. He received the father's greeting silently, and disengaging himself, flew with bounding steps up the gravel walk to behold his mother still sitting in her chair and sobbing nervously. As he approached, she rose and staggering to the steps with emotion, stretched forth her arms and received his rushing embrace with a cry of joy.

"Hello, mother, what's up?" shouted the young man, "crying because I've got home?" and whirling her round and round with boisterous love and rudeness, and kissing her at every turn, he soon staid her sobbing and brought from her a cry of reproachful tenderness.

"Oh, Gordie! mercy on me! don't tear me to pieces. There goes my head-dress."

"And down comes your beautiful braids." Ah, my lady mother, you must forgive me; I have just seen my friend Wash received by his sisters, and he was the one that had to cry out. I thought they would tear him to fragments. I am so glad to see you."

"And I am overcome to see you, my son," and sobbing for pure joy, she gathered up her braids and reset her cap.

"How are you, mamma mine?"

"Oh, very well, dear; and you did stay the year out?"

"To be sure I did—by thunder! did you think I was going to balk after I'd promised?"

"Gordie, dear, don't."

"Don't what?"

"Speak so rude."

",W-h-e-w! old gal; call that rude? Why, my most precious mother, that's delicate, refined, high culture with our mess. We never swear by any deity of inferior rank, but if that hurts your tender soul, I will say 'by Jupiter' next time."

"Gordon!"

"What, ma'am."

"I am astonished."

"And so am I, to come home after a year's absence to find you crying and to be lectured in the first five minutes; d—n it if I am going to put up with it."

"Gordon, my child, my only child," shrieked the mother, "you are drunk. Oh! God have mercy on me."

"Drunk? do you dare to call me drunk? you old

fool; and giving the almost paralyzed form a heavy push, the agonized mother fell prostrate upon the floor, just as his father, who had waited by the stage coach to receive his baggage, gained the door.

"It's nothing to me, Mr. Rand," said the driver, "but it's my notion if you don't see to that boy of yourn he'll be doing mischief. He's been awful this last ten miles, and if it hadn't been for Hancock's son and another feller, he'd a bin the death of me."

"What, my son, Gordon? You don't tell me that."

"I tell you that Hancock and that other feller had to take away his knife and throw it over the bank, send his brandy flask after it, fire off his pistols, and keep him fast by main force; and down here at Frobish's he got out and took a good half pint."

"Oh, merciful Father!" exclaimed Mr. Rand throwing up his hands in despair.

"You may well say that, sir; I didn't want to hurt ye, but Mr. Hancock said, 'tell you to watch him.' Good by, sir."

The good-hearted driver turned his horses toward the road and the stricken father wended his weary steps towards the house, leaving the baggage lying uncared for in the street. A few rods from the door he heard the cry of the mother, and entered in time to see the rude repulse of his son and his wife's fall. Peter Rand, like a deep, quiet lake, could be smooth as glass in calm weather, but was susceptible of

being wrought into spasmodic fury by the wrath of
the tempest. Now, maddened to frenzy, he seized
his son by the throat and hurled him with the force
of a giant across the room, exclaiming with terrible
vehemence, "Scoundrel! villain! madman! you have
killed your mother."

Gordon staggered and fell upon a sofa, a little
stunned possibly, and muttering incoherent oaths,
did not attempt to rise. His last dram of brandy at
the Oxbow tavern now rendered him wholly insensible.

Mr. Rand called for help and had him removed
to his chamber. Mrs. Rand was with difficulty
restored to consciousness, which seemed a cruel
boon to her suffering soul. Her husband bent over
her with ceaseless assiduity, almost amounting to
tenderness; and in their deep and unexpected trial
—this calamity never dreamed of—they were brought
nearer together than ever before in their lives.

"Och, lackaday now, but here's an awful to do;"
said Bridget, "it's meself may well say that. And
the likes of that dinner niver before lifted in the
house, and nobody to be atin' a bite of it."

"Sure, now," said Pat, insinuatingly, "its the
quarest thing alive, mavourneen, that Misther Rand
and his leddy should be taking on so, and graving
their two selves to death about this little bit of indiscreetness of Masther Gordie. Haven't I seen
him in the like fix many a time afore to-day and hid
him in the hay mow, and kept him out of harm's
way to chate them.

"And a baste ye were, Pat, for that same. But I'll go straight now and be asking what shall be done with all this victual, it's stone cold it's gettin', and it's me own dinner I'm wantin'."

Bridget soon returned with the cheerful information that the master said, " Eat it or throw it away," and that he was beside himself with grief.

Straightway the family servants—the cook, chambermaid and gardener—were gathered into the kitchen, where over the first cuts of a delicious roast they discussed with savage censure the "wakeness of American men and women."

"And Master Gordie will be all right the morry, and what for should my lady be screechin' and faintin'. It's only a bit of indiscreetness which down at the tavern would be laughed at," said the housekeeper.

" Och, Miss Maloney, it's niver your own boy you've seen come home to ye the likes of that, or you'd niver be sayin' 'what for would she be screechin' and faintin'.'"

" Well, well," said Pat, "it's no more than could be expected, not a whit, not a whit. If the father ·gives all his days to the makin' of the broth d'ye think the childer will not drink it?"

"And d'ye think ye'd be any the less grieved if ye'd poisonod your own with your own hand, now?" asked Bridget, sharply.

"It's not like I would, and whin I know and reason that he's not pizened and will be like as smart and bright as afore, I be thinkin' there's no reason in the world for such takin's on. Haven't I been the worse for a dram meself before this?"

" Indade, then, ye have, and are ye the better for it now, ye spalpeen?"

" It's none the worse I am, sure."

" Not worse is it? when ye had to pay the twenty dollars fine out of your wages yesterday, for that bit of a spree down at the Oxbow, and half puttin' out Tommy Owens' eye and layin' him up for his old mother to wait on. How can ye sit there tellin' ye're none the worse for it?"

" Hoit, Bridget, gal, don't be insultin' your betters now. It was your own father that went off in the liquor."

" Hould your tongue, Patrick, man, it's trouble enough the house be's in the day, that ye needs to be makin' it worse with your—"

" Then don't be yourself doing that same. Give us another cut of the roast, Mrs. Maloney."

CHAPTER VI.

DIE IN TROUBLE.

WE left Die half an hour ago taking a delicious and refreshing nap in the shady arbor.

Half an hour ago, dear reader, half an hour ago;—a short space of time to the guileless, true heart of the little maiden, but a long weary age to the souls of the father and mother. Long enough to blight the hope of a life, long enough to change the hues of heaven into blackness.

Truly

> "We live in deeds, not years.
> In actions, not in figures on the dial.
> We should count life by heart throbs."

"Oh, Die! Die Dinmont! where are you?" sounded in the ears of the young sleeper, and with a bound she sprang from her recumbent posture almost into the arms of Nettie.

"Nettie, dear Nettie, will you forgive me," exclaimed the half awakened girl.

"Forgive you; why I was just hunting you to forgive me; you haven't done anything."

"I was *so* cross."

" No, you wasn't : Oh it's funny. Ruth told me all about it, and all about Mary's sore eyes, and how she run on about sore eyes six weeks in the month of August, and all that just to make Olivia mad and get you out till you'd get over your cry."

" But, Nettie —"

"Now you dear Die; I can't be happy if you aren't happy, and Wash has come and Mr. Max Carter with him, and we're all so glad; and would you believe it, I forgot all about what he wrote in his last letter; that I must have a nice vase of flow-ers in his room for him; wasn't it mean in me to forget. Now, Die, you make the nicest boquet you ever made in your life and when you hear them all go down to dinner, you slip up the back stairs and put it in his vase; you will, won't you ?"

"Of course I will, and Nettie, tell your mother my eyes aint sore one bit."

" I will,—there's the dinner bell. You love me now, Die, don't you ?"

" Yes, Nettie, indeed I love you, but you musn't talk to Washington one bit about me," and the children separated; the one to revel in the joys of wealth, home and friends; the other, to the perform-ance of duty, oppressed and saddened with a newly awakened consciousness, that was at once an exqui-site pleasure and a stinging pain. As soon as Nettie left her, Die sought the most beautiful flowers of the gardens, and as if by intuition gave them their proper places for a boquet. Soon her hands were full; and studiously escaping observation, she sought the room of the young sophomore. Attempting to set them in the vase without disarrangement, she found some of the stems too long; holding them closely in her hands she was cutting them to the required length, with her back to the door and her face to the mirror, and did not hear the step of an intruder, until a voice cried out cheerily,

"Who are you?'" and before Die could anticipate the action, he caught her head between his hands, bent it back to meet his tall form, and left a hearty kiss upon her lips, exclaiming:

"You're a beauty, and how could I help it? Forgive me, sweet one."

Die dropped the flowers upon the floor and fled like a startled deer from the room.

"There!" exclaimed the daring young man, "always my luck! I'll bet a red apple that delicate piece of mortality is Nettie's favorite nurse girl that she's been writing me about for these two years past. Hang me for a dunce as I am. I must pluck my apple at once and see what's come of it. That beautiful boquet in ruins upon my nice new carpet, and my fairy bird flown and will not enter my room for a month again I'll be bound. George Washingtan Hancock, you must take lessons in experience and wisdom from your honored namesake. He never rushed into battle to be defeated—always acted on the defensive, and gained his victories by a 'masterly inactivity,' as our great statesmen say."

4*

So soliloquizing, the young gentleman gathered
up the scattered treasures, placed them all in confusion in the vase, obtained the 'kerchief for which
he had come, and hastened back to the dining hall.
During the long formal dinner hour, he cast furtive
glances toward all the opening doors, hoping to see
the object that had so enchanted him; but she did
not appear.

There is no love like a genuine boy love at first
sight, for unwise enthusiasm, setting the brain in a
whirl, and starting the whole machinery of nature
and feeling into a fevered commotion. Our young
student had had touches of this heart fever many
times, but nothing so intense as this. The paroxysm
rendered him so nervous, that he made divers mis-
takes and inexcusable blunders, dropped his potatoe
from his fork into his lap, upset his goblet of water
and handed his soup plate for a second supply, sur-
prising his lady mother and eliciting sundry half
ejaculated remonstrances from his fastidious sister
Olivia.

"'Why brother Wash! how agitated you are."

" Why brother, what a mistake."

" Wash, dear, I declare! was heard in remonstrance,
all of which increased instead of diminished the
excitement. When at last he tipped his dessert dish
over the edge of the table, even his quiet mother
could no longer keep silence.

" Washington, my love," she said gently, "do
calm yourself."

"Indeed, mother mine, I am very much ashamed of myself, but how can I be calm on the very instant of my arrival, after a two years' absence from the · dear old home; you should have given me until night to get cool, but here I am set down to dinner with every nerve quivering with joy over the meeting with father, mother and sisters, and Nero," said the jolly boy, patting the head of a favorite Newfoundland, that had stolen to his young master's chair and lain his huge muzzle upon his knee.

"Why, Wash, did I ever! 'sisters and Nero' in the same breath," exclaimed Olivia indignantly.

"Oh! now don't; I really did not mean any disrespect; but having no brother to fill up the gap, our good old faithful Nero came in of himself; bless you old boy," turning to the dog, we have had many a jolly day with one another, have we not?"

"There I declare, you have bettered the matter talking to the dog at the dinner table."

"Olivia, my dear," said the Judge, who had been seeing and hearing, while seemingly busy with the young stranger, Max Carter, "I don't see that you are likely to make much out of your brother to-day; suppose you spare all farther reproof and let him have time to finish his dinner in his own way and get cool afterward."

The Judge was evidently a little disturbed, and as Olivia never ventured to contradict her father, there was an imposed and almost painful silence, only broken by the remarks and questions of young Max,

and the answers of the Judge. Wash, feeling himself the unintentional cause of all this embarrassment at his first home dinner, felt vexed and hurt ;
his face flushed, and he bent over his plate in entire
silence.

Die, in the meantime, excluded from both dining
room and nursery by her imagined sore eyes, fled
once more to the garden with throbbing heart and
glowing cheek. She had seen him, the ideal of her
childish dreams ; she had heard his voice, sounding
to her ears as sweet and wild as the rushing of
laughing brooks in spring time ; she had felt his
warm glowing lips pressed to her own, and her ears
tingled with the pressure of his soft hands ;—her
whole life dilated. Something new, strange and unde-
finable, took possession of her being ; the language
of the passing winds, the song of birds, and the
glow of flowers, had but one language, " henceforth
and forever I live to love !" There was a fresher
glow upon the roses, the white lilies were more holy
and pure, the pansies looked up from their bed, as
though they knew and felt her secret, and were
ready to say, " Oh! we knew it long ago, pretty
one." The golden oriole hung upon the marigold
tops, and whistled his sweetest notes unenvied ; the
robin among the cherry trees, sung vehemently, " I
know it, I know it—trilla-la, trilla-la, to my darling ;"
but Diana felt brighter than the flowers, and happier,
(for this one brief moment of her life), than the
brightest and happiest of them all. Sweet, pure,

beautiful, artless child, she felt his warm kiss still upon her lips, and her untutored soul went out to him in all the fullness of girlish love.

What knew she of proprieties, of castes? why should she not worship freely? who had a right to interfere with her delicious sensations? She did not know, or understand—she only felt and dreamed —until the musical voice of Ruth recalled her to the reality that there were dishes to wash and work to do.

All things are said to come to an end, and so did this sumptuous dinner. The fatted calf had been literally slaughtered, though the returning son was not a prodigal. A feast of fat things had tempted the young student, but it was not enjoyed; more than once he had thought to himself "better is a dinner of herbs where love is."

Ruth missed the busy fingers and busier mind of Die, ever so ready to help with the one and to arrange with the other.

" Now, where's dat young one gone to?" said she, standing in the back doorway among the honeysuckles and fanning herself vigorously with the two corners of her apron.

" She's out there, somewhere; I saw her running down the walk, while they were at dinner," answered Mary.

" She's clean gone mad about dat are Wash, I do b'lieve."

" Indade, Ruth, it's not Master Wash, but yourself that's put her by so."

" Oh, go 'long! what's old Ruth done to de chile ?"

" You're always teasing her about being a nurse and scrub, and all that, in the kitchen with black folks."

" And where's the differ, I'd like to know, if white folks puts themselves and their chillen into the kitchen, 'long of black folks, they must put up with black folk's sass, I reckon;" said Ruth, with a toss of her turbaned head that showed how much she felt herself superior in place and position to the red armed Hibernian by her side.

" Och, Ruth thin, ye needn't be throwing out your hints and insinuations; it's not the snapping of my finger I cares for ye'es, no how, but it's meself knows," said Mary, " that when ye reminded her of it she just set to howling, and then the mistress above, what should she do but take it into her head the maid had sore eyes, and Miss Livy was cranky and driv her out; youve only to call her in, and she's sweet tempered as a lamb, Die is, and she'll do your bidding."

" Lord a massy!" exclaimed Ruth, " what a muss!" and she called Die from the steps and turned to her work, giving out a low, jolly laugh that went croaking over the house like the turning of a coffee mill.

Ruth had once been a slave in some branch of the maternal ancestry in Virginia, and had been trans-ported into a state of freedom for her eminent vir-tues, and to the care of Mrs. Hancock's mother in early life. She had been with the family from its beginning—been nurse and almost mother to all the older children, and loved them as well as she could love anything but her own. There *was* one—the child of her own childhood, born to her in slavery, taken from her arms at three years old, and never after seen or heard from, who remained to her affectionate heart the lone star of life's horizon. " My little boy was a beauty," she used to say to those who gained her confidence, " 'twas as white as you, and had pretty, soft-brown hair, and it curled cunning—why, *I* ain't black; my father was a white man, mammy told me, 'fore she died, and my Neptune was whiter yet."

" And who was his father, Ruth ?"

" It's long ago, long ago; mor'n fifty year, and I was only a little gal, when the darling pickaninny came to me; didn't know nothing only to lub him day and night. One Christmas night, we folks had a frolic in the quarter, and Pomp played the banjo, and we danced purty nigh till morning, and I got awful tired; for I was spry then, and all the boys wanted to dance with me," and the old cook would straighten herself proudly—" and I got awful tired. 'Twas agin rules to stay up so long, and I sneaked home to my cabin, just as the morning was coming over the mountain, and into my straw in the corner, where I had left ' Nepy ' fast asleep when I went out, and my baby wa'nt there. I hunted the cabin over, and he war'nt nowhere. I ran to my mother to see if she had come in the night and fetched him, and she said 'No.' I screamed and cried, and called up everybody, but nobody had seen my chile. By and by old Lucy, the granny of us all, she come to me, as I was raving 'round."

"Ruth," said she, "don't take on so; he'll never come agin; he was too white and too purty to live 'mong us niggers, and they've took him away, I know; I had lots in my day, more'n I have got fingers and toes, and they took 'em all, all, every one, way to the markets, some when dey got big, some when dey was little."

"Oh, Lucy!" I screamed, loud as I could yell, loud as painter in the woods, you think the've tuk him for good?"

"Yes, chile, tuk him for good; he'll **nebber** come back no more."

"Oh, Lucy, and they tuk all yourn?"

"Ebery one, ebery one; Sambo he was first, Caroline and Venus, Tom and Jerry, Mat and Harry, Sue and Jenny, Bill and Steve, Nanny and Nellie, she was the purtiest one, as white as your'n, and little Eli, Cyrus and John, all, all, all."

"All gone? what did they tuk all your'n for, and leave Betsy all her'n?"

"I was most white, you know, and Betsy ain't, and mine was whiter," and old Lucy put her head down to my ear, and whispered, 'old massa's children, ebery one of 'em, ebery one, ebery one, too white, too purty.'"

" Where does they tuk 'em ?" I asked.

" I was mistress's maid, you know, and once when she tuk me with her to Washington, when master was a representor or something, the hotel was full of yaller boys and gals a waitin' on table, and doing all sorts of things, and then I knowed where they'd all gone to. Ruth, honey, don't take on, the Lord knows what's best for you and me, and we're only niggers, if we is half white folks."

"I will have my child, I will have my child," I yelled louder and louder.

" No use, chile, no use, him gone foreber ; but don't hab no more white ones, gal ; they's purty, but they makes heaps of trouble."

" I cried and pouted, and took the sulks, and wouldn't work, and I got an awful whipping, and massa swore he'd sell me to the traders ; but young mas'r coaxed him up to gib me to missus's mother ; his sister and her man moved out of Virginy, way up in Maine, and she tuk me 'long, and then come a law that made me free ; but my purty baby—I love mas'r Wash, now, better than anything on airth, 'cept him, and I wouldn't love Jesus if I wasn't sure he'd give me back my chile, some time."

Such was Ruth's humble narrative, now and then told with sobs and tears, to some one she loved and trusted ; "must tell somebody," she used to say, "to keep the old heart from bursting."

Ruth stood in the kitchen door, and feeling tender towards the faithful, merry maiden, whom she had helped into trouble, she turned and waddled down the alley, to what she knew was the children's favorite retreat, and clapped her hand on Die's shoulder before she was aware of her proximity.

"What's the matter now, you little, sucking, bossy calf, crying your eyes out 'cause old Ruth jest got funny about ye? I'm sorry, and ye musn't lay it up against old Ruth."

"Oh, Ruth, will they tell me to go to Jessie?"

"Never mind, never mind, come now and help me wash all dem dishes, Mary will take care of Jessie; never think a bit more about it, chile, old Ruth fix it all right."

Die sprang to her feet, as thoughts of her duty entered her brain once more. "Yes, I will, aunty, I want to help you; it's so warm, and I know you are tired."

"Laws help the chile, she's good as ever, and her eyes ain't red a specck; why, Die Dinmont, you're the purtyest gal I ever did see; your eyes sore, dem purty eyes, brown as chestnuts, and bright as Wenus, when she comes out at night, as Wash told me they call her up there in the sky. Just like of missus' tantrums and Livey's swells, big squeal for little wool, as somebody said, you know, when he sheared de pig," and another hearty laugh shook the mountain of fat.

"What makes you laugh, Ruth?" asked Die.

"Laws, to think what a hubbub got kicked up, just 'cause poor old me called you scrub and nuss gal."

"Oh, don't!" gasped Die, catching Ruth by the arm, as if to avert impending danger.

The dream was gone, broken, scattered by a word, as a beautiful bubble, upon which are mirrored the bright forms of cloud and sky, of flower and tree, in the gorgeous hues of the rainbow, is annihilated with a breath. Gone, all gone, was the beautiful vision of the hour, and the disenchanted maiden followed Ruth with slow, mechanical steps to the kitchen.

She had fallen, even Aunt Ruth's strong arm could not uphold her, fallen from hope, happiness and love, into the depths of conscious degradation; fallen from the side of the fair-faced youth, who for an hour had been to her an angel of light, down beneath his scorn as a menial, his mother's nurse, one that worked out for old clothes and cold victuals, whose father was almost a vagabond, whose whole life was a disgrace. Like an intuition she saw and felt the whole truth; but she worked on, and by no word or sign revealed to those about her the fearful change that one short day had wrought in her whole nature. She worked on as speedily and neatly as she ever did, neglecting no minute duty until the last task of the kitchen was completed, and Ruth said:

"Now it's all righted up, honey, and since they won't let you up stairs for fear of them sore eyes," and Ruth laughed again, "I'll fill your basket heaping, chile, and you may just go 'long home and send Tom for more, 'cause I hain't got one splinter of kindling."

" Oh, Ruth, not all that," exclaimed Die, as nearly the whole great roast went into the basket.

" Oh, go long now, you jest look at all them vittles cooked up to waste. Didn't eat nuthin, and this hot weather," and in went a turkey minus a wing and leg and a bit of breast, and a large piece of fish followed.

" But Ruth—"

" No use in this tarnal world, all spile fore morning," and in went a dish loaded with bits of pie and a huge bowl of pudding to keep it company.

Die lifted her hands again in remonstrance.

" Lord a massa, chile ! what do you know about it ? There's more vittles in the house than ud keep you'ns a week, and you think old Ruth's going to let it all spile and go to them pigs ?"

Die was silent, for she felt the truth and knew well that the supplies had been close at home for many days.

" And Die, honey, I'se awful sorry, I fretted you this morning, for you is the best gal and the very purtyest one I ever did see in all my life, and the smartest too. I jest wish missis had one like you ; but them chillen, oh, go long, what 'em good for."

" Nettie is good, Ruth," spoke up Die, earnestly.

" Well so she be, good as common, but there's Miss Livey, she's no manner of count, and Miss Emma's just as sweet as pinks and posies she is, but that's all, every mite, can't do nothin', and they'll spile my pickaninny sending him all about alone, and he on'y a boy—and getting up these here big doings every time he comes; don't old Ruth know? don't she? hain't she seen 'um go down, these rich 'uns, down, down, down, with their wine and things, down, down, down, till the dust of the valley covered their wickedness? And Wash was my boy, I nursed him in my bosom night and day, cold and hot, and I lubbed him, and now he's been home five long hours and never come down to see his old mammy."

Here the faithful old servant broke down with a great sob that seemed like an earthquake in a small mountain. Ruth could talk pretty good English when she chose, and fall back to the dialect of the plantation, mixing things ludicrously at times. She was grieved now, and gathering her kitchen apron over her head, she bade Die, in a voice choked with emotion, " Go 'long, chile, and send Tom with them kindlin'."

Die took up her heavy load and went her way; the sun was yet above the horizon ; at another time her step would have been buoyant and her burden light. There would have been but one leading thought—how happy they will all be with this feast of things which has fallen from the rich man's table. Now far other and sadder reflections , made her young brain ache to bursting, and her load seemed heavy; why was she so miserable? She had done no wrong. Why were the Hancocks so rich and the Dinmonts so poor? What could she do for her father? and here rushed in a thought that put to

flight all others, and for the moment engrossed her.
" Father," she said to herself, " is too good and tender a man to be a drunkard; how happy we could
all be if he would not buy whisky ; how wicked he is
when he does get it.   Dear, good mother toiling and
wasting her days in such a place. I have taught
them to read, and they can read the Bible I got for
them of Nettie out of the old closet, and they are
better; and how Tom studies.   Oh, it is only a little
step upward, and how shall I go higher, what shall
I do, what shall I do?" Setting her basket down
upon the grass in a fence corner, and seating herself upon a stone among the elder bushes full of
berries, she leaned her weary, aching head against
the rails, and her tearful eyes fell upon a violet in
full bloom in the hollow of a fence rail, bright, sweet
and cheerful.   The thought took possession of her,
" God put it there in that humble place instead of in
the rich ground of the garden bed, and it has struggled and grown and done its best, and so will I.
No vain regrets shall waste my strength or make my
head ache any more to-night.   Sweet little violet,
good bye," and raising her basket, she rose and
walked speedily and resolutely on towards her
home.

Tom had not come from his work, and two
younger ones were sent with each a load of kindlings, and a half dozen pints of wild June berries
from the hillside for Aunt Ruth.

The deal table, white and clear as a marble slab

(Mary Dinmont was neat to a fault) was set out under the trees at the back door, the dishes arranged and the feast prepared. Not until the little hands of the younger ones had been filled and little hearts and stomachs staid with the broken bits that had been sent in profusion in the basket, did Die allow herself time to chat and cheer her mother's sad heart. They were waiting for Tom and hoping for the father, and meantime the boys returned with burdens as heavy as they could bear; for Ruth, good soul, all mellowed into kindness by Die's ready help and the thoughtful present of the mother, had spared no pains to make their little arms ache.

" Mother," said Die, " sit up and have your cup of tea. You look so tired."

" Wait for him, wait for him."

" No, mother, dear, you know he may be very late; take a cup now and then when he comes."

" Die, he didn't come last night."

" Mother, didn't come home at all ?"

" No; there's trouble, dear, a coming."

" You don't think he is—" Die could not say the words.

" True as you live; it's all over. He's tired of the books and brings home the jug again, and we are almost starved."

" Well, we have learned to bear and suffer, mother. This is a terrible disappointment, but we've had many months of better times, and all is not lost, so drink your cup of tea, and eat a bit of this nice buttered rusk."

With a ready hand the tea was poured, and **the** discouraged woman, cheered and strengthened, roused herself and began to ask questions.

"What kept you last night?"

"You know, mother, they were expecting young Mr. Hancock to-day."

"That needn't have kept you."

The quick eye of Mary Dinmont detected the blush that mounted to the very roots of Die's hair at the bare allusion to the cause of her detention.

"They had a great deal to do and wanted a big dinner to-day to honor his return, and Ruth wanted me late."

"Did he come?"

"Yes, at one this afternoon."

"Is he nice?"

"I only saw him a moment; he was good looking." Die said this as she stooped by the fire to arrange the tea-pot.

"Die," said Mary, "it's a great thing to have learning; I never could have lived this summer through if I hadn't had my Bible that you have taught me how to read."

"We are doing a good deal better, mother, dear. Tom is getting along nicely, and I have got so I can play beautiful tunes on the piano; and while I am tending baby, scouring knives and picking over peas and beans, I lay the books and papers beside me and keep reading and learning verses. And all the boys learn so fast. and father now reads the paper. Oh, mother if he would quit going there."

" He never will, Die, because he thinks it's right
to go; he says if it's wrong to drink it, it's wrong for
Judge Hancock to make it, and he needs a whisky
bitters just as much as the Judge needs wine."

Both were silent for a time; the shades of evening
were falling; Tom did not get home; all the younger
children were given their supper, and a new paper
that Ruth had sent, a large lettered handbill for a
quack medicine, had been duly paraded and read
through and spelled out, even little Luly shouting
and clapping her hands at the red, green and blue,
with which it was ornamented. Quietly Die moved
her mother's old rocking chair with its half broken
seat out into the moonlight, and her own little bench
beside it, and gathering the children about her, she
sang for them the sweet tunes she had learned so
readily from the ladies of the "Lodge." Soon all
were asleep but herself and the waiting wife and
mother; and but for that relentless sting, that terrible pain that never dies in the heart of wife or daughter when the loved ones are tempted and falling,
even they in their fullness of love might have been
happy; but there was a wearing pain that none can
ever feel until some dear one has been sacrificed
beneath the wheels of the crushing Juggernaut of
all civilized lands—the worshipped idol, Alcohol,
dragging at their heart-strings.

" Die," said the mother, after a long silence.

" What, mother."

" Your father said last night," here she choked and

her voice almost refused to utter the coming words, "your father said last night that he wasn't going to let you stay at Judge Hancock's any longer, that Mrs. Frobish, down at the Oxbow, said she'd give you high wages, and I know he'll want you to go."

"Never, mother, never; anything but that."

"He says you don't get wages."

"I get more than wages mother; meat, drink, clothes, books, and chances to learn; money could not buy the half they give me."

"I know that, but if he says you must what will you do?"

"He won't be so cruel as to take me from Nettie, from the beautiful garden, the house so nice and clean, and good old Ruth and my sweet baby. Oh, mother, don't let him; help me," and the terrified girl clung to her mother's hand in agony.

CHAPTER VII.

MORE TROUBLE.

IT was a scene that might have inspired the pencil of Raphael, so pure, so calm, and yet so full of light and life, because so full of human love. The pale-faced mother, with her weary, aching head against the one high part of the broken chair, at her feet the devoted daughter, with features of a Madonna, her large, deep, loving, brown eyes swimming in tears that she held back with a stern will, her long hair beautifully plaited and wound like a shining crown around her head ; while resting her curly pate upon her shoulder, her little dimpled face turned outward in the moonlight, and supported by the loving arm, slept Luly. At her feet, nestled as close to the motherly sister as possible, lay the younger boys: One had thrown a pretty foot up against her knee, whils the other had stretched up his chubby hand and clasped the fingers of his mother's as they lay listlessly upon her lap.

The moon rode high, and sent her beams down through the foliage of he clms in silvery flecks, transfiguring and illuminating the whole scene.

Mother and daughter had been silent for several moments, when the shrill notes of a whip-poor-will that had fluttered into the branches of the tree overhead startled Luly, and she turned her peachy cheek to the lips of Die with a childish, dreamy laugh that seemed like an echo to the note of the bird.

" So you won't go to Frobish's, Diana?" said the mother.

" No, mother."

" Wouldn't it be better in some ways !"

" No ways, mother."

" Why won't you go? You would be more like folks there. Mrs. Frobish was once his mother's hired girl."

" And that's one of the reasons why I would never go there. She has grown into her place, and she would expect all those who were her help to do as she once did, to live and be what she once was."

" She seems a nice woman now."

" Yes, at the parlor door, but I have seen her in the bar-room, I have heard her in the kitchen, and I have watched in the hall; they send me there of errands, and I see and know."

" But the wages?"

" I know they pay well; and she once said if I would come and be chamber-girl, in the best rooms, answer the front door bell, and wait on lady and gentlemen travellers, she would give me two dollars a week ; and the gentlemen would give me lots of pretty things, and the little boys could come down and get enough to keep us."

" That's so Die, and we're *so* poor."

" Mother, I saw and felt all she meant—I will not go. I go there?" and the aroused girl laid Luly down upon her knees, the sweet face turned upward in the moonlight. " Go there and have these little darling brothers coming daily into that back yard and bar-room, to see the sights and hear the sounds I once heard and saw there? To have Tom, our dear Tom, coming there to see me, and perhaps fall-ing into the ways of the place."

" Well, well child, let's put these children to bed."

" More than all, mother, to stay there of nights, to be called to draw liquor for—"

" Oh ! child," almost shrieked Mary, " I don't want you to go, I only wanted to see if you was sure you wouldn't ; I'd rather see you lay dead at my feet, than to have you go there and live as Julia Lee does."

" I never will."

" That's what I told him day before yesterday, and he went away awful huffy ; he said you'd worked up there at the " Lodge " nigh three years for noth-ing, and he wouldn't stand it ; that he'd been to Squire Lyman, and he said that he had a right in law to bind you to Frobish, just as I was bound to old Bent, and to keep you there and use your wages till you was eighteen, and he swore he'd do it."

Die rose without another word and carried Luly into the house, while the mother wakened the boys

and led them to their resting places. The bell of
Oxbow church was sounding nine, and mechanically
the hands of the two women began to clear away
the food and dishes from the table under the tree,
that had been waiting for Heckel Dinmont.   Just as
they were carrying it between them silently to the
place, they were startled by a sound that both knew
too well.   A wild, drunken screech, halfway between
pain and joy, came echoing round the point of the
hill, and then the voice of the man talking, laughing
and hallooing, for Heck had a way of duplicating
himself when in his cups.   He was always two, and
sometimes three or more, and carried on conversations that were as ludicrous as they were sad.   It
was but a little way from the point of the hill to the
cottage, and his words were soon intelligible to the
listeners, and ran as follows:

"Heigho, whoa! hold on, Heck, don't go to scar-
ing them shemales of your'n. Lord Harry, won't
the old woman be mad, won't you catch it, Heck?
Well, (hic) ain't you a pretty fellow, anyhow; two
days of drunk. Hold on, Dinmont, you don't say
I'm drunk? You are, old fellow, whew! yes you
are, all day in them pig styes for a dollar. D—n!
Hold up, Heck, don't swear, you promised her you
wouldn't. And I won't, Dinmont; whew! Dinmont,
you're a gentleman, *you* are; stick to your words.
Where in the d—l Heck—dont you use bad words,
where's that gate? It used to be here, it's got lost.
Stop Heck, stop right where you are, no use hunting

a gate when you can't find it; whew!—will you call
somebody now, Dinmont, *you're* a gentleman, sing
out."

"D-i-a-n-a!" called out the maudlin man in the
softest tones he could control, "Diana!" Diana did
not answer.

"You Die!" yelled the maniac, "Why don't you
come and find the gate, you—hussy, the gate, the
gate, don't you hear? the gate, find me the gate, or
I'll—. Hush Heck, don't swear, you said you
wouldn't and that gal of yours is a jewel, Heck, if
you are an old drunken cuss, and that's just what
you are, by—there you are again—Diana dear, come
and find the gate for your father. There, Mr. Dinmont, that's what I call doing things like a gentleman. Diana, you devilish young one, come and
find"—"I'm coming, father," answered Die, still
three or four rods above the spot where the hapless
victim was groping about in the fence corner hunting for a gate that he had always been promising to
make, but had never completed. She bounded over
the rails that gave no other sign of an entrance
than their well-worn smoothness, and the absence
of one upon the top which had been thrown off, and
rested half way down upon the outside on a log of
wood, while, upon the inside a frail attempt at a stile
accelerated the passage to the road.

"There, father, there is no gate you know."

"No gate? where's the gate gone, my sweety,
who's stole the gate?"

"You forgot to make it, don't you remember. You couldn't find the rails."

"Whe-e-w! but ain't that jolly? ho, ho, ho, forgot to make the gate, ho, ho, ho. Heck, you old rantankerous obfusticated scalliwag; hunting for a gate and there wan't no gate." Roaring and shouting, Heck followed the moving impulse—the hands Diana gave, until he had reached the log which supported the rail, then stumbling against it, he sat down and broke out into a bacchanalian song:

" It's past the art of man,
  Let him do the best he can,
  To make a scolding woman hold her tongue, tongue, tongue,
  To make a scolding woman hold her tongue, tongue, tongue."

" Father, can you get over the fence?"

"No," shouted the man with emphasis. "Sit down here, I ain't a going in there. She'll scold," whispered he, "but I'll preach you a sermon, by Jupiter I will. That ain't swearing, is it?"

Die had never seen her father so drunk before; she had found him silly and maudlin, but always tender and full of love speeches and witless exclamations, only a fool. Now he seemed both fool and madman, idiotic, and lunatic. She urged: but he would not get up or make one effort towards the house; the night dews were falling, and the shrieks and drunken yells had startled the dogs, whose,—

" Loud mouthed roar
  Re-echoed from the other shore."

People came out on the other side of the river with their lights, and the nearest neighbors were startled by the unearthly sounds. "Please, father, do come in the house, you frighten the people, some-body will be coming to see what is the matter."

"Let 'em come," said Heck, "let 'em come, Die!" and he broke into a hysterical cry, "they'll find Mr. Dinmont,—and he's a gentleman, Die, he's a gentle-man, they'll find him pretty badly used up."

At this pathetic break down Die was joined by her mother.

"Heckel Dinmont," said the wife sharply.

"Good gracious, Die," exclaimed the besotted husband, "she's coming, don't you let her know, I'll get right up, we'll find the gate, I swear—no, I won't, Die, I won't swear, but I went down there, and he said, yes he did, he'd give you two dollars a week, and he offered to treat, and you know sweety I haven't had a drop for a long time, and I did, I drank it, and I cleaned his pig styes and he give me a dollar,—and I got five drinks for twenty cents,—that wan't much, or, let me see, I got twenty drinks for five cents, which was it, but Die, he got it all back, every cent, and then Die, that woman of his— I tell you the Devil is a woman; that woman came out and drove me off with a cowhide."

"Father it's damp out here. Come in, I brought you some supper, some of the feast that was got up to welcome home young Hancock and his college chum; roast turkey, bread and butter and cake, and a good cup of tea, come let us help you."

Dinmont tried to rise, but he was too far gone, he rolled off beside the log into the dead leaves and corn husks that had blown into the recess and usually made a bed for the hogs on the street, and there he lay muttering his incoherent thoughts, utterly unable to rise. Diana, almost paralyzed with painful emotion, led her mother back, saying softly, " It's no use, he is too bad to get up, and too heavy for us to lift. I will bring out a blanket and cover him, and set beside him in my old cloak till he comes to,—dear mother, go to bed."

" Oh, my husband, my child, my God!" were the only words forced up from the suffering heart, and throwing herself beside her little girl, she promised to sleep if she could.

Before Die returned to the fence corner her father was fast asleep. Covering him carefully, and laying his hat over his brow, she wrapped her own covering about her and sat down to watch away the night at the other end of the log, her back against the fence.

May we apply the words of the poet to this child of sorrow ? May we change them to suit this case ?

> " In that lone and long night watching,
>   Skies above and earth below,
>   She was taught a higher wisdom
>   Than your babbling schoolmen know ;
> God, stars and silence taught her, as His angels only can,
> That the one sole, sacred thing beneath the cope of heaven is
>   man."

Now to her newly awakened consciousness of the rights of the human being, came the clear impression of the constant wrong that was being perpetrated upon all the people by that great piece of machinery called the still-house; and there, while she choked down the tide of woe, that asked relief in tears silently, under the starry dome of heaven, she resolved to faint not and fail not in her endeavors to save her father from the grasp of the liquor dealer, from the temptations of the intoxicating cup.

Men of the nation, do you see her there? this girl whom you profess to protect, this child for whom you have made laws, sitting alone by the highway, watching the father whom you in your wisdom have constituted her natural protection,—her father whom your licensed rumseller has poisoned, whom your tolerated and protected manufactories have converted into a senseless, helpless *animal*. There they are, look at them; there they will remain till the night dews shall dampen the locks of the maiden, and the terrors of her lonely unprotected life snall cause her heart to throb with agonies, to which the physical tortures of the inquisitions were luxuries, and you will not raise your hands to help her though she die. And he that lies groveling in the nest of the brute, shall rise from his debauch and go forth to add his voice to yours, in ruling a nation. He will stand by you as an equal, and you will all unite your strength to make the curse more potent, the road to perdition more swift and sure for yourselves, your

children, and your children's children, until the nation
shall travail in sorrow and the cry of mourning go
forth at noonday, at eve, and in the precious hours of
the sun's rising, for there shall be one dead in every
house, and there shall be none left to bury this ruin
from your sight.

Heckel Dinmont slept deeply, muttering incoherently now and then, all the while seeming to be
burthened with a nightmare consciousness that he
had done his daughter an immense wrong.

Diana kept the solemn watch until the clock
chimed one; the sound partially awoke the sleeper,
and he aroused himself and sat upright, looking
around him, above and below, at the stars and the
green hills; he rubbed his forehead and seemed
struggling to recall the incidents that had brought
him to the position he seemed to be occupying.
"God of mercy," he at last spoke in a low voice,
"how came I here? I have been drunk again after
all, all her goodness to me, all her teaching, all her
trying, and I swore here under this very moonlight,
on my bended knees, that I would never again get
drunk. ˙Oh! Heckel Dinmont, how low you have
brought yourself, lying in the fence corner with the
hogs. Well," and here the jovial nature of the man
(only partly sobered) asserted itself, "they do say
the wheel of fortune is round, and when a fellow
gets top, whichever way it goes, he must come down,
and if he gets to the bottom he must come up.
Here I am out at midnight, drunk in a fence corner

among the hogs; drunk on old Frobish's cheap whisky, paid for with money earned by cleaning pig styes. Ugh! if I ain't at the bottom, who is, I'd like to know?" and he chuckled a low miserable laugh and attempted to rise; "and right by my own door too,—I'm not sober—I'll not go in. She'd—well who'd blame her, and I couldn't bear it; it would make me mad, and I—I won't; Die would hear me, poor girl, poor girl, poor girl; I love her better'n my eyes. I won't go in; they shan't know what a wretch I've been." Gaining, after several struggles an upright posture, steadying himself by the fence corner, he at last struck out toward the road in the direction of Oxbow, muttering, "she shall never know, she shall never know."

Die stepped quickly after him and laid her hand on his shoulder. "Father, I do know all, and so does mother."

"Oh! my good God!" exclaimed the frightened man. "My child! my girl, is it you or your ghost?"

"It is me; come in with me, father; I have watched you long, and now I want to sleep, and so must you," and drawing him gently in the right direction, he yielded implicitly to her impulse, climbed the fence and was soon asleep beside his wife, whose eyes had not been closed through all these weary hours.

Die dropped herself upon the mattress of straw, by the side of her brothers, and burdened as was her soul with the terrors of the night, the relief was so great that she soon fell asleep and did not waken until the song of the birds, and the crowing of the cocks aroused her to her daily task. Her father was already up and dressed, and was bringing in wood for the morning fire. He did not look at Die or speak to her, but moodily went on with his work, kneeling upon the hearth and trying to blow into a blaze with bits of straw a half extinguished coal. Die ran out to the spring, bathed her face and hands and entered all glowing with health and youth, which throws off sorrow with the first opportunity. She was not happy; but the pressure of last night's misery had been lessened.

"Here, father, dear, is a basin of fresh water for you. What a nice fire you have started."

"Die," said Heck, in a subdued tone.

"What is it, father?"

"Will she scold me?"

"No, I guess not."

"Will you kiss me, Die?"

"Yes, indeed I will," and suiting the action to the word, she put both arms around his neck and kissed him tenderly. At the same moment Mary came from behind the partition that screened her bed and said, with as cheery a voice as she could control, "Good morning, glad you are at home again."

Heck was humbled and subdued, and without speaking another word he took the bucket from its shelf and went for water to make the tea. There was abundance of the last night's feast to serve for the breakfast of the household, and while all hearts were troubled and beating with suppressed emotion, each one was striving in some way to lift the cloud and let in the light.

"There," said Die, "I must go. Ruth said I must come early."

"I'll go with you to the corner."

"Won't you hoe out the potatoes this morning, Heckel?" said Mary, kindly, "and fix my leach, too?"

"Yes, pretty soon; it's too wet yet."

"To-night, mother," said Die, gaily, "I'll bring a new book—such a nice story, 'Pilgrim's Progress,' —and I'll read it all aloud to you. You'll be here, father, won't you?"

"Yes, I will, Die."

"And Tom is coming to-night," shouted one of the boys, as father and Die climbed the stile and took their way toward the "Lodge."

"Die," said the father, "how long have you lived up there?"

"Two years and a half."

"Have they ever paid you any thing?"

"Oh, yes, indeed, *so* much of everything, victuals and clothes, and books and—"

"I know all that, but money, have they paid you any money?"

"No, but so many things that money could not buy; why, father, I read as well as Nettie, and Miss Jones, the teacher, says I play the piano better."

"I know, I know, but—"

"And, father, my slippers and cushion took **the** premium at the fair, if they did go in Miss Olivia's name."

"But that ain't money."

"Isn't it better? We should spend the money, but I shall always know how to read, sing and play, and work nice things, and one of these days, oh, father, if you only will help us, I'll make all these things worth money to us all."

"Die, how can I help you?"

"Shall I tell you? Won't you be angry with me?"

"No, child," and the poor victim of rum, trembling in every nerve, overcome by shame and contrition and softened by love, turned his face away to hide the gushing tears, that despite himself were rolling down his cheeks.

"Go right back now, father, fix up mother's leach so she can work to-day, and then Mr. Harris left word yesterday that he wanted you to shingle his barn. Mother will let the potatoes wait till to-morrow, or Tom and I will hoe them to-night by moonlight. Come home to-night."

"Diana, I will," and he turned and went his **way** with bowed head. Die sped on to her work.

CHAPTER VIII.

GORDON PENITENT.

As the lightning darts upon the object that inter-
cepts its path, and in an instant rives it asunder,
scattering and blighting all things near, even so did
that one fiery glance of the inebriate eye of a beloved
son enter the soul of the mother, and at once fell her
to the floor.

It was the unseen, unthought of cloud in the
noonday of hope and joy that shone in the throbbing heart of the woman and the mother.   Gordon's
absence of a year, the continued good reports,
coupled with the fact that he had never before so
long maintained any position of credit, had filled the
minds of the parents with a hope that in the bosom
of Mrs. Rand, amounted to an almost frantic joy.
Deep as was her love, fertile and ingenious as was
her fund of excuses, and her theories of the reasons
and causes of Gordon's shortcomings, down in her
heart of hearts there was ever a consciousness of his
wrong habits and a fear of the ultimate consequences
of his untrained early life.   Her love was the
mother's instinct ungoverned by reason.   She could

have borne any amount of physical pain without an outcry for this love's sake; she could have been nailed to the cross for him and died, that he might live and be happy. But there was a crucifixion of her spiritual tenderness that she could not bear. To make him even temporarily unhappy, to see him suffer even the slightest disappointment or inconvenience, was to her far more excruciating than physical torture. Fearfully had this reckless, high-spirited, indulged boy tried her. Co-equal with fear and anxiety on his behalf, was the all-pervading happiness that soothed and calmed her as she read his filial letters, and heard from time to time of his progress and good behavior,—and now he was coming—he was near. This pleasure amounted to almost an unbearable pain in its intensity. She had seen him, in her imagination, spring from the stage coach, bound from his father's embrace to her own; and all this had changed with one look, one grasp of the hand. She had felt instead upon her expectant lips the kiss of a drunkard. It was too terrible. Well hath it been sung:

"There is no pain like a mother's pain,
  When the children of her love
Go forth to the world in the ways of sin.
  She mourns like a wounded dove,
Her heart is withered her hope is crushed,
And her wail goes forth till her voice is hushed."

All that long, weary afternoon and night did Peter Rand bear his burden of agony alone by the bedside,

of his wife. Indifferent as were his feelings on the
wedding day, or made up as they were of pride in
the beauty, yet unfaded, of the stately woman, and
admiration of her learning and position; his good,
amiable nature could not resist the influences of her
calm, dutiful life. He had respected and esteemed
her and at the last loved her, not with that passion-
ate glow that might blaze into enthusiasm in a
younger nature, but with a steady and enduring
warmth that burned on, though little oil was ever
poured into the lamp to increase the light. He
could not tell her of this growing feeling, nor could
she find language to make him comprehend how
much he had become to her in the absence of Gordon, who for so many years had absorbed her
emotions and energies. Now he thought she was
dying and all the pent up fires burst forth. "Would
she die?" he asked himself as he knelt by her bed.
She had aroused herself to speak but one sentence,
"Let no one into the house; call no help for me,"
and thus she lay hour after hour with closed eyes,
white as the pillow beneath her head. Without the
motion of a finger, her pulse yet beat, her lips
quivered and the eyelids seemed trying to lift themselves, when a deeper moan than usual burst from
the heart of her husband and reached her ear.

The servants were ordered to watch the chamber
of the young man with assiduous care, while Mrs.
Maloney, who was at once a kind of nurse and
doctor, performed all necessary functions for her
patrons, though not without remonstrance.

"Indade, Mr. Rand, I think it's running in the face of Providence not to have the doctor. It's an ignorant body I am myself, and barrin common sickness and the rheumatics and the fevers, I'd not turn a hand, but the misthress is in a bad way, and the likes of it is past me."

"We will wait till morning, Mrs. Maloney, then if she is no better we will call a doctor."

"No," came from the parched lips of the invalid, and that "No" was decisive and the doctor was not called. From morn till eve, from eve till midnight, from midnight till morning, the watcher kept his place; possibly Peter Rand slept hasty naps as he stood upon his knees, by the bedside of his inanimate wife, holding her hand in his, or pressing his palm upon her brow, sometimes dropping his head upon her pillow, while the one earnest prayer unspoken, but none the less felt, went forth continually, "Oh Father, be merciful."

At last, after the long hours, as the sun rose in the sky, Gordon aroused from his stupid slumber,— aroused as such young ardent natures will, sobered and somewhat refreshed, though still weak and trembling. As soon as he was sufficiently awake to comprehend his situation he sprang from his bed with a bound. To say that the recollection shocked him would not be exactly the truth; that he was really repentant is equally wanting foundation in fact. He knew only that he did not mean to, that it **was** not him, not the *man* that had behaved so badly, but the vile stuff he had drank, and he **was** ashamed.

" By Jupiter," he exclaimed mentally, " must a fellow be blamed for what he does when he is tight? but I'll be good now, I've had my spree. If it were not for *her*, I would not care."

As with a lightning shock, the light and life had almost passed from the body of Helen Rand, so with a flash it returned to thrill every nerve with pain and fear. With his first step upon the floor, over her head, she had returned to consciousness. Through board, beam and plaster she felt the force of his magnetism, opened her eyes, and laying her hand on her husband's brow, as it rested near her on the pillow, she said whisperingly:

" Go to him, dear; tell him I forgive him, and bring him to me."

" Can you bear it now?" answered Mr. Rand in questioning alarm.

" I cannot bear his absence. Call Mrs. Maloney, and tell Bridget to have his coffee ready."

Mr. Rand left the room, joyful that his wife had spoken, yet failing in the slightest degree to comprehend the subtle influence that could so operate on her nature. To him it seemed only *not hypocrisy*, of that he knew her incapable. It was all a mystery, and as such he received it and let it pass, saying to himself, " Nobody ever did or ever will understand a woman." Every feeling of his soul revolted against a compromise with his unruly boy; and shaken by contending emotion, by love, respect and pity for his wife, and indignation against Gordon for making so much trouble, he did not think of the sin to be repented of. He paused in the hall, and strode up and down the long room, to equalize his temper before he would ascend to the culprit. "*I* do not forgive; no, not one jot. I will not say I do, but I will tell him his mother is better and asks for him, and they may settle it between them." Thus resolving he sought the misguided youth.

Gordon had dressed hastily and was about to descend. He knew he had been overcome, but not a vestige of recollection of the scene at home remained in his mind. His encounter with Max in the stage coach, the firing off his pistol, throwing his knife over the bank into the river, having his arms pinioned down by the strong force of Wash, were all remembered; then his sleep, then calling for a drink at the Oxbow, (aye, he cursed himself for that), and after that—nothing. So he was ready to go below without a blush, and in doing so he met his father on the stairs.

"Good morning father," said the youth reaching out his hand. "I'm afraid I have been behaving very badly, but I hope, sir, you will pardon me for this once. I had been steady so long that a little indulgence unsettled me; I certainly did not think I should be so affected."

"Yes sir," said the father sternly, "we were all aware of your unsettled condition. My forgiveness

will depend on your future good behaviour. Your
mother wishes to see you; neither she nor I have
slept during the night, and I fear she will die; you
have nearly killed—"

"Father, what have I done?" cried Gordon in
alarm.

"Done, you reckless scapegrace! come home and
thrown yourself into your mother's arms drunk,
drunk as a beast—but go to her room. If you can
soothe her by prayers of penitence and resolutions
of better conduct in the future, in Heaven's name
do so."

Gordon felt himself a man, at least so near it as
to be entitled to more respect from his father. He
had seen men older than himself, and wiser than he
was expected to be—men holding high positions of
honor and trust—every day of their lives drinking
more than *he* had indulged in, disguised before the
world, and making fools of themselves, and yet
called honorable men; he had seen the first and best
women of society giving the hand, and passing the
jest with the reeling wine drinkers; he had found
that the indulgence of appetite, even to the most
disgusting excess, was only called a weakness among
those who aspired to higher callings and were received in the ranks of more elevated social circles,
than he, Gordon Rand, ever hoped to gain; and why
should he, though a boy, be thus sternly met, after
he had asked forgiveness? With the bearing of a
lord he passed down the stairs without another word,

and banged the door that separated the hall and the
entrance to his mother's room behind him. No
sooner did he find himself in her presence than all
his angry philosophy gave way, and with a cry of
grief, not over his sin but over her prostrate and
death-like form, he fell upon his knees beside her,
clasping her cold almost lifeless hand between his
own, sobbed out his penitence and was forgiven.
There is no sanctum so sacred as that where the sinner, and sinned against, meet and mingle their tears
of penitence and love. Truly has it been said,
" There is joy over one sinner that repenteth, more
than over ninety and nine that need no repentance."

Mr. Rand and Gordon met at the breakfast table
an hour after the interview on the stairs. It was a
cold, constrained meeting. Few words were spoken
and very little was eaten.

" And sure you're missing the mistress at the head
of the table," said Bridget, as she placed the plate
of well browned waffles before the pair, " Come,
cheer up, sir, she'll be better for the dinner I'm
thinking; you usen to be liken' the waffles before
you went, master Gordon, take this one, now, and
the honey is beautiful."

" No more, thank you, Bridget."

" Not one? and what's come over me boy? not
one! an' I call yer a boy axing yer pardon, and yer
taller nor yer father the-day, an' a crop on your chin
this blessed minit, an' we all so happy yesterday
thinking of yer comin,' and now your poor mother
sick in the bed. taken so sudden like."

Mr. Rand left the table, and Gordon recalled to all the bitterness of his position by the careless loving words of the old familiar servant, leaned his head on the table and sobbed like a child.

"Oh now Gordie, darling, don't be takin' on, its better your mother'll be by the dinner, I'm sure, for I never seed her so bright. Just a young gal she was, with her pink flowers in her cap yesterday. It's the joy that killed her entirely, she'll be herself in no time, wid ye's to love and care for her."

"It was I that killed her," sobbed out Gordon.

"Och for ye's now, since ye says it yourself, it was the whisky, my boy, that broke her heart, but what does it signify; ye're not worse than the rest, they're all at it, big and little, and will, while it's poured out in streams that would float the flat boat down the Alleghany. It's Pat tells me all about it, there, don't be spillin' yerself."

Gordon could stand no more, and pushing back his chair went back again to his room and shut himself from sight, resolving and re-resolving as millions have done before him, never again to so anger his kind father, or wring with sorrow, his loving, indulgent, forgiving mother. Gordon never let his sprees, as he called them, last more than one or two days; once duly sober, he would remain so for weeks, yet, when he allowed himself to be tempted, he seldom stopped short of a most disgraceful carousal. Alcoholic beverages drove him into maniac madness.

6

Three long tedious weeks of the vacation passed ere Mrs. Rand was able to join her husband and Gordon at the table in the dining room. In the meantime Gordie had behaved well. With a deep oath he had sworn not to taste anything that would intoxicate while his vacation lasted. Such a vow the high spirited boy would keep. At college he had learned to control his temper. Subject to the continual friction with minds like his own, petted and spoiled by indulgence as he had been, he had seen and felt the preposterousness of his own habits, and apart from the yielding influence of his mother, and under the direct calming power of Maxwell Carter, he was fast gaining the mastery of those passions that embittered much of his life. He would have his " good times," his evenings among the boys when they " elevated the ancient Henry " to their heart's content. Max always went home to his mother at night and left them. He read his chapter for her, and heard her sweet humble voice lifted in prayer or joined his own in earnest entreaty to her silent aspirations. As a tutor in some of the minor classes, by which he earned his own tuition, he had gained an almost controlling influence over the boys, and over Gordon with the rest. Perhaps there was no drop more bitter in the cup which Gordon had mixed for his own lips on that journey home, than the knowledge that Max had seen his madness. To atone now was his determination.

CHAPTER IX.

AGNES FROBISH.

THE front entrance of Oxbow Hotel, or that part
occupied by the family as parlors, bed rooms and
sitting room for respectable people, opened upon a
long street, shaded with elms, which street made the
main part of the village fronting the river. On the
end of the house, or the "L," as it was called, was
the entrance for common travellers, or comers and
goers; while at the back, opening into the stable
yards and sheds for coaches and wagons, was the
bar-room entrance. Over the wagon sheds were
rooms finished and furnished for 'ostlers, coach
drivers and roving travelers, such as made up much
of the custom and profit of the old house.

Between this attractive front and the busy, bustling, noisy rear, there was no more communion than
upon two different blocks of the village; nor did
those who inhabited the neatly kept bed-rooms and
parlors understand any more of the fearful conditions sometimes found under the same roof, than do
the dwellers of the sumptuous apartments of the
Astor, to the lewd rowdyism of the Five Points.

Into these shady rooms Mrs. Frobish (who went herself, for Agnes, to the railroad station, lest she should meet ought that was contaminating,) ushered her darling, and watched her with sedulous care, lest, by any means, she should come to know of the vices that were growing thrivingly under her father's eye.   They had their own pretty tea table, and if Mr. Frobish preferred to eat in the long dining room, and by his jolly jest and loud laughter cheer his guests, he left a vacant place in his stomach, and a spare minute from his duties as landlord, to enjoy a pleasant meal and chat with his snug little household, often repeating, in his own breezy way,

> " There's six cakes for four of us,
> And thank the Lord there's no more of us."

For there was always Mr. Frobish and wife, Agnes, and a sister of the father, that had taken the place of humble companion in the house when Agnes was only a baby, a still, prim maiden of two score, that kept the parlors in the best of order, and never meddled, as she averred, with other people's affairs.

Three days after the arrival of the three college students in the neighborhood of Oxbow, the landlord burst like a southwest breeze into the parlor where Aggie, mother and aunt were at work, and seizing Aggie round the waist whirled her around the ample room in a merry waltz, while he whistled to his own footsteps.

"Hi, Aggie, my bird, got something to tell you," he cried, as soon as he could gain breath to speak.

" And what is it, papa mine ?"

" What will you give to know ?"

" Three kisses and my best tune on the piano."

" Good," exclaimed the happy father, " give me my fee in advance."

" Not I ; you don't make your travelers pay before they eat, or settle for lodging before bed time."

" Can't help it, I lose by it, and I'm going to turn a new leaf."

" Not on me," said Aggie, pouting prettily.

" Well, then, give me the first installment and I'll treat you to the first part of the news."

" Three kisses were given with a will ; the tall father lifting his little dot of a daughter each time to a level with his own jolly face.

" Now, what is it ?"

" Gordon Rand has got home."

" Oh, papa ! is that all ?" and the little lips pretended dissatisfaction, while the red blood mounted to her very temples.

" And is not that enough, you gypsy ; are you not going to ask after your old playmate ?"

Aggie was across the room, flying to hide her emotion, and already touching the keys of her father's favorite air.

" I must pay my last installment," answered back the merry maiden.

" Have you seen him ?" asked Mrs. Frobish.

" Yes, he was down this morning."

" And how did he look ?"

"Wait till Aggie gets through; look at them fingers, though, can't she go it?" And the happy father laughed all over his face in his pride and joy.

"Now tell," said the mother, as Aggie joined the circle again.

"Tell what?"

"How Gordon looks after a year at Yale among the aristocracy."

"Just as he always did, the handsomest chap in these diggins, only more so."

"Has he grown?"

"About a head; he stands six feet, every inch of it, and he's played base ball and rowed boats till every inch of the six feet shows a man; has a moustache on his chin, Aggie."

"Well, what's that to me?" responded the young coquette.

"Oh, papa, don't plague puss, she can't bear it." This was said aside, and then with a louder voice: "What's that story they've got about that he drinks?"

"Who tells it," asked the landlord.

"They said the driver had been telling some such thing."

"What! Gordie, mother?" asked Aggie in alarm.

"All nonsense, some of Mike Pheelan's yarns; he's always blacking somebody."

"Hancock's son came in the same coach and another young man that's a graduate, and they say

the three are going out into the mountains geolo-
gizing."

" Who is the other, what's his name?" asked Aggie,
who was trembling like an aspen at the mere suspicion that her old familiar playmate was guilty of a
wrong action.

" His name is Maxwell Carter. Of a good family,
I am told, but his father took the wine cup too freely,
ran in debt, lost his position as a lawyer, before his
boy was ten years old, and so to get himself out of
trouble he blew his brains out like a man, and left
his wife to get herself and boy out of trouble as well
as she could.

" That's an idea, papa mine, 'like a man.' "

" Yes, duck, precisely like a *man*. Did you ever
know a woman do such a trick? Kill herself and
leave her child to starve?"

" Oh, that's what you mean. Good, now go on,
what else do you know?"

" That his mother, who had been reared a lady and
had married this man against her father's will, earned
her own and her little boy's bread by washing for the
students, and young Max, as they called him, came
for and carried home the clothes, went to the common school, studied his lessons, chopped his mother's
wood, built fires and blacked boots for the lazy
drones, and got lots of dimes and learning, made
everybody his friend, worked his way through college, and has come out first best of the whole class."

" Oh, isn't that grand," cried Aggie, clapping her
hands.

" Have you seen him?" asked Mrs. Frobish.

" Yes, he and Wash drove round just now, and called and shook hands."

" Is he good looking, papa?"

" Oh, you puss; good looking?   No."

" Oh, fie! papa, you know what I mean; does he look as smart as you say he is?"

" Well, I've seen better looking chaps than he, and I should never have picked him out for a genius at first sight; but he has a bright, keen eye, and eyebrows that arch over them as the old rocks do yonder over the Alleghany—dark hair and eyes—well, I can't tell you much about him, for he had such a stream of merry talk and wit that I only remember his voice, way and laugh.   Don't wonder he got along."

" The boys will have a happy time the next eight weeks," said Mrs. Frobish, uneasily looking up at Aggie to see what impression the news had made; but Aggie was busy with her embroidery and seemed already to have forgotten the young student, whose voice, way and laugh had made such an impression. A rap at the door called the host of the Oxbow to his duty, but not until Mrs. Frobish had propounded one more question to her husband.

" Frobish, is he rich?"

" What, Carter?   Poor as a shad in July."

" How in the world came the Hancocks to take up with such a man as that?" queried the shrewd landlady, as she followed her husband from the room.

Aggie kept on with her work, singing in a low tone scraps of favorite airs, while quiet Aunt Phebe industriously mended the rents in sheets and darned the breaking table-cloths, or rehemmed the failing napkins. Half an hour had passed without a word.

"Aunt Phebe, don't you think Oxbow is a queer place?" asked Aggie, looking up from her work and away out of the window and over the hill tops, as if she saw in the glowing sky something that startled her.

"Why, yes, I think it may be rather queer."

"And ain't Judge Hancock a queer man? owns all Oxbow, don't he, pretty nearly?"

"He's very rich and respectable, your ma says."

"I was only a little girl when I went away, and didn't think much. Now when I go along the streets of Pittsburg, walking out with Miss Gold-thwaite, I see all over the city warehouses, tavern stands, and signs on the sides of doors, 'Best Han-cock.' One day I ventured to ask what it meant and they told me it meant whisky manufactured at Oxbow and branded 'Hancock,' because he owned all the distillery and workshops, and people, too, soul and body, and that his whisky was the ruin of the working people."

"Well, Aggie, I reckon that was about it; Oxbow *is* awful."

"And then one night we went to hear a temper-ance lecture, and the man said he'd been to the Oxbow distillery, and he told how many millions of

6*

gallons were made every year, and how many men in the place were drinking men, and, oh! Aunt Phebe, right there before everybody he told of the Oxbow tavern, and described my father and mother, and told how they kept liquor and enticed people into drunkenness, and how the men were stowed away in the sheds over the stables. Oh, Aunt Phebe, the tale he told was dreadful."

"You don't say," said the little woman, with up-raised hands and eyes.

"Yes, and that was not all. He told about Hiram Nelson, that awful boy, you know, that killed Mr. Johnson, (I read it in the newspapers) how Hiram worked for the Judge and supported his widowed mother, and was such a good, steady boy, till he was induced to take whisky bitters by the minister's wife when he had the toothache, and then he got to drinking more and more, and they turned him out of the church for drinking after the minister had advised him not to join a temperance society; that he played cards and drank with the lawyers and jurymen at Oxbow, and when he got wild and cross with whisky and committed that murder in his frenzy, they hung him for it, and that Judge Hancock made the whisky, licensed the tavern, and the jury voted him the right to do so, and then because this boy, as he called him, did exactly what they gave him a chance to do—drink to madness—they took his life."

"It's jest so," said Aunt Phebe.

"Aunt Phebe, my father sells whisky, and makes drunkards?"

"He sells whisky and the drunkards make themselves. Child, no man needn't drink that ain't a mind to. Men ought to be moderate, your ma says."

The rich blood was leaving Aggie's cheek, but she pressed on with her simple earnest questions, though every answer seemed tearing away the foundations of her innocent happiness.

"And he said too that my grandfather died a —".

"Drunkard: yes, he did," said Phebe.

"And his father before him?"

"Yes, Aggie, and five boys; and four girls have married drunkards and are all dead now."

"My great grandfather and three great uncles, my grandfather and two uncles, and my four aunts; he said just that—that temperance lecturer—and I said it was a lie, and you say it was true."

"Yes, but don't tell your ma. You ought to know, you ought to know, Aggie."

The quiet woman had spoken out. In a few short sentences she had revealed great agonies, and frightened at her own temerity, trembling from head to foot, she relapsed once more into her usual silence and took up her darning, leaving the great secret which had blighted her own life untold. But we will tell it.

Her lover had been killed by a drunkard before her face in that tavern bar-room, and after years of confinement in a lunatic asylum the poor broken-hearted girl came back to mend and darn and dust under the kindly supervision of her brother.

Once more almost gasping with the weight that had so suddenly fallen upon her, the young girl queried:

"Aunt Phebe, does my father drink whisky?"

"No, never drank a drop, since,—since he married your ma." She essayed to say, "since my lover was killed," but the words died in her throat. "And your mother would die before she would taste the accursed stuff."

Choking with the dreadful lump that had raised in her windpipe, Phebe gathered up her basket and left the room only saying:

"Don't tell your ma, never, that I told you, but your pa would have died a drunkard like the rest, if she hadn't made him quit."

The room occupied by the two young men at "Hancock Lodge," looked out over the garden and upon the mountain sides as they rose in majesty in the distance, the river, the sweeping hills and valleys of the opposite shore above, and a bow window had been thrown out upon the wall and hung like a bird's nest opening into the chamber. Upon this balcony, shaded with vines and odorous with summer flowers, the two young men had withdrawn one morning after their arrival and sat familiarly conversing.

Perhaps we had better give the reader a little

deeper insight into the character of Max before we proceed farther. It has already been stated that he had graduated with uncommon honors, and yet under extreme difficulties. His progress had been slow and sure; with the assistance he felt compelled to give his mother his days of freedom had been delayed, yet every hour of his time had been employed. One year before he had completed his college studies, he had stood by her bedside and received her dying blessing, and the assurance that in his whole life he had never by any dereliction of duty given her lasting pain. His grief was deep; but it was for himself. He knew well that she was only taken up higher from a bodily trouble that weighed upon her and caused constant suffering, therefore he had bowed his head with a true submissiveness to the hand of wisdom laid so heavily upon him, saying: "Thy will be done, oh! Father, not mine." Resolved to follow his father's profession, he had, in those intervals when he was kept by the side of his mother, read and studied his Blackstone, Bacon, Kent, &c., and when he left the shades of the ancient elms at twenty-three, knew more of law than many a student that is admitted with high commendations to that roll of honor—a legalized member of the Bar. To George (as the students of Yale called George W. Hancock) he had been so closely and intimately allied, that he had become as an elder brother. George knowing that Max wished to push on toward the west, locate himself in some thriving town, pursue the requisite study and enter at once into the business of life, had negotiated with his father, asking a position for his friend as a clerk and writer in his office, where he could fill the time required and come out under the excellent auspices of the influential Judge. The Judge who happened to need such an appendage, acceded to the proposal, and Max accompanied his friend home with the intention, all other things answering to his needs, to commence his life-work in the growing town of Oxbow, which had long been the seat of justice (so called) in the county.

The two young men had been sitting silent, the young heir of those splendid mountains and valleys tipped back in his easy chair, his feet only a few inches above his head, enjoying the fragrance of a perfumed Havana. His companion who had never used the weed, sat upright in all the energy of conscious manhood, taking in large draughts of life, light and beauty, that were satisfying his inner self with extreme pleasure. At last, as if he could not contain within himself all that inspiring prospect, he turned to his drowsy, smoking friend, and addressed him:

"George, my boy, (he always called him George) do you know you are a very happy fellow?"

"Why so, Max?" answered the boy addressed, springing to an upright position.

"There, now, I can afford to talk to you since you assume the bearing of a live man."

"Go ahead," said George, pitching his cigar out among the dewy grasses.

"Well, sir, first you have plenty of good brain and brawn."

"Granted, my most respectable and wise tutor."

"Second, you have a splendid education for your years."

"Granted, again, my most honored friend."

"Thirdly, you have youth and health."

"Precisely what I esteem hugely."

"Fourthly, a very desirable social position."

"Never were truer words spoken."

"Fifthly, untold influence to help you on in the world."

"More than I am thankful for."

"Sixthly, you are the heir to all this beauty and wealth, all this outspread glory of God's heritage, and you ought to be ashamed of yourself."

"Thank you, my very good friend and most excellent mentor, what particular one of all these enumerated blessings am I to blush for."

"For the depravity, my dear fellow, that leads you to throw yourself into your easy chair and indulge in that demoralizing employment from which I have just aroused you."

"Humph! the same old story, Max. You're fanatical on the tobacco line."

"Not a particle, sir; here you are surrounded with all this immensity of blessings, and a seventhly which I forgot to mention."

"Pray what may that be? I have no conception what link you can add to the golden chain already wrought."

"Your good looks."

"Rather a detriment to a man."

"A mistake, sir; but let me go on; here you are surrounded with all this immensity of good fortune, and should guard as sedulously as you would the apple of your eye from harm, every fibre of your young body, for the great work which it will bring to you by and by—searching as with a lighted candle into the uses of every atom, of every nerve, muscle, bone and sinew, of this wonderful fabric which you own—how you may preserve it for the best good of the whole manhood; and instead, you are already vitiating the brain, which is the seat of life and strength, with your poison stimulant— tobacco."

"Are you sure it is a poison?"

"As sure as I am that you told me the exact truth when you described to me your sensations with your first cigar."

"Did I tell you?" said the smoker coloring.

"You told me how your knees trembled, your head swam, you vomited and fell prostrate upon the ground and lay without sense or motion. Was it not poison?"

George did not reply.

"Your father said last evening, when he saw you smoking upon the lawn, 'I deeply regret that my son has taken hold of that fashionable folly. I ruined my health by it while young, and am convinced that I am not the man I should have been had I never indulged in what is falsely called the luxury of a cigar.'"

"Go on," said George, with a sickly attempt at a smile.

"And your mother added her regret to your father's, 'I am so sorry,' she said, 'that Washington has fallen into that bad habit. Tobacco is very unpleasant and always oppressive to me.'"

"Did my mother say that?"

"She did, and I do not know how you can ever carry that unpleasant odor into her presence again, and oppress that fragile, loving being that you call mother, for your own momentary indulgence with the weed, even if it were not injurious."

"You put the matter pretty strong, Max. A habit so universal that one can hardly be comfortable in any company of gentlemen without joining in its enjoyment, seems to me need not call out quite so hearty a denunciation."

"To tell you the plain simple truth, my dear fellow, you never come into my presence with your cigar or meerschaum all asmoke, that I do not feel that I am made less a man by your presence."

"Will you explain?"

"Most willingly. If you smoke and smoke near me, you throw out into the atmosphere a contaminating odor that I must breathe whether I will or no, or I must leave your presence. Even your hair and your clothes carry the perfume. Have I not heard you railing bitterly against the deplorable practice among young ladies of perfuming their hair and kerchiefs, till they suffocated you in church or parlor beyond endurance?"

The culprit winced.

"And many a day, George, while I have bent over you as your preceptor, your perfumes have sickened me to loathing."

"You did not say so."

"Your professors said all I thought necessary, and you were surrounded by associates that would have broken down any attempt toward reformation; besides it will require all your physical force, all your mental resolution, all there is of you, George, for a little while, to resist this overbearing tyrant that is carrying you along to your own injury."

"And now you think I have leisure for the conflict?'

"That's it exactly, my fine fellow. I'm not going to ask you to quit, not I, but I am going to tell you exactly what I think about it, and let your own sense of right and justice do the rest."

"I am sure I ought to be very much obliged for your excellent effort," answered the young heir, at the same time looking away as if to hide the perturbed and troubled look that clouded his face.

"But I am not done with you," resumed Max, "you are guilty once more, and must be reprimanded."

"What now? oh! most unmerciful of men," exclaimed George, throwing up his hands in a deprecating manner.

"Three months ago, at our spring vacation, you accompanied Walters, you remember, to Hartford."

"I remember, and a splendid week we made of it."

"No doubt; well, no sooner were the school days ended, than Gordon, with three others, took a run down to New York. He came home the fourth day, with the other boys, in much the same condition as when he returned here. It took the whole force to get him back and up to his room. It was after nightfall, and when they got him there, his howling and raving were likely to expose the whole party, for they were none of them too sober.

"Max, you don't tell me that Jerome Walters and Sydenham were on a spree?"

"Nothing short of it, George, and a disgraceful one, too."

George was all attention now.

"Well, they smuggled Gordon up to his room after bribing a drayman not to tell, and sent for me. He was raving; his sensitive nervous system all unhinged in a fair fit of delirium tremens, or as near it as possible; four days and nights without sleep, eating gluttonously and drinking day and night, till he went down a mere raving, howling madfellow."

"It was horrible."

"Yes, you may well say it was horrible. He wanted

drink, and when we refused him, his madness was such that to secure the windows, books, looking-glass and furniture we were obliged to tie him down by main force to his bedstead."

"Max, why did you not tell me this before?"

"I sent the others away; they were too drunk and too tired to help me, and I took charge of the poor fellow myself, and from Thursday eve until Sunday morning I stood by him, night and day, and brought him through."

"And saved him from eternal disgrace, for if he had been exposed, and expelled, as he would have been, he would have drank himself to death; I know him."

"You are right; but I, too, knew him, knew him as the most sensitive genius of the school, knew him as one overflowing with the very best of yielding human nature, a jewel in himself, too full of the genial suavity that intemperate men are made of. I knew that they had all four fallen in with demons in human shape that had drugged them with the worst of wines, and robbed them of nearly every dime they carried away with them. Gordon's diamond pin and watch, with curious forethought, he had left in the care of the landlord of the 'Continental,' when they went out the first night, and saved them. It was a horrible spree, but before I unlocked the door or let him out he was duly sober and repentant, promising that he would not touch, taste or handle one drop of alcoholic beverage, wine, beer or cider until the term ended."

" Has he kept his promise?"

" Yes, until the term was out, when you, George, tempted him at our dinner the other day, he lifted his glass, and you know what followed, and what a trial he was all the way home."

" If you had only told me."

" How could I without breaking my trust with him?"

" Max, you are a grand fellow; give us your hand."

" Here it is, my trusty friend," and he clasped in his broad palm the more delicate one of the tall scion of aristocracy with a wrench that was felt. " And now, George, I want you to help me save that gifted boy; we are to be here at home with him for eight weeks. Let us swear to each other, like the children of Rechab, that we will drink no more wine, and that we go to-morrow to this fallen sheep of the flock, and if the work is not already done, help to wash the fleece from the filth and mire into which he has fallen."

" I'll do all I can."

" You will not again lead him into temptation?"

" Not if I know myself."

" Enough, I will trust you. Gordon is too great and good a soul to be lost; he has been petted, humored and spoiled, but the real, sterling stuff is there, if only it can be saved from this consuming fire."

And so the conversation ended, and the two young

men wandered forth and found Gordon already repentant, and in evident alarm lest by some word or action or inuendo, they might reveal more to his father than he already knew of his former departures from duty. He took a walk with them to the hills, and in a few words, but deeply humbled, asked them to deal gently with him, and promised total abstinence while his vacation should last. Falling behind with Max he told him of his repeated and maddening dram at the Oxbow, of his mother's illness, of his own fearful retribution of pain and misery. Max promised help, and left Gordon somewhat lighter of heart than before they came, for he had said to himself with every miserable hour, " I've lost my two best friends."

*   *   *   *   *   *   *

George met Diana that evening in attendance upon Jessie in the garden, and frankly apologized for his rudeness, alleging that he was so overjoyed to get home, that he hardly knew what he was doing, and that Nettie had so often spoke of her as " her sister Die," that he almost felt he might claim the same relationship.

Die stammered a few awkward words of reply, and immediately withdrew with her charge.

She found her father at home, according to promise, her mother's hope renewed, Tom true to his appointment, and a few chapters of Pilgrim's Progress cheered them all. The potatoes had been hilled up.

So the week ended better than might have been
expected, because the actors that we have introduced
in our drama ceased to do evil and learned to do
well, which is the only true repentance for an erring
soul. But to no one of these actors was life the
same. There were spots upon the raiment of some
that could never be washed out, there were experiences for others that had opened up the vistas of life
in long, dim aisles, ending only in darkness. To
Diana, hope and despair seemed to join hands and
wave over her pinions of strangely contrasted hues.
Would her father ever be reclaimed? Could she
ever remove him from the influence of that distillery? Would he grow furious again, and use the
authority of law? Could she escape if such a fearful emergency should arise? Could she obliterate
that new image from her life, that seemed to have
taken possession of every avenue and to obtrude
upon her every thought? She could answer none
of these questions satisfactorily to her own soul, but
she could promise herself to be true and faithful
and do her best, and with this promise, looking up
into the clear, blue sky, studded with stars, ever
faithful, ever true, she felt the voice speaking to her,
" Maiden, be of good cheer," and hope triumphed.
Mary Dinmont was comforted. It took very little
t ɔ lift up her broken and bruised life. To see her
children fed, and happy; to see her husband once
more sober, was enough to calm and harmonize after
such severe trial. As the tortured limb feels easy

for the hour, when the weight that crushed it is removed, so Mary Dinmont felt the relief which had come after her despairing days.

Mrs. Rand saw her son dutiful and loving, and was comforted.

Poor little Aggie! on her gentle spirit had fallen a cloud, almost too dark and heavy to be penetrated. She did not weep, her mother had taught her from babyhood self-control, she did not cry out, but looking to the right and left, before and behind, she had no hope of escape from the tavern; she laid her load before Him who alone can comfort, and grew calmer. Had her prayer taken words, we should have heard the moan, " Oh, merciful Father, deliver me from the body of this death."

CHAPTER X.

THE LOVERS.

THE impression made upon the heart of the young heir of the Hancock estate by the face and form of Diana Dinmont, on the first day of his return home, had only been deepened and intensified by the daily interviews which chance and occasion presented for further acquaintance. True, he had met her as a servant girl, but that seemed only to enhance her beauty and add to the charm of her interesting character, as detailed day by day by the partial lips of Nettie. Her wonderful ability for learning, her exceedingly useful feats of housewifery, her adroitness with her needle, her exquisite taste in arranging and planning, and lastly her splendid voice and magic execution on the piano, all of which could hardly be exaggerated, were so much fuel added to a flame burning all too fiercely and unwisely. Almost daily they met somewhere in hall, garden or nursery, but only with timid glances as a servant did she allow herself to recognize the acquaintance begun so strangely. Nettie soon brought them into more affable terms. He came at last to call her

"Die," chatted with her when he found her setting
the parlor or dining room in order,—and he was
pretty sure to find her,—and by a hundred little
tokens, unseen and unfelt by others, let her know
that he was pleased to be near her and chat with her.
She persisted in being cold. Though her cheeks
would burn and her heart leap at the sound of his
footfall, yet she never encouraged the slightest
familiarity. When called to the parlor to exhibit
her almost intuitive power in music, by Nettie and
Emma, she complied with that blushing modesty
and unassuming grace which charmed every listener.

Rides on horseback, boat parties, fishing excursions, mountain explorations, and greenwood pic-
nics were the order of the day. Judge Hancock,
with his usual largeness of heart, proposed that Max
should give himself an entire relaxation from all
study and care for the vacation days, asserting that
ten years of such uninterrupted labor of body and
mind as his had been, deserved this unimportant reward; especially as George, who felt deeply his
indebtedness to Max, insisted that the latter should
share the sports and festivities of the vacation. The
recipient of all this generous kindness accepted and
felt no compunctions in accepting such agreeable
favors, particularly as he was assured in his own
mind that he needed the recruiting energies of sport
and leisure to enable him to take hold of his new
life with the vigor required.

Max, George and Gordon found merry and willing companions for all their excursions in Emma, Nettie and Agnes Frobish.

The cords of Miss Olivia's "facial predominance" seemed to contract visibly, drawing that already upturned member a little heavenward, whenever the idea intruded itself upon her troubled senses that Miss Agnes was *only* a tavern keeper's daughter, and Maxwell Carter the son of a woman known as one who earned her bread for years as a *wash-woman*. " How *could* brother Washington so lower himself." To escape all contamination, this most discreet young person took herself and her ascending nose off to Saratoga, where she found dignified representatives of illustrious households in plenty, where foreign Counts and doughty Dukes were in abundance, and where there was not the least danger of lowering her social position. Here she allowed her olfactory nerves to become sufficiently yielding to let her said nose down to its natural position of a snub. No one was very sorry of course at the absence of this discordant chord of the family harp, and no one was even for once heard to sing,—

> " The instrument hath lost a strand,
> The sweetest strand among them all."

Merry as Christmas bells the gay party went out at morn and returned at eve, spent the summer twilight in the spacious parlors of the Lodge, dancing quadrilles to Die's emphasized measures or Nettie's passable music, or on the front veranda of the superintendent's house on the hill, or in Mrs. Frobish's exquisitely kept drawing-room, planning each day the round of pleasure that should vivify the rainbow lustres of the next twenty-four hours.

Mrs. Frobish was joyful because Aggie was so happy. There was not a shade of suspicion in her mind that there could be any element in these out-goings or incomings to work evil to her darling. Mothers, in the intensity of their love, have been just as blind, many a time before, mayhap will be many a time again Could she have watched for an hour the great blue eyes of Gordon Rand, as they followed the lithe little figure of the quiet maiden, as it glided hither and thither, adding to every one's comfort and enhancing every one's happiness, or could she have seen the soft sweet look of contented pleasure that crept over the plain features and out of the dove-like orbs of her one precious jewel, as she sat by the side of Gordon at the boat-ride and pulled the opposite oar, his brawny hand encroach-ing upon her side, and covering her little palm and doing her work, always under a protest and reproof for his mischievous interference, possibly she might have taken the alarm and withdrawn her fluttering nestling from the basilisk proximity. But she saw nothing except that Aggie was enjoying the holidays extremely, and that her happiness cast a halo over her home life at the tavern which made it more charming. Yet Aggie did not forget all she had heard and many a tear stained her pillow when alone at night; she remembered Aunt Phebe's story.

Mrs. Frobish would have made no objection to the most devoted attentions of the Superintendent's only son and heir, if Aggie had been two years older. She had married herself at sixteen, and like most prudent mothers at forty was set against such baby marriages. "Let them wait till they have got through with their school books, outgrown their pinafores, can spell crucifixion without missing a letter," was her decided opinion, expressed to Mr. Frobish when talking of such matters.

"Rather guess, Rena," said the jolly landlord, "if we were back to that place we should do just so again."

"I rather guess we wouldn't," answered the dame emphatically.

He only remembered his pleasant hours, while her mother heart went back over long years and looked down into three little graves filled before their time, as she always insisted, because of the ignorant helplessness of the child mother, into whose hands the good Father gave them.

The mother was so happy in her daughter's happiness, so gratified that the Hancocks had opened their circle to her child, and so engrossed in the outfit that was to carry her without trouble through the coming year, that she did not see nor hear, and the blue eyes and brown eyes flashed secrets at will; the little hand had been laid confidingly in the brawny palm, and the pouting lips had given promise of eternal love and received the assurance

of many an uttered oath, that stars might be blotted
out, moons forget to wax and wane, but never
should the love that had been given fail in one jot
or tittle.   Gordie and Aggie were sworn lovers;
this love was not of to-day; it began long years ago,
when he drew her up hill on his sled in winter days,
that he might hold her before him in his arms as he
coasted down; when he divided with her his rich
juicy turnover that his mother made for his noonday lunch, and gave her his slate pencils and helped
her over the muddy ditches.   He was never petulant if Aggie was by, never exacting if she said
"don't Gordie."   His bad moods were when she was
not in the school, and his excuses found ready lodg-
ment in her open ears.   It was a child love growing
with their growth and strengthening with their
strength.   Will it last?   We shall see.

As easily and unresistingly Gordon and Agnes
allowed themselves to drop into love's tranquil sea
and be drowned in its sweet waters, so manfully
did George Hancock resist the waves into which he
had fallen, and resolve to wrestle with every surge
until he should gain the shore, and stand once more
a free man.   Resolves of the morning were forgotten before night.   To leave Die out of all his
arrangements; to eat the excellent pastry, the cold
meats, the pickles and preserves she had prepared,
to remember her at home, toiling out the hours for
old clothes and victuals—*Good God!* how should he
bear it? yet he must bear and suffer.   One slightest

hint of the internal commotion into which his boyish fancy was leading him, would have raised a
tumult that would have resulted in the expulsion of
Die from the house—probably from the neighborhood. The Judge would have paid heavy damages
to the landholder by sufferance—Heckel Dinmont—
rather than have had him as a near neighbor, if but
a hint of the real state of affairs had been revealed.
It is not sure that Heck himself, and his wife Mary
with him, with their intuitive perception of the fitness of things, would not have fled as from an impending ruin, had they known of the state of George
Hancock's thoughts and feelings toward their favorite child. They did not know, and so no storms
were raised either at the white house on the hill, or
the brown weather-stained domicil in the valley.

"Max come with me," said George with a disturbed look and manner one rainy evening, when
from sheer weariness of dissipation all parties had
decided to stay at home and rest.

"Not a walk this rainy night?"

"Only on the long veranda overlooking the garden."

The two young men sallied out, arm in arm.
They walked up and down, listening to the gurgling
music of the little streams which emptied themselves into sewers that traversed the well kept
grounds. The soft dropping of the rain upon the
vine leaves, the distant surly roll of thunder that
answered the flashes of lightning far away to the

west, all had their effect to induce gloom and sadness. As they were taking their turn on the end of
the walk overlooking the kitchen and business parts
of the house, the door opened and let out a sudden
flood of light upon the sombre starless dark.

"Take the umbrell', honey, you'll get wet to the
skin."

It was the kind voice of Ruth, as Die emerged
from the door with a basket upon one arm and a
pail of milk held by the opposite hand. A clear
rippling laugh went out over the dripping flowers
and leaves, as bright and cheery as the flashing
lamplight that revealed the shining beauty and
waked the birds and set them to twittering over
their guarded nests.

"The idea!" said the cheery voice, "of carrying
an umbrella ; where and how, Aunt Ruth, in my
teeth, as Nero carries my basket sometimes?"

"Pshaw now, so you can't, chile, and you'll get
soaking."

"No I won't, aunty. My hood is thick and this
good old cloak will not wet through, and I can run
like a quail you know. Good night."

"Good night, honey, the Lord bless you."

Before the old woman's prayer had fairly passed
her lips, the nimble footed maiden had turned into
a path among the shrubbery and was out of sight.
Ruth held up her light and watched as she disappeared, muttering—

"There ain't her match in this created world—the

purty cretur—and jest as good as she is purty, can't
see for my part what makes the difference. Here's
Die, just the best, turned out in this ere storm to
tramp wid dem heavy things (here Ruth let down
her language and love) to dat old cabin. Her
mother's good enough, and dem's mighty purty
picaninnies, but him's miserablest kind of white
trash, the miserablest kind him is. Gorry, wouldn't
Aunt Ruth like to wring him old neck?" And
twirling her lantern after the manner of taking off
a chicken's head, she stepped back into her kitchen
and closed the door, shutting out all the light from
the young men's eyes as suddenly as Diana had
taken all the life from the heart of one.

Whirling impetuously on his heel and carrying
his companion with him by his force, George strode
to the opposite end of the balcony, setting down his
boot heels with the tramp of a Grenadier. Not a
word had been uttered. After following his lead
three or more turns up and down, Max stopped
short—

" See here, young man, I've done about enough of
this stamping it back and forth on these sounding
boards in the damp and drizzle. If you have anything to say to me out with it."

" It's damnable!" exclaimed George with a vehemence that startled his companion.

" May I ask to what particular 'it' you would
apply your elegant expletive?"

" Max, for God's sake don't chafe me, I am dis-
7*

tracted; I want your advice, your help, your—"
George paused as wanting in words and strength to
finish his sentence.

Max answered soothingly, "My dear fellow, I
have seen and felt for many days that your spirit was
terribly galled, and have patiently waited your own
good time to reveal the irritants that were wounding
you. Let me know in what way I can comfort you;
what is it that looks to you so reprehensible as to
call out the unmanly words you have just spoken?"

"To see that girl," George answered impetuously,
"with her beauty, her genius, her talent, strength
and energy condemned to such a life."

"It is the fate of the masses," replied Max.

"No, I ask your pardon; the masses labor and
bear their burden contentedly without a struggle
or care, and live and die slaves to themselves, and
their own want of desire to elevate themselves.
But—"

"But here is a girl born for better things, you
fancy, than to work with her hands, to carry loads
upon her arms, and brave a warm evening shower,
to bear comfort and cheer to her mother, brothers
and sisters."

"You've a cool way of putting things."

"Is not that the proper way? If I am to soothe
your ruffled feathers or do you any good, I must
take the poetry out of this passion before I can
move you."

"Let me put the poetry into the matter first;

listen to me and understand me, for I am very wretched."

" I will wait your pleasure."

" The case is here; if I were to love the daughter of some purse proud millionaire, flashing with diamonds and gold and arrayed in costly garments, but having no more brains than a peacock, my father, mother and sisters, and that contemptible personage, Mrs. Grundy—I must call things by right names—would clap their hands and shout with enthusiasm. I should not find a straw to intercept my path."

" That is a clear statement, no poetry there."

" No, sir, but the hardest kind of prose."

" Now let's have the opposite picture."

" Well, here is a young girl that holds within herself all the requirements of a true and eloquent womanhood—minus only the diamonds and gold, the silks and laces. I love her, Max, with every nerve and tissue of my body and soul. I am rich at the attainment of my majority. I come into possession in my own right of a huge fortune, left me by my mother's brother, with a prospect of more in other directions than any prudent man can ever use, and yet here I am bound hand and foot like a galley slave by the conventionalisms and fashions of society."

" I do not see it."

" Would this Mrs. Grundy allow me in my own right to help this hapless girl?"

" Let me ask you would this hapless girl, as you call her, allow you in your own right to help her?"

" If the conventionalisms of society would permit, yes, I think she would."

" Permit me to say I think you vastly underrate that young lady's sterling worth if you do."

" Why should I not ?"

" Because it would be neither just or right on the broad scale. It might gratify you, and add to her already uncommon privileges for the time being."

" Please let me more fully comprehend your logic."

" Let us go back a little to strengthen my logic as you call it. You know we have been taught that all old adages have their foundations somewhere in truth, and though I am free to confess there are palpable wrongs to be felt in the organizations of society, the foundations of the social fabric rest as yet upon a pretty firm basis ; and all partial repairs only show the universal weakness of the frame work erected by our new Republicanism on the old weak walls."

" I confess I do not see where you are drifting, and I feel impatient with all the fine spun theories of the age about blood and—"

" Far be it from me, George, to throw one such flimsy rag into the scale to weigh down your sincerly good intentions with regard to this peerless young lady."

" What would you have me do?"

" Just nothing at all."

" Max, you villain, what are you driving at ?"

" Come with me to our room out of this bad air, and I will elaborate to your heart's content."

George yielded to his friend's suggestion, and seated in their pleasant room, the lamplight chasing out the shadows of night, Max resumed.

" According to the history given by Nettie and Emma, it is nearly three years since a frowsy headed, barefooted child of twelve or thirteen ˙years of age, in tattered garments, with uncultivated manners, presented herself at the kitchen door of this " Lodge," asking for charity, which she received. Following up her advantage, this little girl, finding the cook in straits now and then, offered to pick over the beans, gather the currants, grub the potatoes, scour knives and run errands. By and by, she made herself so generally useful that the autocrat of the lower cabinet besought the higher powers to instal her permanently, to become an assistant in whatever department her ready skill and willing hands were most needed; and that, as a return for those services, she should receive the cast off surplus of this lordly house."

" Good heavens ! to think of it; working two years or more for cold victuals and cast off clothes. Max, it makes my blood boil; it shall not be."

" Be patient—in this capacity of nurse and maid of all work she persuaded Nettie to teach her the alphabet, and having mastered that conquering key of knowledge she carries her treasure home and

divides with a whole household, teaches father,
mother and brothers how to read."

"It is wonderful."

"Right there; it *is* wonderful; but this child goes
on, learns of Ruth the art, trade and mastery of the
culinary department, and makes herself so useful
that it is a thing of joy to teach her. By way of
relieving Miss Olivia of her duties and headaches,
she grasps the niceties of *her* occupations and out-
grows her patron; catches the lessons of the music
teacher and appropriates to her own use that subtle
art which thousands toil for but never gain; waiting
upon well-bred ladies and listening to educated
gentlemen, she has caught the passing manners of
the age, and appropriated to her own use without
theft or intrusion, the artistic and subtle intricacies
of genteel refinement and breeding, and won the
love and confidence of every one of the household."

"And yet I am not to relieve—"

"Let me finish, if you please. In the two years,
or, at the most, three, in which this young lady has
been toiling for cold victuals and cast off garments,
has she taken no little steps upward? has she not, in
fact, under this spur of necessity, driven farther and
gone higher than could have been expected under
the most favorable circumstances!"

"I confess you speak the truth as it reveals itself
to me under your showing."

"And you say you love her?"

"As my own life."

" But let me put you on the witness stand and we will see if from your own lips you do not condemn yourself."

" I am ready for any examination."

" If this young girl had not been beautiful, had her hair been stiff and coarse, her skin brown, her eyes grey, her cheek bones high and angular and her mouth wide, would you have fallen in love at first sight ?"

" Probably not."

" Yet some plain-faced girl might be as worthy of your love; therefore it is hardly just to give help to those whom fortune has already favored and forget those for whom fate has done little."

" Then we are to have no personal partialities, no exclusiveness, no selfish loves."

" I did not say that. I only spoke of abstract justice, and in that light only have you any right to interfere with or disturb the relations of that girl's life."

" That may be good philosophy, but hang me if it's not execrable humanity."

" Not at all ; Diana is not yet sixteen, and you, my dear fellow, not yet twenty. Suppose you go to her to-morrow and declare your passion, and find it is returned in ample measure, could you propose marriage?"

" Of course not ; we are both too young."

" Suppose you offer her money?"

" There comes in the abhorrent system of society."

"Are you sure you are right there? is it society that ties your hands?"

"What else, what else?"

"Analyze yourself, my dear boy; is it not Diana herself that you are afraid of? If she were an ordinary beauty, vain of her face, shallow in her judgment, easily wooed, ready to meet you half way, would society, Mrs. Grundy, or all her satellites, have held you to your allegiance? Would you not weeks ago have laid your hand upon your wild flower; have perhaps soiled its beauty by offers of gifts and helps, which accepted, would have destroyed even to your own nostrils the matchless odor, and impelled you to cast it from you, though there might have been no broken law; you would have brought down the anathemas of Mrs. Grundy on your sinless head, and perpetrated a wrong upon your friend for which a lifetime would hardly atone—"

"Maxwell Carter, what do you take me for?"

"The honorable fellow that I know you to be. It is Diana Dinmont in her own matchless purity and dignity you fear, and not your father or mother, your stately sisters, or the critics of the social circle in which you move. Leave her as you would an unplucked lily, to her destiny; breathe into her unwilling ears no word of your love; ere two years have passed you may have outlived its fragrance."

"Never! never!"

"'Never' is a long year. Rest assured if this

uneducated, or *self*-educated girl is made of the stuff we give her credit for, she will climb higher in an accelerated ratio according to the momentum she has already gained."

" And I may lose her!"

" Never fear. If you remain of the same mind, and she is equally worthy, there will be a magnetic telegram somewhere quivering over the wires of life that will bring you together."

." But why not tell her now how much I love her? why not secure my prize while in reach?"

" George, believe me you could not do a more wicked thing; it would only be touching the vibrating wire so roughly as to snap it asunder. Perhaps, to put an end to all this effort, she could not in honor to herself or fidelity to her friends and benefactors, receive the slightest advance on your part. Be brave and true."

" Max, you have never loved."

" Haven't I, George? haven't I dared to look up, as far as you have looked down? Has not my whole soul quivered with torture, when I have remembered myself as the poor boy, blacking boots for money to buy a loaf of bread? thought of my gentle mother, the patient worker? of my almost unknown parentage? George, I have felt it *all*, and it was not society that bound me, but a chain of honesty and honor as strong as steel—enduring as the·everlasting mountains."

" Max," said George, rising to retire, "good night; I will think of all this—"

"Stay a moment. Now I am in the mood, let us go on. This idea of caste—the difference between rich and poor—will work itself out in time, and the man who has brains and hands, and is ready and willing to use them, will find his place and be honored among men. The only distinction that should be made among a free people is the distinction of worth. The Bible contains no truer aphorism than that the sins of the fathers shall be visited upon the children. In despotic Europe, hereditary descent makes the law of caste; but in our own glorious Republic, where every man stands as the representative of himself,—or will when we have outgrown our love of titles—only the brand of shame and dishonor will mar the bright escutcheon of the hero that worthily builds his own temple. I have seen the idol that I worshipped thrown down; have outgrown what I thought an enduring love; have lived to see and know,—that though I looked up as to a star to one, to brighten my path, the time will come when I shall look down and pass by what to me was once so high, so grandly beautiful. She loved me— I knew it—but she sold her young soul for gold and position; I am cured."

"God forbid that I should have your experience."

"You can't, for you are rich and strong. Diana, if she feels like selling her charms, can keep them for no higher market. Take comfort in that. Let her grow, if she has the force and power in her own soul to lift herself out of the 'slough of despond' and keep her face steadily turned toward the house 'Beautiful.' At the end of your college term, when you are your own man, and can afford with strong arm to walk by the side of the one you have chosen as your mate, then there will not be on the broad earth a voice that will bid you God speed more heartily than mine. Until then, keep your love like an acorn, to be planted in the future."

"And she in the meantime must labor and suffer in poverty."

"Is there not a soul-satisfying happiness in it? You pampered babes of wealth can never know the luxury of striving and winning, of suffering and growing strong."

"But she is a woman, and wealth and privilege locks and double locks its doors against the sex, and poverty for them has no keys to the entrances to its privileges."

"There, you have touched a chord that vibrates to my very soul, and I am ready to reiterate the words which opened our conversation. The restrictions upon the sex *are* damnable. Now, good night. I stand side by side in poverty and ignoble birth with your lady love; I have pulled through to manhood, and mean to go on, and by little steps upward reach a goal higher than I dare dream of to-night. Yes, I have 'hoed my own row,' and solemnly affirm to you that there has never been a time in my life when an offer of charity would not have hurt me. I have faith in Diana; the dove has no right to rest in the eyrie of the eagle. If she cannot soar to your side, you do not need her. I know her trials and I will be her friend; trust me."

"God bless you, Max, for these words. Good night; I will do as you say."

CHAPTER XI.

MARRIAGE OF OLIVIA.

The merry college vacation was ended. Wash and Gordon had returned to their studies. Nettie, who thought she loved Die as a sister, found when her hours were devoted to one moving in the same grade of society—one that could enter into and share all her amusements, could talk by the hour about dress and comprehend its importance as she did herself, and especially tattle about the house and entertain her with the exquisite bits of history of school-girl life—its fun and mischief, its jealousies and triumphs, its intrigues and conquests—that such a companion was, to say the least, very delightful. Gradually sister Die, who was nice when no one else was by, slipped into the background, and Aggie Frobish became the "dear love" of the maiden. Under the magic influence of Aggie, the bashful Nettie, just blossoming into sweet sixteen, was attacked with an uncontrollable desire to be sent to a boarding school; to go with Aggie, to room with her and share with her all the labors and joys of the year. Aided by the persuasion of Wash, father and mother gave consent, and the same coach carried four beating hearts, half sad, half joyful, from the "Lodge" gate on the same September morning.

Die was lonely; possibly there was a little heartache, but by no outward sign or token, did she allow the outside world to understand her inward struggles. What if George—as she preferred to call him—had gone without a word, she knew it was best; for what could he ever be to her. She loved him as she loved the clear starlight of evening, or the bloom of the flower, the gorgeous beauty and grandeur of the mountain sides—loved him because he was altogether loveable. She could no more help the feeling that thrilled her with pleasure when he was near, and left in her soul a sense of loneliness when he departed, than she could shut out of her nostrils the fragrance of the rosebud in her hands. Why should she blush for such a love. She did not, nor did she try in the least to exclude it from her heart as an unwelcome guest; she knew it was pure and true, and felt

> "'Twas better to have loved and lost,
> Than never to have loved at all."

And so she went on her way, quietly performing all her duties with a skillful and untiring hand.

Max who had rested till he longed for labor, entered upon his new life with that persevering energy which had marked all his years. Olivia surprised her father and mother, a few days after the

departure of George and Nettie, by a letter announcing her return the following week, and that
she should be accompanied by Col. Vandyke, a retired officer of wealth and station whom she had
met, and from whom she had received proposals of
marriage. He was not young but fine looking, re-
markably *distingue* in appearance, and belonged to
the very best society. "A perfect gentleman."

He had some urgent business to transact for the
Government which would require him to cross the
ocean immediately, and as he was to spend some
months in Europe, he urged a speedy consummation
of the marriage that she might accompany him.
She hoped her parents would make no objections as
she had fully made up her mind to marry the
Colonel, and hinted that as her own fortune was at
her disposal, she might now be supposed to have
arrived at years of discretion.

The Judge read the letter aloud, drew the fingers
of his left hand through his long grey whiskers, and
whistled a low tune, as if he thought there was some
doubt about the "years of discretion" having been
arrived at.

Mrs. Hancock covered her eyes and wept, while
Emma plied her father with questions.

"Oh, papa, whatever shall we do? Olivia going
to be married, and only think of it, in three weeks."

"That is the very thing she has kept us all thinking of this seven years," said the Judge with the
least bit of a tinge of censoriousness in his voice.

"Oh, papa, that's too bad for you to say‧ did you ever see Col. Vandyke?"

"Yes, I have met him in public."

"Do tell us about him, is he nice?"

"What do you mean, pussy, nice in his habits?

"No, of course not, is he good looking?"

"He used to be."

"Why, is he so old?"

"About my age I should think."

"And going to marry our Livia and she only twenty-five," exclaimed the agitated mother.

"She has chosen for herself, you see mother, and politely gives me to understand that this time she is her own mistress; we can only acquiesce."

"Poor Olivia," moaned the mother.

"We saved her once, dear," said the Judge, his voice a little husky in spite of his assumed indifference, and going over to the side of his wife, he laid his hand gently upon her brow and smoothed her hair with his long white fingers. "Mothers will be mothers," said he soothingly, "but we have kept our children a long time and must be willing they should do as we have done."

"But such an old man," said Emma.

It's her own choice, my pet. I must go now to the office. Don't let this trouble you, mother."

"It's so sudden."

"Good night!"

"Good night, papa. Oh I wish Nettie was here, or somebody to talk to. Dear me! what a time

we'll have getting up the wedding things; I shall
have to have a new dress and things. I wonder if
she'll want me to go to New York with her? will
we send for Nettie and Washington? won't Ruth be
in her glory making cake?" And the simple hearted Emma ran on in her childish way asking questions; each question like the stab of a sharp instru-
ment to the worn and weary heart beside her, until
a deep groan startled her into the consciousness
that her mother was thinking of something beyond
the dressing and cake-making—thinking back over
her own unsatisfied life.

It is a theory among philosophers that all earnest,
natural longings will somewhere or somehow meet
with a response—that in the economies of nature,
means are adapted to ends, and that all things work
and move in harmony, governed by the wise and
enduring laws of God. Yet they tell us in the same
breath that woman is made to love and man to reason. If this be so, can there be any true and
harmonious adaptation between man and woman?
Is men's love to be as evanescent as the spring with
its bursting buds and beauty, and woman's as enduring as the breath of her life? Can man's reason
ever satisfy woman's love? Is there not wrong
somewhere? Else why should we find at every turn
mismated hearts like those we have just parted.
Are not women taught to base too much of life's
happiness on love, while men are led out into all
minor likes to fill the measures of longing with

8

variety, with the swift race after wealth, fame and ambition, with all their thousand adjuncts that satisfy from the inherent force demanded to attain them.   Women, especially wealthy women, are thrown by the customs and laws of society out of the pale of usefulness.   Driven in upon themselves, they waste themselves in sighs and groans for want of something better to do.

"There, mamma dear, don't cry," said Emma, springing from her low stool to her mother's side and stooping to kiss her forehead.   "We'll get along with the wedding well enough, don't worry about it."

Entirely misunderstood by both husband and child, the mother could do no more than to suggest that she would like to be left alone to write to Olivia ; and Emma, gay as a butterfly, kissed her good night and flew on wings of hope to find companions in some other part of the house.

There was a commotion in the kitchen the next morning when, according to orders from headquarters, the announcement of the approaching wedding was made to the grand "sultana" of the cook stove.

"What's that you say, you Die, Miss Livy coming home to be married ?"

"Yes, Ruth, in three weeks."

"Dat old critter."

"Hush, Ruth, she's only twenty-five."

"Only twenty-five ! laws a massy, Die, it's twenty-five years if it's one since she's been cluckin' round, settin' up her feathers to try and git a beau."

"Oh, no, Ruth, not more than ten."

"Laws, chile, it seems twenty, she's so onpleasant, and now she's going! ho, ho, ho, ho—I shall split laughing, ha, ha, ha, ha, ha."

"Why, Ruth, are you really so glad?"

"Ain't I though, ha, ha, ha, to have her clean done gone out of the way with her neuralgia, her headache, her toothache and rheumatics, and pain in her back, or nervousness, ha, ha, ha, I laugh some of dis fat off sure 'fore I get through that wedding, ha, ha, ha."

"Poor Mrs. Hancock don't feel like laughing; she says it has made her down sick."

"I tell you what it is, Die, them folks what haint got no purpose under the light of the blessed sun, gits sick mighty easy. If missus hadn't Ruth in the kitchen and Mary in the parlor and nursery, and Die (bless ye) all over the house, she'd git up and do something; dat's it, chile. What 'em wants is a purpose, something to stir 'em up and keep 'em moving. Laws! too much money is a cuss, so it is."

"And what do you say to too little," said Die, laughing.

"Got me dere, chile," said the old woman, "and so Miss Livy's going to marry an old man, ha, ha, ha. Won't he have a sweet time of it?"

"Won't *she?* you mean."

"No I don't nither; haint I had her ever since she was born; don't I know he wants her money you see, goin' to Europe! Well, she's gone and done it at last," and with another convulsion of the huge body, the old cook went on with her preparations for dinner.

When Max came home at one he was informed of the new turn in affairs, and joined gayly with Emma in laying plans and suggesting arrangements. Letters came daily, full of orders, which were promptly carried out. Olivia informed them that her wardrobe would all be attended to in the city; Emma must send measures and directions to Madame Demorest, No. —, Broadway, immediately. Of course, Emma was delighted, and the Judge gave consent.

On the following day came news that cousin Montrose and wife, of Madison Avenue, and Miss Lilly Draper and Capt. Broadhead would be of the wedding party.

Then came a pressing note :

" Emma, you have always wanted a trip on the continent, wny not go with us? Col. V. says it's the thing. Don't think about getting ready, nothing we can get in this country will be fit to be seen over there. Tease papa and he will let you go, Die will take care of mamma—you *must* go.

" P. S.—I've just seen in the paper that father is to be the Republican choice for U. S. Senator. Col. V. says he'll be sure to get the election, then he and mamma can winter in Washington, and leave Die and Ruth with the little ones. Col. V. says you *must* go.   OLIVIA."

A new sensation went through the house like a whirlwind. Mrs. Hancock, she scarce knew why, wept afresh, though she plead that Emma might go; Wash wrote home, putting his request by the side of Olivia's; the Judge looked more sombre than ever, but matters of great national interest were pressing heavily upon his brain; no wonder his brow wore frowns. He ventured a few remonstrances, but was met with such a decided majority in the affirmative that he only said: "Fix it to suit yourselves, my dears," and walked off, as though a trip to Europe was of as little moment as a ride to Oxbow.

Emma having decided to go, Ruth laughed out of the wrong corner of her mouth, for she loved Emma.

The weeks glided swiftly away; the wedding party arrived; Wash came home for one day, and Nettie for a half week; moire antiques, pearls and satins, lace and orange blossoms floated through the old ancestral halls in sumptuous profusion; the words were spoken that blotted forever Olivia Hancock from the records of living things, and ushered into light and life Mrs. Col. Vandyke, at half-past ten on Thursday morning. The lunch was eaten, wine drank, the party said their farewells and took their departure at 12 M.

While the guests were receiving refreshments, Max had stood beside the clergyman, who had tied the knot; they were daintily tasting cakes and sweet meats, when wine was presented—the man of God took his glass, but Max bowed and refused.

"What, Mr. Carter, refuse wine on a wedding day?"

" I have never drank a glass of wine, Mr. Duncan,
and with God's blessing, I never will," replied Max
energetically.

" Considering our Savior's example at the wedding of Cana," resumed the Reverend, " it seems to
me you might indulge at such a time as this."

" I suppose," said Max, " all such wines as those
in your glass are fermented liquors?"

" Undoubtedly, the Judge is a connoisseur, and
keeps the best in market."

" It takes time to create fermentation," continued
Max, " and water that was turned into wine in a
moment could not have been the fermented juice of
the grape."

" Hem,—ha,—yes,—that's a thought, but what
objection have you to a good glass of wine?"

" My Bible teaches me that 'wine is a mocker,
strong drink is raging, and whosoever is deceived
thereby is not wise.' "

" Ah, true, but to take it in moderation?"

" I think the command stands 'touch not, taste
not, handle not the accursed thing.' "

" I remember the passage, yes; ahem, but we
have numerous others that speak of its use approv-
ingly."

" Such as," said Max, looking the advocate of wine
bibbing boldly in the face with his deep, searching,
gray eyes, " 'look not upon the wine when it is red,
when it sparkleth in the cup, when it worketh itself
aright,' as I see your glass of the Judge's best **is**
doing at this moment."

A move was now made by the party, and Max was obliged to leave his wine-drinking parson to attend to the departures. Passing that way a moment after, he saw the glass refilled, and the shepherd of the flock of Oxbow leading his lambs on in "moderation."

Judge Hancock, Washington and Nettie escorted the sisters to New York, leaving Die and Max to fill up the vacancies as best they could.

Die stood over the sobbing mother and soothed her grief with kind words and loving ways, cheering her with hopes and bright visions until, under the manipulation of her faithful hands, the weary woman fell asleep.

As soon as Die had quieted the mistress, she flew to the maids, finding Ruth in one of her fits of rare grumbling discontent.

"You see dem are eyes a shining, Diana?"

Ruth thought she must be very dignified on the first wedding of the household.

"What eyes, Ruth?"

"Dat old man's, what ain't got no hair on the top of him's head, on the place where the hair ought to grow."

"Col. Vandyke, you mean. Did his eyes shine?"

"Better guess 'em did."

"He was happy in his young bride."

"Oh, go 'long, didn't old Ruth stand right there looking at'em, through that hall door, and didn't I ree him fll his glass three times, and then run back and got a fourth while they was all kissing 'by-bys round?' "

"Die," said Ruth, with emphasis, "as sure as you're a born chile Miss Olivia has done gone married an old drunkard."

"Oh, Ruth!" exclaimed Die, clasping her hands together, "and Emma gone with them."

"Old Ruth ain't blind." The old faithful nurse covered her face with her apron and sobbed as if her heart would break.

"I didn't—want—that," she uttered in broken sentences, "I didn't want that, poor thing, poor thing, it's the Hancock fate."

"Be comforted, Ruth, may be it will not be as bad as you think."

The two arose, and under the stress of labor that awaited their hands set aside, if they did not forget, the black cloud that rested over the house. As the shadows of evening fell over the valley, Die filled her basket with fragments and sought the home of a sick woman who lived beyond her father's cottage.

CHAPTER XII.

THE DRUNKARD'S WIFE.

In a low, mud-plastered log-house, the windows only four lights in a frame, and half of those covered with paper and filled in with old rags, the roof looking as though any saucy wind might land it upon the hillside, lived the sick woman. Stooping as she entered the low door, Die was greeted by a feeble voice.

"Good evening, Miss Dinmont; come to the fire."

"Good evening, Mrs. Bishop; are you any better to-night?"

"No, dear; the wind is cold and chill, and I have coughed more than usual."

"I hope I have something to cheer you. You know we have had a grand wedding at our house to-day, and Mrs. Hancock and Ruth have sent you a share of the good things."

Mrs. Bishop sat in an old chair in the corner, which had neither arms nor rockers and only part of a low back left to support her feeble, wasting form. She was leaning against the wall by the fire-

8*

place, and around her hung the pieced and tattered remains of two or three old shawls and quilts. Three timid children had hid out of sight upon the entrance of a stranger, but the sight of the basket soon brought them from their hiding places, with eager looks and questionings, hopping up and clapping their hands for very joy. A fire made of old stumps and bits of boards and drift from the river, burned feebly on the broad hearth, over which the ashes were strewn in profusion. The largest child —a girl of some eight years—instinctively took the old scratch of broom corn from the corner and tried to clear a spot for Die to warm her feet.

"They have had nothing to eat but parched corn, and have been roasting it in the ashes, poor things," said the invalid, apologetically.

"Oh, this good bread and butter won't hurt them then," and Die opened her load of fragments and dealt them out generously, remembering a similar occasion when her own little brothers and sisters were made joyful by a like feast. Tears of gratitude choked the dying woman and set her to coughing. After a fearful paroxysm, she partook with the children.

"Your cough is very bad, Mrs. Bishop; have you nothing to relieve it ?"

"I don't take anything now. The doctor says it will do no good. It's most over with me, Diana."

"But it seems to me you might be made easier— There are so many remedies. Don't despair yet; doctors don't always know."

" If I had a warmer bed and food to eat, it would be all I need—all I would ask. Diana, I have not touched one mouthful of food since yesterday until now." She glanced as she spoke at the wretched framework of boards that held a handful of straw in a broken case. All the bed clothes were around her in the chair; not another chair in the house with even the pretence of a back—two or three benches, boxes or home-made stools were all the seats. In one corner of the leaky cabin, or hut, stood a loom for weaving rag carpets, by which employment Myra Bishop had sustained herself and children for years.

" Oh, Die, if I could sell my loom. Your mother used to come and help me when I first took this cough. She knows how to weave, and everybody would help her; she'd get plenty to do.".

" What is your loom worth, Mrs. Bishop?" Die's thoughts were already planning relief for the stricken family.

" He made it himself, you know, and I don't know rightly—maybe ten dollars. Oh, if I could only get that it would keep me in bread till I die—it won't be long."

The poor creature leaned forward and lifted her eyes imploringly and seemed waiting for an answer.

" Gilbert, you mean, made it. Where is he now?" asked Die, getting up and taking the bony hands of the invalid in her own warm palms.

A long coughing spell, a sob and a struggle had

to be gone through with before an answer could be spoken. " I wish I knew. He left us starving yesterday, and took our last decent quilt to buy corn. Hettie set on that little pot to boil it when he should return, and filled it with water brought in that broken gourd from the spring, and there it has been waiting, filled up as it boiled dry, waiting, waiting, —waiting for the husband and father, and he does not come."

Exhausted by her effort and emotion her head sank upon her friend's bosom. Die drew the shawl from her own shoulders and wound it around the shivering form, and, while her own tears dropped unbidden, comforted her with kind words. It was a chilly night.

"The children," resumed the woman, "went to hunt for him at the mill and shop, and picked up these kernels of corn on the ground where they had been unloading a wagon, but they did not find him."

Did you ever know a woman, reader, who had a drunken husband, that ever liked to call him by his name,—to speak the synonym by which she knew him in brighter and better days?—the " Tom," " Harry," or " Joe," who walked with her in the moonlight, who breathed in the young listening ears the words she loved best to hear, who wreathed the rosebuds in her hair, and promised to love, cherish and protect her till death. That name is too sacred to her soul and memory to be associated with the fallen caricature of manhood that staggers and swears and talks fustian to his own shadow. Oh, that ominous "He or him,"—that shade of the past— what a tale it tells.

"Now, my dear," said Die, soothingly, "you are very tired. Let me fix you in bed, and I will run and see what I can do. I can get you a cup of tea at least, and send some one to find Gilbert."

The old quilts were arranged as well as possible, and the frail woman laid upon and under them, Die disrobing herself as far as she could to add to the warmth of the perishing woman. "There, now you can be comfortable for an hour."

"Oh, yes, but see the children all fast asleep, my poor little starvlings. Could you place them on the bed with me?" Die picked them up one at a time and bestowed them to the best advantage before and behind, at the foot and under the corners of the rags, so that their little bodies, yet full of life and vitality, might give warmth and magnetism to the sufferer; said a hasty good night and almost flew back to the Lodge, saying to herself: "I will ask Mr. Max for the money, and Mrs. Hancock will not deny me a bed and bedding for that dying woman. Ruth will help me carry some tea and comforts,—how brave I feel to beg and work for others; how I shrink from asking for myself,—yes, I will ask, and I can get all I need."

She found Max in the library, as Mrs. Hancock had begged he should stay in the house evenings, during her husband's absence.

Die knocked at the door and, flushed by her rapid
walk, and a little chilled by the night air, presented
to the young man in his easy chair before the glowing grate, a startling picture of beauty. In a few
hasty words she let him directly into the interest of
her work,—"You must send some one to find that
man and help me to get some comforts and conveniences into that hut."   She said must, not like a servant, but like a woman determined to do good.

" Anything,—everything that I can do I will do,
Miss Diana, and here and now let me say a word,
which I have long been wishing to say,—consider
me as your friend ;—we are servants alike to people
who need us and our work ; they can no more live
without our services than we without theirs; let us
be friends and equals." He reached out his hand.
Die took it as if it were her right, and said, " I accept your offer.   Can you let me have ten dollars, or
shall I call upon Mrs. Hancock ?"

" Call upon Mrs. Hancock.   It will do her good
to have an object for her thoughts just now.   I pity
her too."

" So do I, Mr. Carter."

" Call me Max, please."

" I will; but we must hurry. I will go to Mrs.
Hancock, while you order the team for bed and
bedding and set measures going to find Gilbert."

Max was already drawing on his overcoat. Die
flew to the kitchen, aroused Ruth and set her great
heart to throbbing in behalf of " dem children." Mrs.
Hancock opened her purse without a word.

" Don't talk of pay, Die, let your mother have the loom ; you earned it long ago and ought to have had wages. How thoughtless we've all been, you shall have twelve dollars a month after this."

Die was joyful. It had come at last without her asking ; she had no time now to speak more than—

"Oh, thank you, dear Mrs. Hancock, I will try and earn it," and she bent down and for the first time touched her lips to the lady's brow. "I will fill the place of Emma and Nettie as well as I know how."

" Go to the store room and take all the things you need. If you do not find a comfortable bed for that poor woman, take one from the bedsteads in the chambers; they will lie idle all winter." Then re-membering *her* absent ones she fell to weeping as was her wont, while Die rushed away to carry for-ward her errand of mercy.

Mrs. Bishop refreshed with food and made warm in bed, knowing that her children were fed and cov-ered, and that Gilbert would be looked after, fell quietly to sleep and did not waken until the shout of Martin, the man of all work, " Whoa! there, back; stand still now, you pesky old varmint. Whoa! there, I tell you." Before she could com-prehend the sounds or her own condition of warmth and absence of hunger, Die's gentle knock and entrance had assured her all was right. Ruth wad-dled in after Die to prepare the " yarb drinks and fix up the beds with her own hands."

Martin had brought ax and saw, and the first thing was to set the cabin aglow with a roaring fire. By the time that was done Max arrived with the news that Gilbert had been found dead drunk—he whispered this to Die—by the side of a jug in the cooper's yard in one of the big distillery casks of his own making, which was yet minus a head, (Gilbert was a cooper by trade.) He had been carried into a back room in the office, safely housed for the night, and strict orders given that he should have no more whisky. Frobish hated drunken men with as much consistency as most men. He believed in drinking with moderation, and, of course, Gilbert Bishop the drunken dog would get no more there—not another drop if asked for—until he was sober and able to earn money to buy the privilege of getting drunk again. Was Frobish any more inconsiderate than his patron, the Judge, or his law-givers—the men of honor in the nation who make moderate drinking lawful and respectable?

Max and Martin with strong hands made quick work removing the loom from the most sheltered part in the room and setting in its place the old fashioned high post bedstead. Die had found in the garret mattress and feathers both soft and warm for the worn and fleshless limbs. Sheets, pillows, blankets and comfortables were soon in place and a huge awning of cotton cloth, which the merry-makers of August had used for their wildwood parties, was thrown over the high posts and securely fastened down to keep out winds and storms, and when the village clock struck ten the work was all done and the poor sufferer helped into her good bed. She wept for joy. "I almost want to live now," she said in whispers—"live to tell you how I thank you."

The loom was loaded into the empty wagon and left on the way inside of Heckel Dinmont's new gate, which glowed in the starlight as if it had been covered with a coat of golden paint. Ruth also enjoyed the starlight ride. Die had put the golden coin which Mrs. Hancock had given her, into the sick woman's hand, whispering:

"For the loom you know; now go to sleep, dear. He's all right and safe and won't be here till morning."

Myra Bishop closed her eyes with an indistinct "God bless you," and our heroine seated herself in the well stuffed and well worn arm chair which had been twenty years wasting itself unused in the same garret with the bedstead, with a candle on the shelf for use as occasion required. The pot of herb tea sending out its aroma, to be drank every time the patient coughed, was on the hearth. The tired girl was soon asleep with the rest of the relieved and gratified household. Towards morning the invalid wakened and called for drink; paroxysm after paroxysm prevented the return of sleep, and Die drew the arm chair to the bed and sat down beside her.

"I can't live long, Diana," she said with feeble

voice, "but I want to tell you or somebody before
I go, of the time when I first knew Gilbert," she
spoke his name softly and kindly now, as if a sweet
memory was stirring within her heart. "He wasn't
as he now is; father kept a grocery and tavern in
Greenfield and Gilbert used to see me serving customers behind the bar sometimes. He never drank
then, but talked temperance. I laughed at him and
mixed and sweetened and persuaded him to drink
his first dram. After that," she paused and covered
her face with her bony hands, "after that he drank
in moderation until we were married. He was good
and kind a long time; until we came here that he
might work at his trade. He made money and we
—oh, that still house, that tavern—don't blame him,
I did it myself." She lay a long time coughing and
weeping and when she grew quiet she lifted the
great blue eyes to Die's face. "I have knelt at the
feet of Jesus, Diana, and prayed by the day and
hour for years, and I feel that I have been forgiven,
but I never shall forgive myself, never! never! until
he ceases to drink. I do not fear death, yet I would
like to stay with my children. Peace has come to
my soul,"—she paused a moment and then looked
up earnestly—" can forgiveness undo wrong done
or take the sting of sin out of the heart while we
see its effects daily before our eyes? Diana, do we
read the scriptures aright. Is not our own self-
accusing conscience ' the worm that never dies,' our
own sins the scars that will never wear away? And

yet I did not know the wrong, for all about me I
heard the words and thoughts of men whose wisdom was taken by the world as pure and good, who
were accounted men of God." Again she struggled
with her agony, and again she spoke her pleading
words for him. "If *he* would but change, if he
could cease to do evil and learn to do well, then like
the Peri I could fly to the gates of Heaven with her
song on my lips bearing that precious burden—a
repentant tear. I could sing as did she her song of
joy—

> 'Farewell, ye odors of earth that die,
>   Passing away like a lover's sigh,
>   My feast is now the Taboo tree
>   Whose scent is the breath of eternity.
>   Farewell, ye vanishing flowers that shone
>   In my fairy wreath so bright and brief,
>   Oh what are the brightest that ere were blown
>   To the late tree-springing by Allah's throne,
>   Whose flowers have a soul in every leaf.
>   Joy, joy, forever, my task is done,
>   The gates are passed and heaven is won.'"

Low and sweet was the voice that intoned those
beautiful words, and when they were ended she sank
again into a torpor which made Die shudder. Was
it the torpor of death? As day dawn broke over the
hills, Mary came to take her place by the sick woman and let Die return to the "Lodge," but not
until she had promised the mother that she would
look after her children when she was gone and try,

oh for her sake, try to make him repent. **Die** promised.

We said Heckel Dinmont's new gate looked in the starlight as if it was covered with golden paint. Die never went through it without feeling that gold could not brighten it, for it burst upon her out of the recollection of that awful night and told her her father had not drank since. The old fence, too, was straitened up, and the logs that lay strewn about in the summer days were chopped into fine wood for winter use. There were steps upward within and without; and when she told her parents that she had paid for the loom with gold given her as honestly her wages, there was great joy, and Heckel was not slow to put it up for his wife in a spare corner of the home room, where every beam and shaft, spring and treadle, ever split in the reed and eye in the harness, were at once prophetic of coming comfort and plenty.

"Mrs. Hancock has been wanting some weaving done for a long time, mother—carpets for the back rooms and kitchen. Ruth and Mary cut the rags long ago, and I sewed them. She will send them to you to-day; won't it be nice? Good bye."

"Ain't it nice to have such a child," said Heckel, musingly. "Mary, *she saved* me."

Mary's eyes were full of tears.

CHAPTER XIII.

THE DRUNKARD'S FAMILY.

Myra Bishop had been well brought up and had received a common education,—had spoken pieces at quarterly exhibitions and dialogues with her school-mates at evening entertainments—read Byron and Moore, Burns and Shakespeare in her gala days, and it was one of those reminisences that had come like a sweet dream to her memory as she thought of her life's spring-time in connection with her husband. Was Myra Bishop's an uncommon case? Not at all; probably there were a hundred households within the reach of the burning stream of death that went out from the village of Oxbow, that were as near starvation, as broken, as miserable and despairing as the one described. A hundred did we say? Multiply by ten and you will have half the number of sufferers, and yet the diabolical work goes on. How could it stop? Was Judge Hancock alone to blame? The farmers must raise corn and rye, and sell it to live; the lumber man his staves and hoops, the cooper make his barrels, the coppersmith ply his skill, the distiller use his science to manufacture, the engineer regulate the machinery, the millwright work at his wheels, the blacksmith swing his hammer, the coal-diggers ply their trade, the teamsters fetch and carry, the common laborers earn their bread, the managers, overseers, and the superintendent hold their book and·pen ready to record. Where shall we end our list? Where begin the work of demolition? Whom shall we censure? Who has done this mighty wrong. Oh, from the most ancient of days it has been going on, and if we look clearly and understandingly upon the matter we shall see it is not the maker and vender alone, not the licensed tavern-keeper and bartender that we have to contend with, but a hydra-headed monster that spawns his progeny in our very household and we warm the eggs of the serpent in our own bosoms and nurture into life with our own selfish loves that which we loathe and despise.

Let every mother rear her sons to shun the inebriate's cup, and every father resolve that though poverty cover him as a mantle, he will not work to make drunkards. Let every man, woman and child bow before the Lord and vow like the children of Rechab of old, that they and their children shall drink no more wine (or intoxicating beverages) forever. Then will come a true reform.

Do you ask when this will be done? Never, until you and I and all those about us, wherever we may be; on the mountain or in the valley, at the east or west, north or south, in the hedge rows or in the work shop, in gilded halls or marble palaces, work for its accomplishment; work as men work to dig channels to the sea, work as they struggle and heave to throw out the foundations of the moun-tains, and lay down the tracks for the iron horse; work as men work for wealth and fame; then it will come,—come as our civilization has come, by slow and sure steps, and the great wrong will disappear as the forests have vanished from the hills and mountains, the valleys and plains. Do you doubt? Will a people who have conquered all kings but King Alcohol, leave *him* on his throne to despoil the fairest and best of their loves and hopes?

> By all the victims of the past,
>   By all the bitter tears
> And groans wailed out upon the blast,
>   Of countless suffering years.
> By all the hopes of mercy given
>   To human hearts to know,
> Of peace on earth or joy in heaven,
>   Let true hearts answer, *No!*

We must work, and through earnest work we shall conquer.

Die, as we said, went home at day dawn; found Ruth already up and driving about to put things to rights, for the wedding had disturbed the tranquility of the kitchen as well as the parlor. Die joined her with willing hands, forgetting, in her exuberant health, the long disturbed night or weary yesterday. To the astonishment of all, Mrs. Hancock's bell

rang an hour earlier than usual, and as the chambermaid was not up and dressed, Die answered it
promptly.   She was prepared to meet Mrs. Hancock
sick, worn out and despairing, and braced her own
nerves to go on with the task of soothing and com-
forting.   Imagine her surprise to find her up and
dressed, and only wanting a ewer of hot water that
she might wash Jessie herself.

"How did you leave poor Mrs. Bishop, Diana?"

"More comfortable, Mrs. Hancock, for your great
kindness, but not any better permanently, I fear."

"It's very strange, Die, that no one knew how sick
and poor she was before."

"Her husband is a drunkard, Mrs. Hancock, and
that you know shuts the hearts of people against
doing for their families what they would in case of
any other misfortune."

"I don't see why it should," answered the lady.

"Because folks say it only encourages a man in
his bad habits.   Gilbert Bishop took the very quilts
off his wife's bed and pawned or sold them for
liquor. His cooking stove, pots and kettles went
long ago, and chairs and tables and everything that
he could trade off went the same way."

"The law ought to be put in force against such a
brute."

"I am told that the law is powerless to help in a
case like this."

"Why, how so?" asked Mrs. Hancock excitedly.

"Because all that belongs to husband and wife is
absolutely his to keep or sell as he pleases."

"I don't believe it. If there were such inhuman laws on the statute books, my husband would know it, and I should have heard of it before this time."

"Bishop sold all her decent clothes last summer, and her breastpin and earrings her father gave her before she was married, and her great family Bible, her mother's wedding gift; and when she was weaving a carpet, would go and get the money from her employer and spend it for whisky."

"Diana Dinmont, what a horrible creature he must be. I'll have my carriage right away after breakfast and go myself and see what can be done. I never heard of such a wretch."

"He is far better than many others, Mrs. Hancock, for he never abuses her or the children as some others do. Sam. Roland whipped his wife a few weeks ago, and put her and his four little children out in the rain at midnight and they staid out until morning."

"And did no one take him in hand?"

"Yes, he was brought before Justice Phelps and fined ten dollars and bound over to keep the peace."

"Was that all?"

"No, not all; they had a cow which she had raised from a little calf,—one that she bought with money earned at house cleaning. She had fed it and kept it at pasture out of her own hard earnings, and now it was keeping her children in milk and she sold enough to buy meal and some meat. As soon as he

Q

was out of the constable's hands he drove off her cow, sold it for fifty dollars—not half its worth— paid his fine with ten of it and gave the other forty to Frobish for a liquor bill."

"It isn't possible," exclaimed Mrs. Hancock, com- ing as near indignation as her subdued and broken nature could reach.

"It is true. She went to lawyer Stiles, and he told her that in law the cow belonged to her hus- band, and she could do nothing."

"Did not their neighbors interfere?"

"Three or four of the women went to him and begged him to get back her cow, but he only cursed them for meddling, and said he'd teach her to com- plain of him to the justice another time."

"Why don't she leave him?"

"He would take away all her children. The law allows him that privilege too, and she will bear starvation and death for her children."

"Don't he work at all? What is his trade?"

"He's a blacksmith—and a good one; often works every day in the week, and takes home liquor at night and drinks and makes hell for her half the night; gets so far gone there that he is stupid and sleeps till morning, works all day again, and drinks at night; so he keeps going."

"Oh what a horrid life for a woman."

"Horrid to think of, more horrid to bear," an- swered Die. "Shall I bring the water now?"

"Yes, please. I will go down to breakfast."

" Oh, will you? that will be delightful for the children."

Die went after the water, trembling and frightened at her own temerity in daring to expound the law to Mrs. Judge Hancock. Where had she found this? She had become an inveterate reader, and every pamphlet and paper that went into the waste basket seemed to furnish food for her longing mind. In a *Tribune* she had read of these laws; from the gossip of the town she had heard them repeated, and her opinion of Sam. Rolands' case was gained from the Judge himself as she waited at dinner, and heard him give the precise right of a husband in such a case to lawyer Stiles himself. Servants have grand opportunities if they would use them.

Mrs. Hancock took her place near the head of the table, but insisted that as Olivia, Emma and Nettie were all gone for the year, that Diana should set at the head of the table and do the honors of its mistress.

After breakfast she was requested to ride with Mrs. Hancock; " but dear me," exclaimed the owner of the elegant silk morning dress and point lace kerchief, fastened at the throat with garnets, " Die, you must have some new clothes, we have neglected you shamefully, child. Can't you wear Emma's dresses?"

" This is one Miss Olivia gave me of hers."

" Hasn't she left a closet full? she said she would not take one old thing with her."

" There are a good many dresses belonging to the three young ladies, in a large trunk, which they told me to fold away."

" Go get something nice, and put on Emma's last spring hat and saque; I know she did not take them —make yourself nice and go with me."

Die obeyed orders and selected a plain grey traveling suit which had been made for Miss Emma in the spring, and a quiet hat to match. She felt a tremor through her whole soul as she encased herself in these stylish garments. She had been commanded, what could she do but obey. She knew, too, that the garments would be lost or useless if laid away, except they might be used as charitable donations, and they would not be thus used, because they were unsuited in their richness and make to the wants of the poor.

Once seated in the carriage, Mrs. Hancock opened upon her a new sensation.

" Die, my girls are all gone, and I must now have a housekeeper and manager to fill their place. Could you do it ?"

" Oh, Mrs. Hancock, I am so young."

" I know you are young, but Olivia and Emma both say that you will do better than any one else; you have been with us three years and know us all, and we all know you and trust you; it will not be hard nor require all your time, and you shall have hours to read and study, and Mrs. Jones, whom I wish to retain, will give you what instructions you need."

"Mrs. Hancock, I can try. If I succeed in satis-fying your requirements I shall only be too glad to retain the place."

"Well, that is all I desire, for the present, so you may consider yourself manager now. Whenever I wish anything special done I will tell you and help you along, and Ruth understands everything, only she can't do all, you know—cannot keep accounts."

"I can't write," answered Die, instantly, while a deep crimson stained her cheeks and brow.

"Well, well, that's bad, but you bring the items to me and I will put them down. I used to keep them. By the by, I don't believe anybody keeps them now. This reminds me that Wash said to me yesterday, 'Mother, can't Mrs. Jones find time to teach Die to write?' I declare, I had quite forgotten it. Wash is *so* thoughtful."

Die blushed deeper and felt pleased and humbled, pleased at being remembered, humbled that she was so ignorant. Mrs. Hancock could never have been so free if her daughter had been present.

At the door of the hut the carriage drew up for them to alight.

"You don't mean to tell me that this is the place?"

"Yes, this is the home of the sick woman."

"This hovel, this hog-pen, this barn," exclaimed the exquisitely dressed wife of the millionare; "Can it be that a human being, a woman, lives here?" and she stepped from her carriage without even seeing Martin's proffered hand, and gathering up her skirts she followed Die into the house.

Mary had left Mrs. Bishop in the care of a neighboring woman, after preparing her breakfast and attending to the wants of the little ones. The woman promised to stay till some other should come to relieve her. This promise had not been kept, and the sick woman had risen from her bed to quiet the cries of her babe, and sat almost gasping for life in the cushioned arm chair, a picture of death in life. No tale can tell the wretchedness of the poor with such minuteness of detail as to make those who have not seen, with their own eyes, realize the woe. Could the children of wealth and pride be induced to see and hear for themselves more frequently the conditions of poverty, would not their charities reach out more broadly, would they not feel and learn to know more understandingly the meaning of those sublime words, "Love God with all thy heart and thy neighbor as thyself."

Mrs. Hancock walked directly to the sufferer, who reached out her attenuated hand with an appealing gesture, and the rich lady forgot to hold up her silks, forgot herself in the squalid misery around her, and dropping into the one old chair took the cold thin fingers in her own.

"Did God send you here, Mrs. Hancock?" said Myra Bishop, looking out of her great clear eyes into the face of her visitor as though she would read the very thoughts of her soul; "I know He did, for

I prayed that He would send some one, some one to hear me, some one to promise me to care for these (she looked at her children), when I am gone. Promise me that you will not see them starve; that you will not let them take them to the poor-house. Oh, lady, you have little ones, you have houses, and lands, and money, more than you can ever use, more than you will ever know; as God gives to you will you not share a little, ever so little, with my babes?"

"I will, I will, Mrs. Bishop, your children shall not suffer," exclaimed Mrs. Hancock with vehemence.

The mother lifted the little gloved hand she held between her own to her lips, raised her eyes in mute thanksgiving, and murmured a few indistinct words of prayer. She let go the clasped hand, laid her head back against the cushions, drew one deep sigh and seemed to breathe no more.

Die sprang to her side with the exclamation, "she has fainted!" and lifting her in her arms as she would a child, laid her upon the bed, chafing her hands and face, while Mrs. Hancock applied her salts—always in her pocket—helping to restore her. After a few seconds there came one more spasmodic gasp, Myra Bishop opened her eyes, smiled, whispered "Tell Him to come, oh, it is beautiful," and passed away without a struggle or a moan.

The two women stood beside the calm, beautiful smiling figure, in silence for a moment.

Die was the first to speak.

Mrs. Hancock seemed petrified with the strangeness of the scene and the emotions it had called up.

"She is dead, Mrs. Hancock. Died of cruelty and wrong."

The words seemed to revive her patroness.

"Oh, Die, run tell Martin to drive for the doctor—stay, don't leave me here, I will lift her head, give me the salts."

"It is useless," responded the girl; but Martin received the order and drove away furiously, and soon found the person he sought, who returned with him in the carriage, only to say as Die had said before:

"She is dead, Mrs. Hancock, died by cruelty and wrong."

"Oh, merciful Father!" exclaimed the rich lady, "whose fault is all this?"

CHAPTER XIV.

MAX AND GILBERT.

Max, prompt and faithful in everything he undertook, rose early and searching to the bottom of his trunk, drew out an old suit of clothes that had served him in the last years of his college life, when he was struggling with manly pride against poverty, and earning his bread by sawing wood and cleaning school rooms, lighting lamps, etc., for his more idle and far less intellectual classmates. He looked at the suit a moment with dewy eyes, as the remembrance of his mother sprang up before him, in all her placid patience and dignity, from a surreptitious patch which she had fitted with motherly care. He remembered one night when he was weary, when his brain was perplexed over the abstruse lessons he must learn, when an indignity offered to his manhood made his proud pulses throb with indignation, when he sat moodily by the cottage fire, almost ready to say, "the way is too dark, the labor too heavy, I must give up;" how *she* came with gentle grace and sat down upon his strong knees, (as she often did), laid her soft cheek upon his brow, and patting his cheeks with her hard worn hands, said

cheerily: "Come, now, Max, my boy, forget it all
for a little, and let us love and talk nonsense as we
used to do; it's a long time since your baby fingers
curled my hair. Can't you make mamma look
pretty once again?" And so he forgot his weariness, his lessons and his insult, and twined her brown
locks, touched with silvery threads, round his fingers, and told her stories, as in his boyish days, and
grew rested and refreshed, and went to his toils with
renewed strength and hope.

Oh, mothers of boys, if you only knew how you
could hold them by such love, how you could purify
them by your own purities, and charm their longing, clamoring boy senses by your sweet caresses
and toying plays, you would not, you could not
throw them from you as you do out into the laby-
rinths of life, to search up and down for what they
need among the painted syrens and bright eyed serpents that lurk in all its secret places to ensnare and
destroy. The grog shop lures its surest supplies
from cheerless homes.

But reader, Max must not be left dreaming over
those old clothes, while Gilbert Bishop waits madly
and faintingly, safely locked in that back office,
starving for food after his two days stupor, burning
with thirst, and his conscience goading him with a
whip of scorpions. He has a dim recollection of
taking his wife's last, best quilt, and rushing down to
old mother Quiggly's, who kept a kind of trade in
all things in Frog lane; of promising Hetty if she'd

fill the pot he would bring the corn; he knew he sold that quilt worth five dollars for one, and a jug of whisky thrown in; he knew he went out into the cooper's yard and behind a high cask took one drink, intending to leave the jug there and go to the mill to buy the corn. Alas for intention when the jug is near. He knew now that something dreadful had happened, or he should not be there; he had no idea that more than one night had passed, and he longed to get out to get one dram—only one. No, by all that was holy he would take but *one* and then fly with fast feet to Myra. "Poor dear Myra and little Belle, Neddie and Hetty, how hungry they must all be; what a brute I am." Then he shook the door, tried the windows, swore fearful oaths, (drunken men are always profane), shouted for help, cried and blubbered like a whipped school boy.

Max wiped the dew from his eyes, "no time now for sentimentalism, I have better things than these to keep for her dear sake," said he to himself, and tying the garments in a bundle he left word that he should not return to breakfast, and hurried away to his prisoner whom he found as described; but when the key turned in the door, Gilbert rose up in wrath determined to annihilate the wretch, even were it the Judge himself, that had locked him away from his starving wife and children.

Max no sooner entered the den of the wild beast, than he was met by the animal himself aiming a blow with his unsteady fist, which the quick ready foil of Max turned aside, and the infuriated prisoner, from the momentum of his own intent, missing his object, went sprawling upon the floor.

" You d——d infernal scoundrel," he shouted as he went down ; what would have followed was suppressed by the fall.   Trying to gather himself up he fell again.   The jar had hurt him, he was so weak.

" Come, my poor fellow," said Max soothingly, " let me help you."

" Mr. Carter, is that you ? how came I here. Give me a little drop just to steady me; I am choking— there was plenty in the jug."

By the time these incoherent sentences had been spoken, Gilbert, by the help of Max, was on his feet again.

" Yes, we found your jug where we found you, in a cask in the cooper's yard, dead drunk, Gilbert Bishop.   Martin, the Judge's man, and myself brought you here last night, and you have been away from home two days. There, you have all the explanation."

" Dead drunk, empty jug, two days," said the bewildered man, clasping his forehead with both hands. " Mr. Carter, could you let me have one dram, just one ? Oh, I am so faint, so weak. *Just one*, Mr. Max, come now, don't be hard on a fellow."

" Not a drop, Bishop, I would not curse you with another dram for the whole worth of yonder distillery.   Here are water and towels, wash the slime of your revel from your face, pull off those filthy rags, and put on this suit, then go with me to the Oxbow and get a good cup of coffee and a steak, you'll be stronger then. Why, my man, you're starving."

"I know that, Mr. Carter, but victuals ain't the thing, if I'd a little sup," and Gilbert burst out sobbing again.

"Hush! you driveler," said Max with authority. "Do as I bid you, your wife is dying; don't talk to me of drams."

Gilbert Bishop obeyed, and with trembling, unsteady hands, helped a little by the kind hearted Max, who had seen and helped many men of higher positions than the poor wretch before him, was soon ready for his short walk.

"Coffee for one, beefsteak for two," was his prompt order as they entered the breakfast room an hour before the usual breakfast time.

More than once Gilbert looked up pleadingly, but there was that in the face of Max which said plainly "It's no use."

He ate like a famished wolf; ate and was refreshed, then rose from the table and started with steadier steps towards the bar room.

"I can go alone now, Mr. Carter, don't want to trouble you sir, never mind me. I can go alone."

"No you can't," answered Max jovially, "we've had a good breakfast and now we'll take a walk to the office, have a little chat about matters, and when you are rested we'll go up and see Myra and the children."

The words "Myra and the children" stung him
like serpents, and yielding to the superior strength
of his companion, they walked away from that curse
of human souls—the tavern bar.   Once in the office
his hunger satisfied, he gave himself to drowsiness
and fell asleep.   He had been nearly starved.

Max took his books and pen and waited patiently
for the second wakening, knowing that he would be
more in his sober senses and better prepared to be
talked to and dealt with.   It was ten o'clock before
he made his appearance from the inner room.

"Now, Bishop, wash your face once more, comb
your hair and look as decent as you can, and we'll
go and see Myra.   She is very sick.   I couldn't let
you go this morning with your red eyes and bloated
face, it would have killed her; but you look more
like a man now."

Bishop obeyed like a spaniel, and the two walked
away to meet the fearful shock in reserve for the
husband and father.

The doctor had told his story as he passed through
the village; how Mrs. Bishop had been found starving by Diana Dinmont the night before, Gilbert dead
drunk for two days, and how she had died an hour
ago in the arms of Mrs. Judge Hancock.

The news flew like wildfire, and the good people,
(they were good people) that had let the drunkard's
cabin and all its inmates alone for weeks, were stirred to the quick with this dreadful report, and before
Max and his charge arrived at the hovel, the room

was full of women earnest to help and standing in each other's way.

Mrs. Hancock had left with the first influx, simply saying " let all things necessary be provided and send the bills to me."

" What does all this mean?" asked Bishop with a look of alarm, as they neared the door and discovered the crowd. Max was silent ; a terrible suspicion flashed into his mind although he had not heard the report. He stepped in before Gilbert and ascertained the whole truth. Laid out at full length on the frame of boards that had been her wretched bed, only a white sheet beneath and thrown over her, lay Myra, her hands folded over her breast, the clear eyes closed and the sweet smile still lingering over the pleasant lips. A murmur ran through the room " he's coming," and all fell back and left an open passage from the door to the bed. Max took in the whole at a glance, and stepping back took the arm of the man that was to meet his fearful doom, and half leading, half forcing their way, led him in sight of the outlined form beneath the folded sheet.

Gilbert stood as one stupefied an instant, his red face lost its color, his eyes stared wildly. He was sobered now ; walking with unfaltering and quick step to the frame he folded back the sheet, looked into the dead face, touched the cold brow with his hand, uttered a fearful cry, " *I have killed her*," and sank to the floor a lifeless mass of suffering humanity.

Heckel Dinmont who had been actively engaged making the hut fit to be entered, caught up the falling man, and with the help of Max bore him out into the cold October air. A wild commotion spread through the house and the doctor was sent for. No sign of life stirred the rigid frame, the hands were purple and the jaws set. Every moment added to the crowd, and the fearful tragedy was repeated from mouth to mouth with immense variations. Exaggerations there could not be, the facts were sufficiently appalling, but the gracious acts of the Hancocks and Dinmonts spread out to the crowd, filling it with astonishment and admiration, increased immensely the desire of every one to help.

The doctor decided that Gilbert was not dead, the terrible shock had suspended animation for a time; he would revive in convulsions. "That hut is not fit for a sick man," said the doctor, and half a dozen neighbors offered to receive him; others to take charge of the children; the minister's wife to give place for the corpse and provide for the funeral.

There were plenty of friends and helpers now. Oh, that they had stretched out their hands to save in the day when Gilbert walked by their doors to that dram shop, when they saw and knew that every rising sun found him nearer the brink of ruin; when they saw without an effort to prevent it the cheek of Myra grow pale; when they gossiped about her toiling life, heard the children cry for bread and gave no heed. Now it was too late.

Before night, under the supervision of Max and Heckel, all things had assumed a solemn quiet.

Myra Bishop, laid in a plain coffin, had been carried to the vestry room of the church.

Gilbert, who found a resting place with a neighbor who knew him in better days, gave no signs of consciousness for many hours.

Mrs. Rand, on the hill, picked up the curly pated Neddie and his dimple-faced little sister, and took them home. She knew Myra Bishop, " she belonged to our church, was a good woman, and these children were born when their father was not a drunkard." Her life was very, very lonely since Gordon went away, and so was Mr. Rand's; she would take the little ones.

Diana had orders to bring Hetty to the " Lodge."

" What shall I do with the things? " asked Die.

' Give them to your mother, they have done their work for me," answered Mrs. Hancock.

The ten dollar gold piece was found tied with a bit of spool cotton into the fold of an inner garment. Myra, weak, faint and dying, wished to hide it from him if he came—hide it to supply bread for her children.

Max had dispersed the crowd with a temperance lecture that made every man and woman feel about himself or herself to see whether it was really so— that they were guilty accomplices of this fearful tragedy, and ending his remarks by asking that they

should all meet him at the church Sunday evening
at 4 P. M., after the funeral.

Mournfully, painfully, through contortion that
racked the body and soul like the wheels of inquisi-
tion in olden time, Gilbert returned to life after
hours of agony. He was not calm nor strong
enough to bear the detail of his misery for many
days. " No wife, no children, no home," groaned
the stricken man, " all gone; gone for whisky," and
he turned his face to the wall and prayed to die.

When Max returned to the " Lodge" at evening,
he found Mrs. Hancock somewhat troubled over a
dispatch from the Judge :

" He would see Nettie to Pittsburg, but must be
absent two weeks."

The day and its incidents had opened a new vein
of thought and feeling to the mistress of Hancock
Lodge, filling, in part, at least, the vacuum made by
the sudden revolution in her own home.

The little maid from the hovel, dressed neatly in
garments improvised out of old and forgotten
stores, was the pet of the evening. Jessie brought
out all her play-things to amuse and cheer, still the
heart of the little mourner was heavy, and in spite
of all their kindness, would lighten itself with sobs
and tears, now and then asking about " mamma."

At Mrs. Hancock's request, Die spent the evening
in the sitting room with the mistress and children,
managed their little plays, and gave pleasure and
comfort to them all ; and in spite of the loneliness

occasioned by the absence of her family, Mrs. Hancock was measurably cheerful, forgot to think much about herself, and went to bed in good season to sleep soundly until the breakfast bell rang; rose refreshed and declared she felt so much better she would ride again; she would take the children and go up and see the other little ones on the hill.

"So Die, dear, get them all ready by nine o'clock, and tell Martin to be punctual," said the lady.

"Laws, chile, didn't I tell yer? missis got a purpose, dat what does it. Oh, go long, dese grand folks have to kill off somebody or do something to keep 'em stirrin'; aint that a purty young one, though? and she's smart, too."

All this and more was said to Mary, as they stood at the door watching the process of filling the carriage, and the lively prancing of the horses, that seemed to feel as if they, too, thought it a Godsend that their mistress had "got a purpose," that they might get out of their close stalls on these breezy October days.

"Ain't our Die getting on stilts, though? riding with my lady and wearing big folks' clothes; and don't she deserve it? Lord a massy! she ought to be a King's daughter, she's so nice and clever," said Ruth with a hearty ha, ha, ha.

CHAPTER XV.

THE FUNERAL.

"Now had the season returned when the nights grew colder
    and longer
And the retreating sun the sign of the scorpion enters.
Birds of passage sailed through the laiden air from the ice-
    bound
Desolate northern bays to the shores of the tropical islands.
Harvests were gathered in and wild with the winds of Sep-
    tember
Wrestled the trees of the forest as Jacob of old with the angel,
Then followed the beautiful season,
Called by the pious Acadian peasants the summer of all saints,
Filled was the air with a dreamy magical light, and the land-
    scape
Lay as if new created in all the freshness of childhood.
Peace seemed to reign upon the earth."
            —*Longfellow's Evangeline.*

On such a day, in the sweet hazy atmosphere of
an October Sabbath, the people gathered to return
dust to dust, ashes to ashes. The hill sides were
robed in glory, and the winds as they gently stirred
the pines and yews of the churchyard, seemed singing a solemn dirge for the dead.

The strange and sudden decease of Myra, the

woeful tale of the husband's crime, and its speedy retribution, had spread far and wide among the people on the hill side; the dwellers in the valley and at the neighboring villages, living quiet lives of dutiful industry, free from excitement, heard of it and wondered how such a thing could be—longed to see and hear all about it—and hastened to the funeral. That church in Oxbow never was so crowded before, and not half of those who came could find places to sit or stand beneath its roof. They had come from miles away, fathers and mothers bringing their young children, that they might look upon the pale still face of the drunkard's wife, who had died of starvation and neglect, while he lay senselessly stupid with his jug beside him; young men that had tampered with the serpent and wasted their strength to slay him at will, were awed into an idea of abstinence, and for the time resolved that they would not be tempted again; they remembered Gilbert Bishop as one like themselves, ouly a little while ago, drinking in moderation, strong and free, cheerful and free-hearted. Excess had never soiled his name or paralyzed his energies, and now so low, so lost, fallen and condemned. Maidens were there by the scores, moved by sweetest pity, not unmixed with curiosity, to look into the coffin of one who had born so much, and yet, through all the suffering, loved on, and died with forgiving words upon her lips. The sad circumstance, with all its details of enduring love and

motherly devotion, had touched, with a holy influence, the hearts of this multitude, and mellowed
them to receive a lesson of truth on temperance, on
that day, that might have crystallized into a life-long
power of self-denial, forming a basis upon which
they could have builded temples of sobriety and
virtue as lasting as time.

Such a discourse they opened their ears to hear
from the Rev. Chas. Duncan, as he took his place in
the desk, with the three helpless children and the
dead mother before him, and the pale broken wretch
that had sacrificed her, lying helpless only a stone's
throw away, to illustrate every sentence of well
pointed rebuke his lips might utter.

The bell tolled in solemn peals the age of the departed—twenty-six years—so young, yet gone to her
account at the bar of God.

The choir sang a mournful voluntary, and the
Reverend Charles Duncan rose, spread wide his
hands, and offered up a beseeching prayer for the
souls of men, after which he read, with slow and
deep intonation, that impressive portion of Scripture, the ninetieth psalm :

" Lord, thou hast been our dwelling place in all
generations.   Before the mountains were brought
forth or ever thou hadst formed the earth and the
world, even from everlasting to everlasting, thou
art God.   Thou turnest man to destruction, and
sayest, return ye children of men.

" For a thousand years in thy sight are but as yesterday when it is past, as a watch in the night.

"Thou carriest them away as with a flood; they are as asleep in the morning; they are like grass which groweth up; in the morning it flourisheth and groweth up, in the evening it is cut down and withereth," etc.

The house was as still as death while the pastor continued to the end of the grand psalm. Still deeper grew the awe as the choir again gave forth that old hymn for the dead,

"Why do we mourn departed friends,"

and the swelling minor notes of "China" surged like an autumn wind through the aisles and galleries. Sobs were heard and the eyes of the multitude grew dim with emotion. Then rose the man of prayer again and announced his text from Philippians, 4th chapter, 5th verse, "Let your moderation be known unto all men. The Lord is at hand."

The reverend gentleman now proceeded to explain his text to the minds of "my hearers," by expatiating on the wisdom and goodness of the Creator. That all events were by his ordering and that the children of darkness must trust in faith. That a dispensation like the present came not as by chance, but hallowed by the love of the Father who saw the end from the beginning.

"It might be asked by the caviling or carnal minded, why God had seen fit to take this mother from her babes in the prime of life, to cut her down like a lily plucked in the time of its blossoming? To this there was but one answer, 'The Lord is at hand.' Perhaps this death was to warn them to repentance, to impel them to seek the Lord while he was near and to call upon him while he might be found."

He warned the people against false doctrines, against those who came to them with other standards of hope than the gospel of the Lord Jesus and him crucified. " Let your moderation be known of all men, the Lord is at hand." The voice of his thundering denunciations against those who would lead them by pledges and signs to accept other guards and guides than the church and its sanctuaries, woke those who were beginning to feel dull under his common places. Now they said to themselves he will give us a thought on the monstrous sin that has brought us together to-day. But no. He branched off again, "Let your moderation be known of all men." All excess was evil, and the Lord was at hand to punish with swift justice the sinner who forgot this wise command: "The way of the transgressor is hard." To totally abstain from that which was in itself useful and agreeable, proved a want of faith in their own strength. To resist temptation was to act the part of a coward, and to distrust the power of God who had said to his saints, " My grace is sufficient for thee."

And so to the end of the sermon did this man, who had given himself to the work of teaching this people, evade and avoid the direct issue of the fearful dispensation that had called them together.

The sisters were exhorted to charity, to look after those little children called by the Providence of God to struggle through life without a mother. The fathers to look well to their outgoings and incomings, to "Let their moderation be known to all men." To the young he gave exhortation that they should lay by all sins that so easily beset them, and put on the whole armor of righteousness, that they might fight the good fight of faith to the end, and receive the crown of glory at the coming of the Lord, never forgetting the solemn words, " Let your moderation be known of all men, the Lord is at hand."

Max sat in the well cushioned pew of the Judge, in the center of the church, and listened intently, keeping his eyes fixed upon the speaker. The advice sanctioned moderate drinking. As he proceeded the brow of the young man darkened; he folded his arms across his breast and set his teeth resolutely together. He knew what the people did not, that this sermon, without point or force against intemperance, was aimed at himself; for he had drawn up in the two days past, constitution and by-laws for a temperance society, had written out a pledge of total abstinence from all intoxicating drinks as a beverage, and had presented it to some of the best citizens and found them ready and willing to sign it. Thus supported he met with no difficulty in getting the names of a half dozen others of the most prominent members of the

10

church. It was a good beginning and he was in hopes that with such a heading he could bring the pastor to join him; but when he had called Saturday evening, asking him for his own name and for that of his wife in the space left at the head of the list, he refused almost rudely and went still farther, denied the use of the church for the proposed meeting, and almost bowed the young lawyer out of his house, by telling him he could not give him another moment of time on account of his imperative ministerial duties.

Max was marshal of the day, and as soon as the exercises were concluded, gave out the order for procedure in a clear manly voice, standing upon the pulpit steps in view of the people, adding close upon his announcement a request that they should tarry a few moments after the ceremonies at the grave were concluded. They had probably observed that the husband of the deceased was not present, they undoubtedly one and all felt an interest in knowing the exact truth in regard to the causes that had called them together. This he wished to give them that there might not be misrepresentations that would militate against the interests of the community.

The Rev. Chas. Duncan turned very red in the face, put his notes into his coat pocket and walked deliberately out of the house.

The funeral ceremonies were continued without further interruption—the parson not even meeting

them at the grave to utter his last benediction over
the remains of the drunkard's wife.

It was a moment of solemn interest; the little
children had looked their last upon the face of their
mother, and bewildered by things about them, were
led away by the kind hands that had guided them
there, as soon as the exercises in the church had
closed.

Max lifted his hat after the coffin was lowered to
its resting place, and thanked the people for their
attention and kindness. Then he alluded to the
circumstances attending the death of Mrs. Bishop,
repeated her last words, descanted upon the love and
trust of such a woman, of the duty of husbands and
fathers, the duty of neighbor toward neighbor in
social relations, and the cruel neglects to which the
poor and needy were subject from those who often
professed to love their neighbors as themselves.
Then he spoke of Gilbert Bishop, of his course during the last few months, of his former character as
detailed by those who had known him for years, his
honesty and upright bearing in business, his industry, his genial habits, his kindness to those about him
or beneath him in the scale of wealth and position,
his worth as a man in the community and his worth
as an immortal soul.

The voice of Max had been low and clear, and
his words were simple, yet they went to the hearts
of the people. As they grew more and more inter-
ested they drew nearer together until they closed

around him in solid phalanx. He told them what Gilbert Bishop was now, and where he was at that moment. Now he had reached the culminating point of his brief impromptu address, and he turned upon the causes of the ruin of this man—the distilleries, the taverns, the licenses given by voters that these things should exist, and the tone thus given by public opinion to make these things respectable. He hurled his anathemas against moderate drinking, arraigned the churches and all professing christians who advocated that view of the subject, as leading the weaker ones of the world into the by and forbidden paths of temptation and wickedness. He looked into the faces of the men that surrounded him, and with words of warning which seared and burnt as they fell predicted *their* fall. Nor did he pause here; on and on like an avalanche rolled the force of his eloquence, scathing distillery and licensed taverns, secret rum holes and home indulgence, until every soul in his auditory felt him or herself in some way or some shape responsible for the new made grave that lay before them.

Never before had the inhabitants of that valley heard such stirring words of truth, and when he ceased the cry went up with a shout—" go on."

Max knew that the enthusiasm could not be long kept up, therefore he declined; but holding the pledge above his head, after he had read it aloud, he said—

" Meet me on Tuesday evening next in the court

room in the village of Oxbow; here it is cold and not fitting that we should remain longer. There, where the jurors who licensed the bar, and the judge that condemns the victim sit, there I will speak to you farther of wrongs which we are one and all inflicting upon ourselves and society."

Had he presented his pledge then and there, like the converted ones at a revival meeting under the power of an inspired teacher, when they fall at the mourner's bench and cry, " Lord help us or we perish," so would these have signed the pledge of total abstinence and cried for deliverance.

He preferred to leave them until Tuesday to reflect. Some he knew who would have bound themselves that day, would have burst their bands ere the week went by, and lay a new sin upon their lives. Such a work illy done would deaden afterinfluence, and he had not taken up these ponderous balls for a moment's play. He meant work; work that should tell on the future prosperity of the people of Oxbow. That day Maxwell Carter learned his own power, and went home resolved to use it for the good of his fellow men.

" I tell you that young lawyer, what do you call him, is a screamer," said Donohue, the shoemaker, as he sat on the back steps of the Oxbow among a dozen of his class, who had dropped round that way as usual for a social Sabbath evening chat.

"It's my notion he does something more than scream," answered old McKay, the teamster, who

bore upon his shoulders the weight of three score
and ten years. "Tell ye what, old chaps, I haint
hearn so much truth as that youngster told in forty
years. I hearn his like once in my life and it's done
me up from that time to this," and the old veteran
lifted his straw hat from his bald pate, and ran his
old withered hand across his head, as though there
was something in the recollection of that time which
gave him pain.

"How was that, uncle?" asked young Robson,
who sat on an old empty whisky barrel, kicking his
heels against the hollow sides, "let us have the
story."

"It's a tarnal bad yarn to tell on a feller's own
self," said the old teamster, "but if I thought the
lesson would bring you up standin' just where you
are, Jake, I'd tell it."

"Well, go ahead; what d'ye say, boys?"

"All 'greed," responded half a dozen of the
younger members of the crowd, who liked to hear
McKay's stories.

"Well, ye see it was when I was about thirty, I
guess, I lived down on Big Beaver. It was the most
almighty mean place ye ever hearn tell on, and I
aint agoin' to dodge the truth. I was just the mean-
est cuss there was there. Whisky was plenty, for
the old stills were stuck under the hills all up and
down, and every feller that didn't keep a canteen in
his pocket was out of fashion. We spent our time
horse racing, fox hunting, at shooting matches,

huskins, and all them darned things, and I don't think I knew half the time whether I was a man or a monkey. Well, there had been a revival, or a protracted meetin' down our way and Bill Stetson, he had a small farm up the Beaver five miles or so, and was a good sort of a feller with a wife and six or seven children. He never got high only when he came down to Riggville—that was our town—to sell his hogs or taters or anything, then we fellers used to git around him and make him drink. Our old parson he talked like Duncan over there about *moderation ;* a man's a fool, I tell ye, to talk that way; can't be did, no sir! moderation to-day means lay in the gutter to-morrow; I know—I've tried it."

" Oh, go on with your story, old hoss, I'm getting hungry," said Jim Moody, the merriest soul in the crowd.

" Well, ye see, Stetson married my sister" (the old man cleared his throat); " he and she somehow got in with this Methody revival and both got religion and jined. This put the devil into us boys, so the next time he cum to town we got him into a bar room, and talked moderation and Scripture till we got him to take one dram. Don't I remember how we pretended pity and anxiousness and all that! He want going to take but a taste, just to warm him up,—it was awful cold,—but when he got one he wanted two, and we soon had him too drunk to go home, and there we kept him fooling for a week, and we a teasing him and making him believe he'd lost

his chance for the good place, and all such stuff till
we got the feller crossy like; well we had our sport
out and let him off and he went home. The minister was purty hard on him, and his wife none the
lovingest. He kept up steam a little—everybody
did in them times—and what should he do but take
it into his head that he was lost and going to hell
forever and his wife too, and the only way to save
the children was to kill em' while they were young
before they had a chance to sin. So the next night
he got pretty raving; they had a big log fire upon
the hearth and while Zilda—that's his wife—was
gone to church, he took the baby out of the cradle,
and threw it into the middle of the roaring hickory
fire among the logs, and burnt it to death, and then
tried to knock the brains out of the next one; I tell
you the truth, he burnt it to death." The old man
stopped a moment to clear his throat and drew his
hand across his eye.

The crowd started, and various ejaculations revealed their intense horror.

"What did they do with him?" asked Moody.

"Why, sir, they took up poor Bill, tried him for
murder and sent him to penitentiary for life, and his
wife was broken-hearted, and his children went vag-
abonds because their father was a murderer. There's
moderation for ye; all because we boys were—"

"Were a set of infernals," roared one of the
crowd.

"But hear the rest, boys; over the funeral of them

children we heard just such a sermon as that lawyer gin us. It wilted us, and four on us swore before Almighty God we'd never be moderate drinkers again ; and, boys, *I've kept my word.* If you want
to live as many years as I have, cuss that doctrine of
moderation ; I've hearn it all these years," and the
old man lifted his right arm toward heaven, "and I
swear to you I have seen it slay my companions till
their grav stuns whiten all the road of my life like
mile stuns on a turnpike road, from then till now."
The old man walked away, and one by one the crowd
followed to their homes, and did not, as usual, slip
nto the Oxbow **bar** for their Sunday night dram.

CHAPTER XVI.

THE BALL IN MOTION.

Tuesday evening came, and brought with it an immense multitude who had heard the ring of the young lawyer's voice from afar. The court room could not contain the half of those desiring to enter. They stood at the windows, crowded the aisle, and hung upon the railings, and yet the cry went out, "they come, they come."

Max turned a little pale and his knees smote together, but in his voice there was no quaver of fear, in his words no faltering, and in his arguments no flaw. His address was short but so forcible that it swayed his hearers to and fro, as the branches of the elms bend to the wind; and when, at the close, he called for those who were willing to stand with him on the platform of *total abstinence*, he found numbers ready to marshal themselves under his banner and follow his lead.

Among the first to take their places in the front were Heckel Dinmont and Mafy, his wife, followed by Die and Tom. Others followed, and as fast as the foremost retired the ranks were filled. Shout after shout made the walls of the house of justice tremble; the meeting was a success, and as such was accepted by all parties. A victory had been gained, but to maintain the position there was needed valiant warriors, and they were found. Young men and maidens, ready to buckle on the armor, those who had seen and felt the evil, but waited for their leader, for a master spirit to move them on. That master spirit they found, fully adequate to their wants, in Maxwell Carter.

Die was installed in the changed household of the Lodge, as the presiding Penate of its various departments, and though Mrs. Hancock did not quite lay down her "purpose"—as Ruth called it—she only carried the small end of the yoke, and let the balance swing light or heavy, as the case might be, or as the mood pleased her, upon the shoulders of her younger and stronger companion. Yet she never went back into her former listless habits and ennui, and Die became her companion in every sense of the word, from the sharer of the evening gossip to the family secrets and arrangements.

Max, having leisure, became her teacher one hour every evening in mathematics, while Mrs. Jones— the governess—carried forward her writing lessons and grammar, and proud they were of the progress of their pupil. Heckel Dinmont arose, under the manipulations of Max and Die and the alphabet, into an expansion of manhood which astonished his friends and confounded his enemies.

Emma and Olivia wrote letters home full to the brim of their admiration and enjoyment of foreign lands, but certain sentences set the home friends to thinking that after all she had not come to "years of discretion," when she gave herself and fortune to an old man, a gambler and a drunkard.

Judge Hancock was elected United States Senator for six years. He said to Max :

"We are running different lines; you go ahead with yours, and if you can reform this community, God be praised. I took things as I found them; they are bad enough, but I have other work to do."

The Judge was busy preparing himself and business for his Washington work when the time should come, and Max became factotum of the Hancock estate in the absence of its owner.

George would graduate the following year, make a short visit at home, and then join his sisters over the sea, to be absent two years at least. Nettie was still at boarding school. She and Aggie Frobish were inseparable friends, spent all their holidays at home, and were becoming accomplished young ladies. Max received letters from George and Gordon very often. George told of Gordon's success in everything he undertook. He was the life of his class, the undoubted genius of the college. "I tremble for him all the time; not a week passes that he does not stimulate himself for some effort, with wine or brandy; so do most of the boys for that matter, but Gordon is as sensitive as a woman

Give him his way and he will go to the d— as most of our brilliant men have done (*vide* Byron, Moore, Poe, Burns and Clark). Is it ever to be the fate of genius?"

At another time he wrote: "Max, what shall I do to save Gordon; he is the pet of the southern bloods and all the northern spendthrifts—and we have plenty of them. Not a meeting or evening party is complete without him. Ply him with wine—not too much—and he's splendid; dramatises equal to Booth, and reads like Fannie Kemble; alas, poor Aggie."

Gordon wrote: "George is a regular old puritan; only needs a white necktie, to comb his hair straight back from his forehead, and take a few lessons in sacerdotal sighing, to be dubbed reverend. By the way, Max, is there not somebody that he loves better than his mother, that is holding a spiritual influence over him that is not of the other world? Something has transformed the careless, jolly, roistering George, into George the jolly, but careful and sober.

Gordon wrote beautiful, soul breathing billets to Aggie every day, or stole away and on the wings of iron and steam, spent a few delicious hours with her every few months, and always met her on his home visits.

Mrs. Frobish, who had been born in the lowest grade of life, transferred into a tavern kitchen in her childhood, taught all the tricks of dishonest servility, had been lifted out of her position by a

sincere love that saw her only as the buxom beauty
who, being well trained for the work, would make a
good wife and landlady, and had commenced her
career as we have stated in a former chapter.

The love of a mother for her children began soon
to draw the good in her soul upward, for a soul she
had which might, with early bias in right paths,
have been led into all that was womanly and beautiful. ▪ Led in an opposite direction by all the
attractions of her early surroundings, shall she be
blamed for failing, where the wisest and best of our
nation and of the world have gone down to rise no
more?

Ere you blame the womanhood so tried and
tempted, ask your own heart, oh! reader of my
words, what you would have been in her place.

It is many a year since she seduced Farmer Paxton with her wiles. It is many a year since the
spirit of good has been calling with winning tones
to her better nature, to turn aside from the old worn
paths of demoralization, and enter those which lead,
by gentle steps upward, toward the gates of the
heavenly kingdom.

Would Aggie ever be what she was now? she
asked herself. She started back from the thought,
as if a skeleton glared in her way. Could she,
would she bear and endure, to see her husband or
the husband of her child a drunkard? A skeleton
more haggard, more terrible confronted her. Long
ago she had refused to enter the bar, long ago she

had said, "The time must come. Ah, how she will hate us when she knows how we make our living. Oh, Aggie, oh, Aggie."

Aggie had gone to her boarding school with a heavy weight upon her young mind. Aunt Phebe's story had troubled her. In the dead of the night she had sobbed over it, and resolved to "ask mother all about it; may be it was not so bad." But when morning came, the joyful spirit, lifted up by the sunshine and cheered by the seeming happy life about her, shrank from the midnight resolves. It was unpleasant; to-morrow would find for her a more convenient season. Have not older heads reasoned in the same way and put off duty until too late?

Mr. Duncan, her minister, said, "to drink in moderation was not wrong;" and did her father and mother do more than others? Somebody must keep a tavern, and there were taverns in every place she knew, and bar-rooms in every tavern.

So advised, so reasoning, the fluttering bird that had promised never to dip its little bill in the wine cup, grew satisfied, and let the sweet love of Gordon cover the aching wound she had received, out of sight for a time. But the skeleton before Mrs. Frobish's eyes would down at no such bidding.

"Have I a right to be an accessory in making of other women's husbands and sons what would blight and deform every particle of my own happiness in life? Have I a right to let any other mortal

mind do my thinking, or assume the moral responsibility of my actions?"

These questions became troublesome guests, demanding answers, and would not away; late in life
it is true, but daily doing their worst. No one in
Oxbow had been more shocked than she, when told
of Sam. Roland's conduct and the law that sustained
it, and it was no soothing ointment laid upon the
raw and smarting wound, to be told by her husband,
"If I had not taken the cow somebody else would."
It did not help matters at all.

She had made the spirited reply, and the jolly
landlord had laughed his acquiescence.

"They say that husband and wife are one, Mr.
Frobish, and that one is the husband. Good; now
I demand that the half of you which is made up of
me, shall order that cow back again, and the me that
is in you will see it is done, as sure as my name is
Rena Frobish."

"Just send Jake out to-night to open the stable
door, and Rose will toss her horns and go straight
home, and there we'll let her stay, wife, we won't
quarrel about it," said the landlord.

"And Sam shan't have any more whisky?"

"Never a drop from me."

"We're one on that score then."

"Be careful you don't prove us two," said Frobish
as he retreated, admiring more and more the spirit
of his wife.

That night a tall figure, muffled in a cloak, might

have been seen to enter the low door of Sam. Roland's domicil, and after a moment's conversation to slip out again, whispering these words at parting :

"Call it the landlord's cow and no one will dare touch it."

Rose, as the cow was called, already stood at the gate chewing her cud contentedly, surrounded by the gladdened children, hanging on her horns and leaning against her smooth sides, and pretty Rose bowed her thanks as the tall figure departed.

By and by had followed the death of Myra Bishop. Mrs. Frobish,was one of the first to answer the call for assistance, and like the piercing of a stiletto that had reached her very vitals, was the answer returned to a neighbor's question which she overheard. "Where do all these men get their drinks? Judge Hancock will not allow any of his people to sell a drop at retail."

"At the Oxbow ; it is the front door to hell," answered a grieved spirit that every day felt the hot breathings of that atmosphere.

Do we call her words unwomanly? The landlord's wife retreated with a sore heart. She heard the appeal of Max over the grave of the victim of whisky. Deeper and deeper, like a surgeon's knife, cutting into the flesh to take thence a poisoned tumor, went the hurt, and before the Christmas days came with their merry bells, that brought home

Aggie to lay her head on her bosom, the Oxbow tavern was kept without a bar.

Reader do not lay the book down crying out this is preposterous. I tell you, No! Every character has had its type in real life

CHAPTER XVII.

HECKEL DINMONT LEAVES OXBOW.

A few weeks after the funeral of Myra Bishop, Max sat by the bedside of the repentant and sorrowing husband, trying to open up to him some light for the guidance of his future life.

Gilbert had spoken but little as he lay helpless, for it was many days before he could even lift his hands, and had never once alluded to the subject of his wife's death, or the fate of his children; deep lines of pain alone told the watchers of his misery. He made no complaint, asked for no favor, nor suggested the slightest improvement in treatment or condition. Some said he was crazed; others, that the shock had paralyzed nerve and brain, that idiocy would follow as the last act of the tragedy.

To-day Max had lifted him up, propped him with pillows, smoothed out his beard, and trimmed his hair; talking to him the while as if he was a mortal man and worthy to be forgiven, though his sins amounted to seventy times seven. To induce him to talk, he threw up the window, into which the clear November sunshine poured like a golden flood.

" There, isn't that grand," said **Max, as** he drew
back the curtain to its utmost limits.

> Was there ever a day so bright as this,
>   Or ever a sky so blue ;
> One fleecy cloud like an angel's wing,
>   With the sunshine glist'ning through?

Max sang cheerily. A groan answered his impromptu madrigal.

" Come, my good fellow, let me set you a little
higher; can you stand that? take a good look;
Rand's house looks fine on the hillside, amid its
Indian-summer glories; those golden maples in
front, and the scarlet leaves of the wild woodbine,
twining around the white columns, are a sight fair
to see."

The invalid turned his eyes wearily toward the
view indicated, but made no response.

" Bishop, did you know Mrs. Rand had taken your
two youngest children home with her?" asked Max,
as if the question was very commonplace.

" Who has taken Hettie?" asked Gilbert, huskily.

" Mrs. Hancock."

" And they are waiting for me to get well enough
to take them off their hands?"

" Roused at last," thought Max.

" No, I guess you will have to work hard to get
them back ; they are the pets of both households."

" Did she—did Myra give them away?"

" No, oh no; but she did ask Mrs. Hancock to
care for them, and I assure you they are in good
hands."

The invalid covered his face with his hands, and for the first time broke into sobs and tears.

Max let the grief have its run, knowing that nothing would be more likely to break up the torpid state of body and mind into which he had fallen; the emotion was fearful for a few moments, and then he grew calm and asked:

"Will you tell me all?"

"Are you able to hear it now?"

"Oh, Mr. Carter, I am not able to bear this horrible suspense; did she curse me?"

"Oh, no, Bishop, she blessed you."

"Oh, tell me all and let me die."

"We're not going to let you die; you have been very weak, and sadly tempted, and fearful results have been the consequences. You must not now be weak enough to die, but brave enough to live—to prove to the world by a true repentance before God and man, that you *can* cease to do evil, and learn to do well; greater criminals than you have done so."

"Never, never, never," moaned out the fainting invalid.

"There can be no sin so deep, no stain so black, that God in His infinite goodness and love will not forgive, if rightly repented of and abandoned."

"Tell me all."

Max detailed the night scene with Diana, and repeated the words of love spoken by the wife, at which Bishop broke forth afresh with tears and groans.

Then the words of the dying " Tell Him to come, oh, it is so beautiful"—were whispered gently in his ear, and the sobbing soul received them as a benediction, only saying:

" Now leave me alone. Oh, those words, those words."

Max laid him down and left him.

After a day or so he was able to sit a few moments in a chair, and to talk freely of his children and his future prospects.

When told of the commotion that had followed his wife's funeral and of the temperance organization, he shook his head and answered bitterly :

" The good and the beautiful crucified for the uplifting of the multitude, and I the Judas Iscariot."

One evening as he bade Max good night he said :

" Give my thanks to those good women who have my children ; some day I will try to repay them by showing them I am worthy to be the father of my own babes."

Twice had Max asked if he wished to see the children, but he answered :

" Not yet, I could not bear it."

On the morning after the message had been sent, the family found his bed and room empty. Search was made to trace him without effect. He was gone, and after much wondering and prophecying, his absence was forgotten, and Oxbow moved on as before.

Spring had come again to gladden the hearts of

men, and with it many changes, the most startling of
which was that Heckel Dinmont had found out that
he had tarried long enough in Oxbow, that it was
time he lived on land he could call his own; he
began to understand too that it was infinitely more
comfortable to do a good rousing day's work for
himself, than two days' work in one day for his
neighbors, and get pay for but one. Reading the
papers had filled his head with these notions. There
were lands to be given to actual settlers in Kansas
and Missouri; why should not he and Mary have a
home some day.

"Why," Mary said, "we can;" so said Die.

Die had laid up four months' wages, and Heck
found fifty dollars in his box, and the loom, which
had clattered merrily all winter, had put a new phase
on many things.

"Will you go along, Die?"

"No, father, my place is a good one in all ways;
I am progressing well with my music and arithme-
tic, grammar, writing and geography. Mrs. Jones
says I am to-day ahead of Nettie; my wages are
good, and the presents I receive would overwhelm
me, if I did not know that it is a charity to use
the surplus of that which is thus thrown upon my
hands."

"You are right, Diana," said Mary Dinmont, "stay
and gain all the knowledge you can. We will pio-
neer, and the boys will find a chance to work as they
grow older, and when the time comes you can teach
us all; I am so strong now."

"That's the ticket, exactly," said Dinmont, clapping his hands; and the boys set up a shout "Hurra for Kansas! Hurra for Die!"

"What does Tom say?" asked Die.

"He's fierce on the track—says he can manage a farm now better than Harris, and he don't want to stay here and be nothing but Tom Dinmont as long as he lives," said Egbert.

"And so he is going to leave *me* here, to be only Die 'as long as I live,'" answered Die, mischievously.

"Oh, you're a born lady—everybody says so—spect you'll marry Mr. Max fore long."

"No, Teddy, I shall never marry Mr. Wash."

"Hurra! Mr. Wash; who said Mr. Wash? your face is as red as a pink, Die."

"Why, Teddy, what do you mean? I meant to say Mr. Max."

"Yes, but you was thinking 'Mr. Wash,'" said the young tease.

Die's cheeks grew redder and hotter as she turned to her father:

"Have you money enough, father, to carry you through? it's a long journey."

"I was thinking, Die, if I left you as security, maybe the Judge would help me."

"Me; how is that?"

"Well, you're getting twelve dollars a month, and you don't seem to need much. I thought you'd like to let me have it, so if I borrow of him you can pay him the interest, and I'll pay the principal when I get started; after that I'll pay you."

"Oh father, I *can* do that, and I am so glad to be able to help you; that would be worth a life time of being 'nuss and scrub.'"

"Who called you that?" asked Heck, indignantly.

So Die told the story of the sore eyes, only leaving out her own little love episode, making a hearty laugh for them all; even little Lulu clapped her hands and joined in the glee.

As Die walked home, beneath the shining stars, she called herself to a strict account—"am I secretly nursing a passion for my patron's son? am I, unconsciously to my better self, giving out the deepest, purest energies of my being to one who will never appreciate them, one who perhaps if he knew them now would laugh them to scorn?"

All these questions ended in convincing herself that she did, more than any other (in a certain way) love George Hancock, and that the sensation had revealed itself more forcibly that day, that his image had been more clearly defined to her vision, and his name brought more closely to her lips, by a letter from Nettie which she had received that morning, and which ran thus:

"Oh Die, Gordon wrote to Aggie the other day that our Wash had a lady love, at whose shrine he worshipped morn, noon and eve; and that, even in the silent watches of the night, he did not cease his devotion. Oh, won't that be grand, to have brother

11

Wash in love; how I'd like to hear Ruth groan when she finds it out; don't tell her till I come. * * * Thirteen weeks now, only thirteen; how funny it will be to see you at the head of the house. Don't you fall in love with Max; if he was rich I'd set my own cap for him; don't you tell him, that's a a dear—goodby."

In spite of her desire to do otherwise Die had to acknowledge to a keen sting of jealousy,—to an aroused sense of right of possession,—to a feeling which always accompanies jealousy. "He is mine; what right has any other to engross his admiration."

Instantly she cast this feeling out of her heart with the imperative command, "get thee behind me, Satan. What shadow of reason have I to lay claim to his affections; true, with a boy's generosity, he was attracted nine months ago with my pretty face, —I know I am pretty,—and he let me know it; but did he not also let me know by the same suppression of himself, which I could see and feel, that he was wrestling down this attraction as unwise and forbidden? Had he in recklessness of consequences told his love, and tried to win from me a confession of return, I could hate him for his weakness; but he has been noble and brave, and I will follow his lead; respect him and love him with respect, as I would one already fixed beyond my reach by a fate that is inexorable, and rejoice if another worthy of it holds him in her love."

But while she resolved, this pure hearted child, but just emerging from the darkened ignorance of poverty,—almost of degradation,—felt the tremor of this hidden life current, this magnetism, as that which carries the thought and words of those thousands of miles apart on the quivering wires.

"I will do right, and every aspiration of the day will ask for guidance that shall lead me safely."

Heckel Dinmont was in earnest, and found Judge Hancock ready and willing, to advise and help him.

There was but little to do, to arrange things for departure, and Heck often rubbed his hands and said in his jolly way, "Blessed be nothing after all, for nothing is easily moved;" and before the May flowers were gemming the velvet robes of the prairies, Heckel Dinmont and his wife and children were on their own quarter section, and in their own house (framed in Pittsburg) on the rolling prairies, by a beautiful river in Kansas. His team, which the Judge had furnished, united with that of a neighbor who lived miles away, was breaking up the matted growth of ages.

Mary was full of hope. Not yet on the summit level of life, buoyant with renewed health and strength, she met her destiny in a new country with joyful anticipation. The suffering of the past had inured her to hardship and bold courage to meet the worst, and resolutely to conquer. Her husband did not drink and her sky was all rainbows.

"If he will keep his pledge—and I will not doubt him—we shall never want. Oh, God be praised for all this beauty, for all this hope," was her daily prayer and thanksgiving. If the starving, toiling millions that gather in, and hang like swarms of flies about our cities, could but know how much less striving it would demand, to place themselves above want in the great open fields of the west, than to live out their days in tenement houses, in slums and alleys, would they not strive? would not God through some benevolent judge, help those who would rise up forcefully to help themselves? Reader, I think so. Heck found precisely the objects in his new farm, to engross all his surplus vigor and talent; his work of the day, left unfinished, yet moving on toward the end, was his own, not his neighbor's; each day stirred in his soul a new hope for to-morrow, which bound him as with iron chains to his purpose. There was no such man on the border to help his neighbors, no man whom neighbors were more ready to help in return. No one knew of his past nor taunted him with former follies. He was a friend and counsellor, and all that was in him was uplifted, strengthened and enlarged. Heckel Dinmont was growing into the stature of a *man*, a man worthy to be the husband of Mary Dinmont and the father of Diana.

CHAPTER XVIII.

LETTER FROM MRS. RAND TO HER SON.

My Dear Gordon: I wrote you in my last, that I had failed to persuade your father to leave his business long enough to visit New Haven, and be a witness of the exercises of your graduating class, in July. This I regretted sincerely, as he has not allowed himself a month's leisure since we have lived together, and I believe that he—and every other business man— needs occasional rest and recreation. He thought he should lose the "run of his work," if he indulged himself as I proposed.

I tried to convince him that Judge Hancock will, in all probability, live out the remainder of his allotted days in peace and plenty, even if one of his humble laborers, after twenty-five years of toil, should lay down for a few weeks, his account books and his pen. I even went to the Judge and received, not only permission, but urgent entreaty that Mr. Rand would comply with my wishes. He assured me that Sherwood, who has been in the office as assistant for some years, is fully competent to take charge.

All was in vain, I could not move the imperturbable rock one hair's breadth. Now you will be astounded—for—*we are coming.*

You know the old saying, "Man proposes; but God disposes." I have a story to tell that will fill you with astonishment, and I hope, give you pleasure.

I have never very fully detailed to you my early history, always intending to do so at some future time. But, you know,

Gordon, dear, that there are some points on which I could never speak without yielding to what is called "woman's weakness,' suffocating sobs and tears. Therefore, those points have been avoided. But I can write about them, and yet repress the surging emotion that in conversation wholly overcomes my womanly dignity.

My mother and her brother, ten years older, were left orphans when mother was but sixteen. Grandfather Walpole left a small property, and after the custom of the English (he was an Englishman by birth) willed it all, as far as the laws would allow, to Uncle Nehemiah, enjoining upon him to care for and educate his sister, and at her marriage to bestow upon her one thousand dollars. All this was done with scrupulous honesty and economy. Not one unnecessary penny was expended in my mother's behalf, although her brother was said to be getting richer with every hour.

He never married. Could not afford the luxury of a wife, or even housekeeper, and when, at the age of twenty, my mother accepted the addresses of my father, Lieut. Gordon, of the U. S. A., Uncle was so offended that he paid her promptly the one thousand dollars, and forbade her his house.

My father was not well calculated, I think, to make the pecuniary wheels of life move easily; and when he died there was not enough left of his possessions to meet the necessary expenses of the funeral. Father had never been willing that mother should make any appeal for aid to her brother; but now, reduced to the utmost straits of poverty, she wrote to him for help.

I was then seven years old. He answered her appeal in person. I remember him well, a cold, silent, stern man. He heaped reproaches upon mother; but my curly hair and brown eyes (they say I was a pretty child) seemed to melt a little of the ice of his heart, and for my sake, he doled out to us a scanty subsistence, until I was old enough to be sent to an academy for young ladies in Harrisburg, where I remained, at his dictation, for six years.

At the death of my mother, he sent me five hundred dollars,

telling me decidedly, that I was now eighteen and must henceforth depend upon my own exertions; that he had not educated
me to become an idler; but to give me the means of working
out my own destiny independently. I thanked him and promised to do my best. I soon found a situation as teacher in the
academy where I had been educated, and remained there until a
visit to Oxbow with one of my pupils made me acquainted with
your father.

I never heard again from my uncle. Indeed, while I was
thankful for the great help he had bestowed, I felt that his letter precluded all continuance of acquaintance and my pride
prevented my writing to him, lest he should think I was har-
boring an idea of becoming his heir.

I have heard, from time to time, of his immense wealth and
his miserly habits; but he has formed no part of my interest in
life and, of late, has been almost wholly blotted from my memory.

Imagine our surprise, then, at receiving a letter, a week since,
dated Nashua, N. H., from his business agent, informing us of
his sudden death, from paralysis, and the subsequent finding
of his will, by which I am made his heir, to an almost incalcu-
lable amount of bank stock, cotton factories, houses, bonds,
and other valuables. The agent requested my immediate presence and that of my husband.

Do you wonder that father has changed his mind? Are you
surprised that he has given up the superintendence of the distillery at Oxbow? Will you be entirely displeased, that we
have made arrangements with Judge Hancock for you to join
his son and Prof. Winthrop in their contemplated journey on
the continent; that we are to be with you commencement week;
accompany you to New York, see you safely on board the
Arago and out to sea; and then turn our faces toward the Gran-
ite hills?

Now, my dear son, before you make any of your enthusiastic
demonstrations over this questionable good news, let me say a
word or two in reference to the bearing of this legacy upon our
future lives. Whether it will make us more happy, or more

miserable, will depend upon ourselves ; on the uses to which we shall appropriate it.

I am glad for your father's sake, because it will release him from the continual drudgery of labor which he has imposed upon himself.   To educate and provide for you, have been the purposes of his life.   These objects are attained and now he can rest.   It will add to my happiness beyond this, only as it will enlarge my means of doing good.   By the way, those pretty children of Myra Bishop's have been to me a source of exceeding enjoyment.   We shall leave them, during our absence with Diana Dinmont and Miss Jones, at the "Lodge."

Diana is improving very much and has been Mrs. Hancock's shadow the last eight months.   Gossip has it that Maxwell Carter is going to marry her.   She is a pretty creature ; but he is entirely too well endowed and cultured, to take one whose whole life has been spent in the position of a servant.

Feeling assured that my budget of news needs no enlargement, I am   Your loving mother,

E. G. RAND.

P. S.—I want to add I am so glad that you are heart-whole, and have made no engagements with the attractions about Oxbow.   I used to be afraid of that little Aggie Frobish.   Be careful, my dear.   The world is wide, and you will have ample time to examine and discriminate, before you are twenty-five.

MOTHER.

The night before Gordon Rand received the above letter he had been indulging in one of his licenses ; or as he himself called them " sprees."   Promising that it should be his last until after Commencement, he had finished his graduating oration, passed triumphantly through his examinations, and with a half dozen others, gave himself up to the convivialities of the club room.

It was late at night when he returned to his room, reeling and almost insensible.   Late when he awoke in the morning, with a terrible headache, and in no condition to be seen. George brought him his letters and sat down by an opposite window to read his own, while the thoughtless, reckless inebriate tried to read his mother's loving words. Two or three times he began the letter and laid it down from sheer weariness and trembling. Laid it down with muttered curses and discontent. At last, when George had read his letters, Gordon hurled his mother's across the room, with the imperative demand, "Read it for me, George;" and hiding his face in the pillow he awaited the contents in silence.

George picked the letter up with no very generous feeling, and proceeded with his task until he came to the revelation of the bequest. Gordon, who had not stirred or spoken before, jumped from the bed like a mad man, hurled his pillow to the ceiling, sprang up and down with a wild hurrah, and then flung himself on his bed panting and exhausted, shouting, "Go on, go on." George continued and read the calm motherly letter to the last words. The reference to Diana shook him like an ague. The words "Going to marry her," glared at him like demons; yet he kept his voice steady, forced the paling coward blood to sustain its flow in his cheeks until he had finished, then laid the letter down and left the room without a word.

Gordon was scarcely less shocked by his mother's allusion to Aggie. The high state of physical excitement into which the news of the legacy had

11*

thrown him, had passed with his gymnastic exercises, and with the reaction came this depressing
allusion to the girl he loved; for he loved Aggie—
as such natures as his do love. Loved her as he
loved himself, when self did not demand some
thoughtless indulgence, and even then with her beside him to council in her sweet voice, he would
have abstained.

The words of his mother aroused his better nature.
What was that fortune to him, if Aggie were not to
share it! What would life be without her! He
sprang from his bed, exclaiming, with vehement
passion and grief:

"What is my life worth to her, to me, to my mother, to my father, to any one, if I continue as I have
begun! What would my mother have felt and said
if she had seen her 'dear son' lying there, too im-
beeile from last night's debauch to read her loving
letter! Oh! Aggie, Aggie, my first, my only love,
what a fate will be yours if I win you! Can I go
on? Can I cheat her pure soul any longer?
Drunk! yes, I was *drunk* last night. What better
am I now. Yes, I am *drunk*, and I am a hypocrite;
false to every soul that loves, or cares for me; false
to George and Max, who love me for the good I
have in me and try to save me.

"Oh! God of mercy, can I be saved? Can the
bent and gnarled young oak become straight? Can
the lightning blasted rock become whole again?
Oh, blackened soul of mine! If I could bear my

burden alone; if I could crush out my life! But
the pure sweet lily that I have dared to call my own,
would blight and die all the same, and all the joy
and light would be blotted from the lives of the
mother that loves me so and of the father whose
failing years have been given all to me.

" And for what do I suffer so and cause such suffering? Because I cannot turn aside from that accursed cup that is bearing me and thousands beside
me to the death—to living death. Oh, mother, my
too loving mother, why did you yield to my cravings,
why indulge my imperious nature? Oh! mothers, everywhere, be wise for your own love's sake."

Groaning in agonies of self torture, this gay, talented, every way richly endowed man, raved up and
down his room, pouring out in incoherent exclamations the misery of his soul.

The coming fortune, the trip to Europe, the opening career, all that would have filled him with intense delight, were buried, for the time, beneath the
avalanche of guilty sorrow that overwhelmed him
in this moment of awakened consciousness. Hour
after hour, his torture continued unabated, for he
felt no strength within himself to sustain an honorable life; but at length he threw himself upon his
knees and clasping his mother's letter in his hands,
he vowed never again to drink anything that could
inebriate. Soothed by this resolve, he threw himself
upon his bed, and fell into the heavy sleep that follows such excitement.

While Gordon sleeps, and George is trying beneath the heavy foliage of the college grounds to
reason himself into patience and a forgiving spirit,
the cool summer winds whispering to him what
a truly manly man should do under the circumstances, we will read his mother's letter :

My dear, dear George :—I have so many things to tell you
to-night that I wish unusually for your very self to talk with.
Writing is such a labor to me. Die should be my amanuensis,
but she and Max have gone to Oxbow to attend a temperance
festival, the proceeds of which are to be given to a public library. They are always doing some good work. I think they
were made for each other, and your father shares the opinion
with me. Speaking of your father, I think he is failing. He
is very far from well, and gives himself no rest; although he
promises to do so this summer, Max having proved such efficient help. He thinks you had better go from college direct to
New York, as Prof. Winthrop wishes to be in Frankfort-on-the
Main in time for some great scientific demonstration, which he
wishes you to attend. You will there obtain introductions to
many great men of the different countries you will visit. So
we shall leave Jessie and Hetty with Die, (we couldn't live if
it were not for Die) take Nettie, and be with you at commencement; go with you to New York, see you off, and then spend
the summer where we can enjoy it best.

Next winter your father will take his place in the Senate and
wants to take us, Nettie, the children, Die, and all, to Washington.

We have had a terrible letter from Emma. She says Olivia
is nearly crazy. That Col. Vandyke is no government agent at
all ; but a gambler, and drinks so that there is no living with
him peaceably. She is very homesick, and wants papa to find
somebody to bring her back. It is horrible, and my heart aches
for my poor suffering children ; but most for Olivia, doomed to
what a dreadful life. Until we can act for them, I try to lose
myself in the demands which are so urgent here.

I had almost forgotten, in my own troubles. Mrs. Rand's good fortune. A miserly uncle has left them a large estate, and they are talking of sending Gordon with you. How will you like it! Aunt Ruth sends "Heaps of love" to her "baby" and hopes you wont't go into that country where they eat frogs and cats, 'cause you will get "pisened." She is a good old soul and quite "set up," she says, with the idea of going to Washington with us. Jessie sends brother Wash a kiss. Nettie was well at last writing. She and Aggie will be home Saturday and we shall all start Tuesday morning next.

Your affectionate mother,
EMILY HANCOCK.

To this motherly letter no especial pang was added by Mrs. Rand's postscript. The words, " They were made for each other," proved rather a salve than an irritant. " Is that so?" George asked of himself. " Had Max an intuition of that fact when he exacted of me the promise to leave Die in ignorance of the true state of my feelings until my return from Europe? Is this the reward of my devotion to her, my trust in him! This the end of all my castle building!"

Deeply pained and disappointed, he was yet outwardly calm. Months of entire suppression and continual reasoning concerning what was best, what ought to be, and what should be, if his energy and continuity of purpose could bring it about, had not been in vain. Yet his thoughts ran on much in this wise. Resign her! Yes, he would, without an outward murmur. Max was far more worthy of her than he could ever be; it was fitting in every way. They were born in the same grade of social life; knew from experience its hardships and trials; could

sympathize and comprehend. Yes, it was the wisest
and best for both. He would write so to Max. No,
he could not. What right had Max thus, without a
word, to win the love which he knew his friend held
above all earthly possessions for himself. Was it
honorable? Was it like a gentleman? No, it was
treachery.

The conflict between self and justice waxed warm,
sometimes wrathful; yet the quiet voice of honor
and reason whispered in the sober, unperverted soul,
" Let Max claim what he can win. If you love truly,
you will rejoice in the happiness of the object of
your love. In just so much as Max Carter is nobler
than you, is he better fitted to be the companion of
the pure minded, beautiful girl, who has wakened
your love."

The college bells rang out their peal for a meeting, in which he was to take a part. With manly
promptness he found his place and, although the
waves of passion and disappointment tossed high, he
kept his hand firmly upon the helm and guided the
bark of his bright manhood safely into its accustomed harbor.

When he returned to his room an hour later he
found Gordon still sleeping, his mother's letter
crushed between his hands, and traces of great blis-
tering tears still upon his face. He had not awakened the sleeper by his gentle entrance; and stood
looking at him with intense pity. We cannot hate
any one whom we thoroughly know, and George

could not find a harsher feeling than pity for this frail sufferer from a violated appetite. Noting the distorted face, so racked with pain and conscious guilt, he could not but recall words written long ago, by one under the influence of a like accusing conscience.

·" Drunk! Parrot, and squabble and swear, and discourse fustian with one's own shadow! O, thou invisible spirit of wine! if thou hast no other name to be known by, let us call thee Devil."

" Oh! that men should put an enemy into their mouths to steal away their brains! That we should with joy, revel and applause, transform ourselves into beasts."

" To be now a sensible man, by and by a fool, and presently a beast. Oh, strange! Every inordinate cup is unblest and the ingredient is a devil."

Still looking upon his prostrate companion, and thinking how aptly the words of the transgressor of olden time applied to the being before him, his thoughts took a new direction, and he exclaimed aloud—

" Oh! Maxwell Carter, but for you I might have been even as he; but for those true searching words of a true and noble man, that roused me to self-control and self-denial. Can any human soul know its influence upon another human soul? Who has a right to condemn another's weakness? Shall I, heir of all the ages of dissipation and death that have gone before me in my family, boast of my strength;

or set myself above this one that has fallen? Only in total abstinence from all that can inebriate, am I made whole and kept from this groveling. Oh! Gordon Rand, would that I—"

George might have quoted Shakespeare by the hour without arousing the sleeper, so accustomed were they to spouting poems and rehearsing lessons, but the moment his own name sounded in his ears, Gordon awakened and sprang up bewildered.

An explanation ensued; all penitence and self-accusation on the one part; all kindness and persuasion and truthful advice on the other.

Imperative duties commanded the time and strength of each, and taking hold of these duties with a will, the interest in them soon soothed their aching hearts. Here let us leave them; their reputations untarnished in the eyes of the world, their prospects unsurpassed, and their firm resolves untried. Leave them with their yet unformed characters, to stamp upon their lives during the next three years the impress which their acts shall give.

Gordon can yet redeem the past and become a shining mark of nobleness among men. George may fall by the wayside, tempted by loving hands into the forbidden paths of self-indulgence.

Reader, would you tempt either of these again? Put "the enemy into their mouths to steal away their brains?" would you crush that mother's hopes, hasten the grey hairs of the father to the grave; blight the life of the maiden who loves; and rob the world of talent and worth? Would you?

CHAPTER XIX.

THE FARM REDEEMED.

"Don't be discouraged, Heckel," said Mary Dinmont to her husband, as he sat by the tea table, leaning his head despondently upon his hands. "Look back four years and see if you really find anything to make you disheartened."

"I know, I know, Mary. You would have me remember what a brute I was; for it's just four years this month since Die watched her wretched father through the long doleful night. But, Mary, what are we to do? Every cent of the money is due and I can't pay it. If the Judge pleases, he can foreclose the mortgage to-morrow and sweep away all the avails of our toil and privations of years."

Mary rose from her seat and standing behind his chair drew his head back against her breast, and whispered softly: "Even then, my dear husband, we s ould be infinitely better off than we were on that dismal night; for our hearts are full of love and sympathy and we have learned to do our best."

"That's true, Mary. But it goes hard to think of losing all this that we love so well."

"I guess, dear, we shall not lose it."

"My wheat will not be worth harvesting. Forty acres of it a loss; and if this drouth continues, our corn will not be sufficient for family use, and if the coming winter should be like the last, our stock must be sold."

"Surely, if we write to Judge Hancock, he will give us another year."

"And if another year should be like this, only more so," said Egbert, "what then?"

"We will wait and trust. But let us hope that another year will not be as this and the last have been."

"Well," said Heckel, rising and unclasping the soothing hands from his brow, and touching the warm cheek so near his own with his lips, " I guess that is the best we can do, Mary. I don't like it. Die has already done so much for us that I hate to ask her influence with the Judge. We'll wait and trust and do our best."

"There's Tom," shouted Egbert, springing from his chair to the door with a bound. " Now we shall have a letter from Die." And away he ran to meet the rumbling cart far away on the prairie.

"It's a good while since we've had one," said Mary stirring about to put things in order for the coming teamster; setting the supper again on the table and preparing his favorite dish of milk, adding thereto all that a tired boy who had tramped all day beside his team over a dusty road would be expected to want.

There was something in Mary's movements that indicated unusual nervousness, even impatience; something in her look that hinted mystery. Heckel watched her, as she moved to and fro, and wondered if the unusual appearance, which he could see but could not analyze, were the result of her efforts to keep up heart against all the discouragements that surrounded them.

"Poor Mary," he thought to himself, "what a hard life I've led her." He went to the door and out upon the porch that shaded his home. Far away under the soft summer moonlight, lay the fields he was so fearful of losing. Beautiful in that silvery light did they look to him with their growing crops, the groups of cattle, the well built fences, the barns, like painted castles in the shimmering light.

Sunlight would have revealed the effects of the drouth, but the calm clearness of the night only enhanced the real beauty; and his heart swelled with painful emotions as he thought of the possibility that it might all pass from his possession as a dream.

One year before he had asked an extension of time of Judge Hancock and received it, and now to ask again! How could he?

Soon Egbert interrupted his thoughts, having out run the weary team with the letters and papers.

"One from Die, one from Die, hurrah! and Tom says there's a big box come by the river steamer."

The letter was for Mrs. Dinmont and she eagerly

broke the seal and devoured the contents. It was full of tender kindness and inquiries, of circumstantial revealings of the daughter's life at Washington. She was no longer scrub and nurse girl, as long ago, but the private Secretary of Judge Hancock, and had been filling that position for over two years. She had not told them before for she had wished to be secure in her place ; to know that she had taken this step upward beyond possibility of return, before she should claim her position in the eyes of those nearest. Then followed family news, the expected return of George, now three years absent; the ways and doings of Max Carter, who had been for two years the successful law partner of the Judge ; sundry anecdotes of good old Ruth in her immense importance and dignity ; cheering words with Lulu and a promise of presents one of these days ; love to all, &c., &c.

Heckel looked grave over an inclosure that had been handed him. Die hoped he would excuse her for the course she had taken; but she could not attempt to secure for him any further favor from Judge Hancock. Having promised to be his security for a reasonable time, she had cheerfully fulfilled her contract, and had so far paid the interest on the debt ; but now, occupying a different position, although she received a higher salary, it cost more to make a proper appearance in the society in which she now moved; and she ended by politely, but positively, declining to pay any more interest to feed grasshoppers and answer the exactions of frost and drouth. She hoped he would feel that she was right, &c., &c.

Heckel laid down the letter with intense pain. Mrs. Dinmont ran her eye over the pages.

"Just as I expected, mother," said he, "City life has spoiled our girl. The farm may go now. It's small loss and pain to that."

"Oh! father, Die must be joking. I'll never believe a word of that letter is in earnest. I have faith in Die."

"And so have I, Mary. But I know that city life and city notions have a great effect on girls."

"And boys too, father."

"Yes, boys too. But on girls more than boys because they are weaker and more dependent."

"Heckel," answered Mary with a deep and startling positiveness in her voice, that sounded a note of censure, "Heckel Dinmont, when has Diana been weaker and more dependent than yourself, or any other man that you can name? When has she trembled before her duty? When has she failed to steady herself by the staff of right? Depend upon it, she has written that letter to you in jest, and there will be an explanation."

"It may be," answered Heckel, "but the jest has come at a sore time and is not agreeable."

"There's a big box in the cart, father," shouted Tom from outside. "If you'll help me, we'll bring it in before I take the cart to the barn."

" Hard, dusty traveling, ain't it ?" asked Heckel.

" About the worst I ever saw."

" The horses look fagged, poor fellows! I'll take care of them. You go in to supper."

" Egbert will do that. I'm awful hungry."

The box was soon tumbled in, too heavy to be lifted, and quickly opened to the eager eyes. Oh! what treasures rolled out before their astonished gaze. Books, maps, charts, pictures, clothing, dry goods, household comforts and conveniences, rich and good, such as never before had served their uses; little luxuries and adornments that threw Lulu into ecstacies and brought tears of thankfulness and pride to the eyes of the mother. There was a set of surveying instruments for Tom, a new black silk dress for mother, and a fresh suit of broad cloth for father, from Judge Hancock, closed the joy-giving revelations.

Happiness pervaded the group as note after note appended to each package gave the name of the donor and intended recipient. Tom was scarcely able to satisfy the little hunger that joy had left him.

" Who in the world could ever have put it into the head of the Judge to send these instruments?" said Tom.

" You wrote to Die that you had been out surveying with the State party."

" So I did, and that I believed I could teach myself if I had the tools. So I did. Die's a brick." •

" Die is a good child," said the mother, with full heart.

Heckel was troubled, sorely, deeply. What were all these gewgaws to his beautiful farm. He walked the floor moodily.

" Why, see here !" exclaimed Tom, " where's that big express package? I gave it to Egbert, I guess, with the letters. What was in it, father?"

" I haven't seen it."

" Where is it then ? He's lost it," and Tom rushed out of the house, with Egbert after him. The paper was soon found and proved to be an express package, as Tom had said, directed to the " care of Henry Jones, Land Agent. To be delivered into the hands of Heckel Dinmont, or his son Thomas Dinmont."

" What can this mean ?" said Heckel, as he examined the date. " Three weeks on the road."

" Jones says it's been there ever since the day I was in before. Came just after I started home."

Slowly, as if afraid of some impending calamity, Heckel broke the seal. First he took out an official paper, which proved to be the mortgage on his farm, given the year before to Judge Hancock. He began to tremble and the great drops of perspiration stood on his forehead. Next he opened a small paper and found a receipt from Judge Hancock for fifteen hundred dollars, and his own notes for the borrowed money. Then a letter from the Judge, saying that Diana had paid the whole amount from her earnings of the last two years, having served him faithfully and efficiently as secretary and amanuensis, and re-

ceived from him a salary of one thousand dollars a
year, and that she had become so necessary to him
that she would receive for the future fifteen hundred.
He added : " Do not hesitate, Mr. Dinmont, to accept this gift from your paragon of a daughter. I
assure you, that she will not be more joyful in seeing that your farm is unencumbered and entirely
yours, than in knowing she has thus saved you from
anxiety, and placed you where future misfortunes
from unavoidable causes, need not oppress you.
Let me congratulate you and Mrs. Dinmont on
being the parents of such a child. She has, indeed,
honored her father and mother, and may her days be
long in the land. She is not only invaluable to me.
in her official capacity, but also a pearl of great
price in my family, having always retained her place
among us as manager of the household affairs, and
having become, indeed, as one of ourselves. I
am glad to hear of Tom's interest in civil engi-
neering, and hope the books sent with the instruments may enable him to go forward with the self-
education already begun." The letter ended with
the assurance that they might at any time make reasonable demands upon his time and purse, their
security being still the competent and faithful girl
who had heretofore held that position.

Dinmont fairly shook with emotion as he read.
He handed the papers to his wife and without a
word went slowly out into the moonlight, that only
the stars of heaven should see his tears of joy and

gratitude; that only the blue vault above, should cover his head as he knelt in prayerful thanksgiving to the God of all goodness and truth, for granting him such a child, such a wife.

"Mother, what is it?" asked Tom, who had noted the emotion of his father.

"Diana has earned the money, has paid the mortgage and here are all the papers."

"Are we all free now?" asked Egbert with intense excitement.

"All free, and Die says this money all belonged to father, for legally, he has the entire right to all her earnings until she was eighteen, and she is only a little over that now."

"Oh! mother," sobbed Tom, his manly young heart overflowing in irrepressible happiness at this sudden relief.

After a few moments with her children, Mrs. Dinmont slipped out to share her joy with her husband.

"Tom, how did you sell your load?" asked Egbert.

"Tip top," answered Tom.

"What did you get for my skins? sell 'em all?"

"Every one."

"And them stuffed birds, rabbits and squirrels?"

"Got cash for the whole. Dr. Skiles says you're a genius and he'll buy all you'll put up."

"What did he think of the bugs?"

"Says he hasn't any finer ones in his whole collection and you must keep on."

12

"I'm bound to do that. Did you see the railroad men?"

"Yes; had a long talk with the superintendent, Mr. Jenkes. He wanted to know all about this part of the country and the road up the river. I told him all I knew and he took it all down in his book."

"Are they going to want you?"

Capt. Wilkes says he'll give me a place as rod-man."

"Will they pay you anything?"

"Yes, but not much at first. He says I must begin at the foot of the ladder and climb up."

"That's it! I believe in that. Let's look at that compass."

Tom dried his eyes, and the two boys took the shining treasure from its box and examined it with earnest care.

"This fixes me all right," said Tom.

"That's so," said Egbert, "and we can study and work and experiment together. How clever it was of Capt. Wilkes to teach you so much."

"If I hadn't been always ready to help through all his hard work, though, he wouldn't have done it. That's the way for a fellow to get a going. Don't be selfish. Help everybody when you can, and always be respectful and kind. It's a sure way to make friends. I brought Harper home to-night in my cart. He's got a big claim up here and wants the lines run. He said Wilkes told him I could do it as well as the county surveyor. I said I could if I only had the ' weapons.' "

" Good! Now you can prove it."

" And I will, too."

" Ain't it grand about Die ?"

" Just the grandest thing out."

" I was sorry for father when her letter made him feel so badly. Won't she be sorry when we tell her how he got her last letter first ?"

" I tell you," said Tom, bringing down his great fist on the table with a bang that started Lulu to her feet, " Die shan't do it all. I'll pay her back part of it, before I'm two years older. You'll see."

The entrance of father and mother put an end to the spirited talk of the two boys, and the happy household soon retired to dream of the peace and plenty that had become theirs.

An hour before the sun had spread his glittering, diamond flecked mantle over the broad swelling fields of Heckel Dinmont, the members of the family were all astir and about their daily duties.

Lulu, gay as a prairie bird, ran out to feed her chickens and display to them and to the meek eyed cow that her mother was milking, her new straw hat; enjoying with the fulness of health and vigor, a pitched battle with the strutting turkey gobbler that took offence at the scarlet streamers.

Mary's laugh at the child was as musical as the oriole's trill, while Teddy startled the colts with his hearty " Ha, ha, ha," as Lulu discomfited her enemy with a cornstalk lance.

Is there a happiness like being out of debt? a peaceful serenity like that of knowing that the roof that shelters us, the land that feeds us, and the labor that bends us, are our own?

" We will pay Die, one of these days, father," said Tom as they were grooming the horses.

" Yes, Tom, and we will rest our hearts in peace until the time comes, and be all the more faithful for her great love and kindness."

" We will," answered Tom heartily, " and father, I would like to join Jenkes' railroad corps again, if you are willing."

" Why, Tom—I don't know—who'll help on the farm?"

" There's Walker and Ellis and Fritz, they are all stronger than me and they'll any of them work for you. My wages will more than pay a man in my place. I will be learning a good business for life."

" Well, I don't know, Tom. Perhaps it's best. One farm can't keep us all many years. Yes, you'd better go."

" Thank you, father. Shall I go into the cornfield to-day?"

" No, it's too dry."

" Then I'll take Egbert and go up to Mr. Harper's and run his claim with my new instruments, if you are willing."

" All right. Do whatever you do, well, my boy. Try to learn that lesson earlier than your father did."

" I will do my best."

" It don't seem quite right, Tom, for me to be taking all your wages.

" Just exactly right, father. Die has helped you until she is eighteen. Why should not I ? Legally I belong to you some years yet. If in that time I don't drive my stakes so as to be able to take good care of myself, and you and mother when you need me, I shall be mistaken, that's all."

" Don't touch liquor, Tom. You know it was my stumbling block all my best days. Stand to total abstinence."

" Father, don't look back at the past. I have had better teaching than you ever had, and shall have much to answer for if I allow myself to be tempted. There is not one in the corps that does not drink but me. I have a hard row to hoe sometimes; but when I think of you and mother and Die and all the misery of the past, I feel brave and think I shall never fail."

" May the good God keep you, my boy," answered the father, as they turned to the house, answering the breakfast bell of the happy and faithful mother.

CHAPTER XX.

BROKEN VOWS AND THE RESULT.

Gordon Rand lived true to his vow, until he had
been some days at sea, when a wild storm arose that
sent all landsmen to their rooms in uncontrollable
sea sickness. Gordon's sensitive and somewhat
reduced organization did not recuperate as rapidly
as is usual, and the physician ordered brandy. From
the moment when he first tasted it, the charm was
broken. Each day found him the gayest of the gay;
the wittiest of the witty; and sometimes the midnight bells warned him to a drunkard's couch,
whither he was conveyed by other strength than his
own. But, as his beverages were mainly wine, he
would sleep away the stupidity of his debauch and
rise fresh and charming by midday.

There were beautiful and interesting women on
board the vessel, such as Gordon had not habitually
met with in society, and they charmed him. The
same circle met daily, read together, worked together,
walked, played, danced, sung; morn, noon and eve,
and none yielded so wholly to the fascinations of the
hour as Gordon.

In vain George cautioned, in vain recalled the painful experience of the past. The possession of wealth that seemed without limit, had partially transformed the young man. Among strangers, free from college restraints, removed from the influence of his father and mother, he made sad havoc of his powers.

One morning, after a deeper revel than usual, he sent for George. He was too sick to rise. One of his bewildering headaches was upon him; his brain reeled and fearful phantoms hung upon the walls and crept in hideous forms upon the ceiling. His spree had won him to imbecility and madness. George bent over him kindly, taking his head and soothing his terrible fancies with gentle and encouraging words.

The physician was called and, as usual, prescribed anodynes and small doses of brandy to sustain the sinking vitality of the patient. The latter, however, George decidedly refused to administer.

But why follow out these wretched details? Why dwell upon what comes before medical men daily and demands of them, trumpet voiced, a wiser and truer system of practice? Who shall measure out unto them, misery and woe as they have meted unto others in their reckless ignorance or heartless greed? After days of torture, such as the reviving inebriate only can know, Gordon grew calm and restful.

"I am a ruined man," he said to George one morning, "a perjured, broken, craven man."

"You may reform, Gordon. Your constitution is not broken, your character is not lost. You have been terribly unwise, but you may regain all by a strict avoidance of the causes that have brought you down."

"Never, never! I have sworn to myself again and again to do better; I have all the guards and helps that man can ask and yet—I have fallen. You say I have not lost my character. . Perhaps I have not lost my reputation; but I feel that my character is undermined, that the bestial elements have gained control."

"Do not despair, Gordon. You are too weak to talk now."

"One thing I will do," continued Gordon, unheeding the suggestion of his friend, "I will write to Aggie," (his voice choked with emotion) "and release her from all engagement to my embruited self. She, at least, shall not be sacrificed."

He groaned aloud and hid his face in the pillow; but George could see how the veins of his forehead swelled with agony as he repeated, "She shall not be sacrificed."

"That mischief is already done, my friend."

"How so?" with a sudden lifting of the agonized face.

"Can you crush her love by this release you speak of?"

"My God! no. Unless I can make her hate me."

"You can do no such thing. You can break her heart and blight her whole life."

" What shall I do ?"

" Reform. Pursue your travels; outgrow your terrible propensity and make her happy."

" I cannot. Oh ! I cannot. If other men would not tempt me, if even women did not tempt me, I might live."

" They tempt me also," said George, "and I refuse. I bear their scorn and contempt. They taunt me with being a bound slave, with having pledged away my freedom; but I will not allow them to move me."

" You are strong, I am weak, trained in weakness."

" Only by abiding in principle can you be strong."

" Do not argue, George. I must drink, though I die."

" Drink ? Gordon. You must drink `and break the hearts of your parents? Drink, and drown in your sparkling glass the happiness, perhaps the life of your betrothed ? Drink, and destroy your health and talents ? Drink, and make your genius a curse and your education a reproach ? Drink, and fill a drunkard's grave ere you have attained the full measure of your manhood?" exclaimed George, in a bitterness of spirit which he could not control.

" You have described my fate," answered Gordon in a tone of utter despair, that struck mournfully upon George's heart and made him repent his impulsive words.

" No, Gordon, it must not be. Cheer up, try once more and you may succeed. Better men than you have struggled and failed, and tried again and again and conquered at last."

"I know," answered the invalid in a faint voice. "But where one has triumphed, ninety and nine have gone down forever."

"Be you the *one*, then, my friend. For the sake of wealth, fame and honor. Think of it, Gordon, think of it and try to get well. We get into port to-morrow."

"To-morrow?"

"Aye, to-morrow, my boy. You must sleep now."

"Sleep," said Gordon, turning his great eyes up to the face of his friend. "Sleep is not for the damned."

"Oh, Gordon. I pray you do not talk so. There! good-by. I must write letters to send back by the first mail after we get ashore."

"Good bye, George," answered Gordon in a hollow voice that seemed to come from unfathomable depths of woe.

George hurried on deck and tried by a brisk walk to throw off the gloom that had settled upon his spirit. "He will be better to-morrow, poor soul," he said to himself as he paced up and down with uneasy heart.

Others joined him and it was some time before he looked in upon Gordon again. He seemed asleep and he retired quietly, knowing that he needed nothing so much as rest.

At day dawn they cast anchor. Not wishing to go ashore until after the crowd had departed, and wearied with the long previous watches by the bed-side of his friend, George slept late. As soon as dressed he hurried to Gordon's room. But he was not there. His trunks were gone, and the servants were already arranging the room and clearing away the evidences of sickness. George's look of aston-ishment and inquiry were answered by the waiter.

"Gone ashore the first load, sir."

"What?"

"Gone ashore, sir, at five this morning."

"Did he leave no note or address?"

"No, sir, not as I've seen."

George searched the room, but his search was vain. The reckless victim of appetite and passion had escaped and would doubtless so secrete himself as to elude all inquiry. He learned further that he had gone with a young man who had attached him-self to him from the beginning of the voyage, and two young ladies who called themselves sisters of the man. These had been companions in his dissi-pation, and had won from him large sums of money at play.

George sought him diligently and gave the mat-ter into the hands of the police, and waited until Prof. Winthrop would wait no longer, affirming that they were well rid of a disgraceful "companion du voyage," and that wherever he was, the sharpers that had enticed him away would not leave him as long as he kept in funds.

A month later, Aggie, who had been deeply

grieved at his abrupt departure, but had forgiven him in the plenitude of her love and trust, and was trying to be cheerful in her home, received the following note, postmarked Liverpool, without date or address:

My Darling Aggie---This is the last note or word you will ever receive from me. I am a drunkard. I have perjured myself by breaking my vows to abstain, Hate me if you can, and let it help you to forget me, that I am unworthy to look upon you or speak your name.   GORDON.

Aggie fell insensible into her mother's arms, and it was many days ere she recovered from the unconsciousness that followed the reading of that terrible message. Then she confessed the engagement and the love that now would sap her life. Max had heard all the fatal story from George and told the poor girl frankly and tenderly, leaving her, as he felt was best, no lingering hope to build falsely upon. A deep cry of anguish escaped the lips of the devoted mother at the conclusion of the terrible recital.

"Oh!" she cried. " Is this my retribution for the many drunkards I have made. Back to my own soul has come the barbed arrow through the heart of my child."

For many weeks Aggie remained an invalid, but a good constitution and loving care prevailed at last, and slowly, wearily, as the fever passed away, health and strength returned. But the cheeks of the mother had grown pale, and the full round form of the once cheery, light-hearted matron wasted to almost skeleton proportions. Educated in careless ignorance of moral obligations to others, shaping her actions to the requirements of her surroundings, doing as others did, not as they should do; she had lived thoughtless of consequences all her early years. She loved her husband and her child absorbingly; lived and moved in their interest only. Now, at middle age to be awakened from this long dream of security, to be aroused from the selfish policy of living only for her own, "letting well enough alone" was an intense pain, and causing an unceasing inward struggle. All night long she would watch beside her patient daughter. A breath or sigh awoke her if she chanced to sleep. In general, she slept only when Aggie slept, and wakened with her as if the spirit of the invalid were shrined in her own body. Could she have gone away to pour forth the pent up agony in penitential tears, she would have become calmer. But she feared the quick eye of the sufferer, hovering between life and death, would note the traces of any such outward manifestation, and all was repressed.

Aggie talked very little and had not as yet spoken Gordon's name. The physician pronounced her convalescent, when three months of fearful suffering had passed, and on a beautiful autumnal day, when hills and vales were flooded with light, Max sat beside her while her mother rested, and tried to win the pallid lips to a smile, by telling all the current news of the village. He said at length:

"Nettie will be home next week."

"Will she?"

"Yes, and we have letters from Emma and **Mrs.** Vandyke." Here a perceptible flush passed over the wan face. "Emma, I suppose, sailed ten days ago. The family expect to meet her in New York, and with the two girls back, we shall be more lively."

Aggie's clear brown eyes rested fixedly on his face as if asking, "What of him?" but her lips did not move. Max interpreted the look, and taking the thin hand that hung over the bedside tenderly within his own, he answered the mute appeal:

"No word from *him*, Aggie. He has evaded all inquiry and we fear he has become the victim of those reckless people."

She made no movement, uttered no word. Her eyes closed wearily and great tears forced themselves between the lids and fell in mournful silence on her pillow.

Max knew they were the first that she had shed and that they would do her good. He did not speak, and at last without raising her eyelids, or making any movement, she whispered:

"Max, I will live for my mother's sake. He loved his wine more than he loved me. Shall I die for such a man, and in dying kill those who are true to me? Leave me now and tell my mother what I say. He has deceived me; but I will try to forgive him."

" You are a brave girl, Aggie. He is, indeed, unworthy, the sacrifice of so good a life as yours. Forgive him and try to forget him."

" I cannot forget; but I can learn to live for others. I have only lived for self. Go now. I want to be alone."

Max delivered his message, and a pale glimmer of hope dawned in the crushed and wearied heart of Rena Frobish. With this hope was born a new love for all humanity, a desire to do good, a yearning of soul to go out among those scattered up and down the streets and alleys of Oxbow and preach to them a new gospel of temperance and love. Cautiously she opened her heart to her daughter as they went forth together, seeking invigoration in the open air, and together they dropped by the wayside many a seed of thoughtful truth that germinated and bore fruit in coming years.

One day they were riding leisurely along the road, when they overtook a boy driving a nice looking cow with a pair of beautiful twin calves by her side, white as snow and full of frisky life that attracted Aggie's attention.

" Oh! mother," she exclaimed with unusual animation, "how I would like to have those pretty creatures for my own. I wonder if they are being driven to market?"

" I will ask," answered Mrs. Frobish, glad to see the slightest interest taken in anything outside their own weary disappointed lives.

" My boy," she said, drawing the reins as they approached, " whose cow is that ? " .

" The landlord's cow, ma'am," answered the little cattle driver, making an attempt at a bow and standing hat in hand.

" What ! the landlord's cow ? "

" Yes'm, that's what we allers call her now. We used to call her Rose."

" Are you Sam Roland's son ? "

" Yes'm. I be."

" Where does he live now ? "

" He lives up there, just the last house you see, out of town, by that willow tree,"

" Are those pretty calves yours ? "

" They belong to mam. Pap says the cow's her'n now, next to the landlord ; he hain't nothing more to do with her."

" What are you going to do with them ? Are you taking them to the butcher ? "

" Taking them to the butcher ? No, sir'ee," answered the boy in astonishment at such a question. " I'm takin' 'em out to Deacon Jones' pastur."

" You'll let the landlord have them, if he wants them, will you not ? " asked Mrs. Frobish.

" Well," said the boy, looking disturbed and pained. " I reckon we'd have to ; but—I reckon— we might pay for 'em now. We'd all hate mightly to part with 'em."

" Never mind, my little fellow. They are very cunning and you may keep them," and she drove on.

"Mother, what did he mean by saying 'the land-lord's cow?'"

Mrs. Frobish told her story and Aggie was amused and actually laughed one of her old happy trills, that sounded joyfully in the ears of her mother.

"Is Roland still drinking?"

"I don't know. I have not heard of them for a long time. He did better, his wife told me, after the prosecution."

"Let us drive up to the door and speak to her."

No suggestion of Aggie's passed unheeded, and Mrs. Roland was surprised in a few moments by an unexpected call. Untying her soiled calico apron and drawing her hands vigorously over her forehead to smooth any ruffled locks, she hastened to the gate, followed by her troup of little ones.

"Good morning, Mrs. Roland," said Mrs. Frobish cheerily. "How are you? It's a long time since I've seen you."

"Pretty well, ma'am, thank ye. And how's yourself?"

"We are getting better, Mrs. Roland; but Aggie has been very ill."

"Yes. We he'rn about it and was mighty sorry, Sam and me."

"You've got a new place, I see."

"Yes'm. I told Sam as how I thought we'd better get a little out of town, and so we rented this piece and planted it, and we've had a right smart crop this year."

" What did you raise ?   I see you have nice corn."

" Can't be beat, nowheres, I 'low—that corn.   I had a nice lot of tomatoes among the corn and I guess nobody ever had such luck.   They grew like all possessed.   Sam says it's 'cause they was so shaded.   The sun burnt out everybody else's and we've sold every bushel for cash.   They just come up theirselves and we let 'em run."

" That was lucky."

" Did you see Jim with the cows down yonder ?"

" We did, and the pretty calves too."

" My gracious ! them calves !   I guess if Sam has had one man arter 'em he has had fifty.   And you'd laugh to hear him, Mrs. Frobish.   He tells 'em they're the landlord's and can't be had for money.   I guess I must tell ye, Mrs. Frobish," and the woman looked down and pushed a cob about vigorously with the toe of her old shoe, " that trick of your'n of letting the cow out, was the making on us.   Sam swore that he'd let you know that he wouldn't be beat out that way, and he hasn't drinked a drop since, more nor once or twice, and now he don't touch it and says he ain't agoin' to agin."

" I'm very glad," was all Mrs. Frobish could say.

" Well, Mrs. Frobish, you say you're very glad ; what do you think I be ?   I bless you every hour in the day, and I never go to bed at night that I don't pray for ye.   And me and Sam together has 'most money enough to pay ye for that ere cow, and I sent ye a lot of things out of my garden when ye was all so sick. I told the gals not to tell ye. I'd tell ye myself when the time came."

"Oh! Mrs. Roland, I thank you very much. You are welcome to the cow, and—"

"I know that, else we'd never had her; but if I lived to be as old as granny Nut, and she's a hundred 'most, I'd never git done paying ye, never. Ye gin more nor a cow."

"What is your name, little curly head?" asked Aggie of a little one that had climbed the fence and was hanging on the top rail.

"Aggie Roland," was the proud answer,

"Aggie Roland? Then you must be my little namesake. My name is Aggie. Won't you get down and bring me one of those pretty long handled gourds lying in the grass?"

The little girl made speedy effort to reach the ground before the others and there was quite a scramble. Tom, the junior, finally seizing and presenting it.

"Den," shouted Aggie, "I'll div her my white kitten. Mayn't I, mammy?"

"She don't want your kitten, keep still."

"Oh! yes, I do, Mrs. Roland. Let her give me the kitten. I love kittens and I love little girls. You'll come and see kitty, won't you?" The child nodded an affirmative, and the mother and daughter drove on, carrying the white kitten and happier for their call.

CHAPTER XXI.

A CHAPTER ON MARRIAGE.

When Judge Hancock assumed his duties as United States Senator, he placed all his monied interests as well as his extensive law business in the care and keeping of Max Carter, establishing him as his legal partner.

At the capital he found it necessary to employ an efficient private secretary, and engaged a talented and educated young man, giving him a salary of fifteen hundred a year.

At the end of a month the senator's right hand was enveloped in that homely but effective compound, a bread and milk poultice, and his secretary was off on an excursion without leave. In this emergency he called upon Die to answer some important letters. Her work was so speedily and accurately done, in every respect so unexceptionable, that he decided at once, with her consent, to exchange the whiskered specimen of the *genus homo*, who smoked, drank wine and indulged in occasional *strong* language, and who had come to him so "highly recommended," for the quiet maiden, who kept his office—a room in his house—in the best of order, never disgusted him . with odors of stale smoke, or roused his temper into fever heat by unpardonable blunders, after an evening of fashionable, gentlemanly exhilaration. In this accidental way our heroine became the private secretary of the influential politician and statesman.

When Diana received her mother's letter detailing the loss of crops and her father's embarrassment; and asking her to solicit an extension of time from the Judge, she went to her ever kind and generous patron and fearlessly made her statement of the facts. The result was as we have seen ; the Judge affirming that for equal labor, equal remuneration should be given, without regard to the sex of the laborer.

Let no one suppose that Diana escaped the persecutions that fall to the lot of pretty women. A Georgia governor had bowed at her feet and offered his hand, his three motherless children, his magnificent Southern home, his widespread plantation of rice and cotton and *one hundred human chattels*, with the stereotyped assurance that she should "never know care or toil within his sheltering arms."

His amazement can be better imagined than described when he received from this " Northern beggar-girl "—as he afterward called her—a decided negative to his suit. He demanded her reason for refusing an offer that any lady might be proud to accept. To which the dignified girl simply replied:

" I have no reason to give, Governor L., save that I do not love you and I therefore cannot be your wife. Nor have you any right to demand other reason than that."

Count Armour, a French nobleman, spending a couple of winters at the capital, was charmed with the easy grace, the brown eyes, sweet voice and rosy lips of Mdle. Dinmont, to whom he was presented at one of the evening reunions in the Senator's parlors, to whom he bowed in the Senator's office, with whom he met and chatted occasionally in the halls of state. He, too, offered heart and hand; but strange to say, the daughter of Heckel Dinmont, born and reared in abject poverty, preferred the position of busy scribe and thoughtful housekeeper, to that of countess with a life in baronial halls.

The discomfited count. knowing that his secret was safe, consoled himself, and six months later, sued for the hand of Miss Emma and was accepted.

" Why is it?" asked the Senator one morning, " that you so persistently bluff off all your suitors, Die ?"

" I have many reasons for not encouraging any special intimacies. If I bluff my suitors, you know, I retain them as fast friends."

" But why don't you encourage some of these truly excellent men ? Most of the mammas that bring their daughters to the capital would be enchanted with your opportunities."

" First, I do not wish to marry for some years."

"What next?"

"I must then be fully persuaded in my own mind that it is best for me to marry at all. Thirdly, I must esteem and love the man I would marry. I esteem many whom I could not love. I cannot love unless I first esteem."

"Go on."

"The man whom I would marry must be free from the bad habits men usually indulge; must not be a wine bibber, a user of tobacco; must not be a sneerer at my own sex; must be, in short, as pure and true in his moral nature as he would expect his wife to be. He must be one who would not assume to be my superior, although his education and position might be above my own. He must consider me his equal, meeting the requirements of his nature, precisely as I should consider him answering, in the wealth of his manhood, the needs of mine. I hold that between husband and wife there should be no reservations; no exclusive privileges for either."

"But suppose," interrupted the Judge, "you were to marry a man worth a million of dollars. How then?"

"I should marry the man, not his dollars; and should have no more right to his money after marriage than before, unless he gives me to understand that we are to share it equally during our lives. Yet, if he exacts of me all my time and energies in any direction, or simply forbids me earning my own

living, he then is bound to place freely at my disposal means enough to meet all my reasonable
wants."

" And how as to the *personale* of your husband ?"

" He must be no shorter than I, no less in weight;
his hair must not be red, and his country must not
be Kamschatka."

The Judge laughed and Die returned to her letters. She had never ceased her earnest endeavors
to supply the deficiencies of her education, and in
her great fear lest she should still fall behind others,
she had really disciplined her mind and stored it
far beyond what is usually required of woman. She
was scrupulously neat in her toilet; never so far
out of the mode as to attract attention, never so far
in advance as to render her conspicuous. She understood what so many ladies do not, that to be well
dressed was to have the whole toilette so harmonized
as to produce no startling effect. She so arranged
her wardrobe as to require the least possible amount
of time in its daily adjustment. All her leisure
hours were given to mental improvement. She
studied both French and German with the best mas-
ters, and during the hours which she saved from
evening dissipation and morning weariness, she became complete mistress of both languages and of
much pertaining to science, history and literature.
In her daily intercourse with all classes, she gleaned
the best thoughts of mature minds, and learned useful lessons of self-respect from the weak, supercil-

ıous and proud. Her life was not without its trials and vexations; but she looked upon these as " hindrances " necessary to further advancement.

" I have no time to fret over mortified pride, or jealous rivalries," she said to her friends. " No time to give a heart beat to an ignoble thought. Day by day I see my duty and the hour in which I accomplish it faithfully, I have gained a treasure which I can never lose. Every new thought makes me richer and wiser."

" You're a strange girl, Die," said the Judge one morning, after watching her adroitly dismiss a gentleman who annoyed her.

" Mr. C. knows that my time is yours, sir, and what right has he to engross it ?"

" It will not do to be too rigid with your friends. I fancied his face showed wounded feelings."

Die looked up, her face sparkling and firm with inward conviction, and answered :

" I have given all my lady friends to understand that my office hours are not to be infringed upon, and not one of them molests me. Men do not encroach upon each other's business hours simply to visit, and if women are to occupy positions of trust, they must also be undisturbed."

" Mr. C. is a gentleman of leisure," said the Judge.

" And supposes all ladies have as little to do as himself. I must teach him better," answered Die.

" Most ladies are at leisure and would gladly entertain Mr. C. as long as he chose to remain."

"I have found, Judge Hancock, and I say it to you as to a father, that there are few men in the upper ranks of our social circles who do not look upon every young lady as lawful prey, ready to fly unhesitatingly into any snare they may set for her, thankful, indeed, for being caught. Mr. C. is an amiable and interesting man ; but he is of that way of thinking. He has proposed marriage to me and been told seriously that I could not entertain the proposition ; and yet returns to the attack with an assurance that convinces me he considers me capable of saying ' no,' when I mean ' yes.' The sooner I undeceive him the better."

"Perhaps you are right."

"My kind friend, I do not wish to marry. There is not one of these men who would not start with dismay if I were to present him to my father and mother. They would consider their social status wholly above my own, and to wed one of them would insure me a life long humiliation. I refuse them from principle. There can be no happiness for me in marriage without perfect oneness of feeling in all things."

"Do you not sometimes misjudge ?"

"I think not, I desire to be just."

"Why did you refuse the Governor ?"

"You have already had my reasons in general. Even if he could consider me his equal, he still drinks, smokes, chews and deals in human chattels. Is not that enough ?"

"Enough, certainly. Why the Count?"

"He was simply infatuated by my beauty and had not one particle of regard for my worthiness of character as a woman. What is to me of most importance, would have been to him of none."

"And what objection to Mr. C.?"

"His face is this morning flushed with wine, and he convinces me in many ways that he has formed a low estimate of woman, and that his wife could never be to him anything beyond that estimate. But Judge Hancock, one sentence will dispose of them all. They are not to me loveable, because they are not true, good men."

The Judge looked at her admiringly and left her to her writing.

CHAPTER XXII.

PREPARING FOR THE PARTY.

"Die, you are really provoking," said Nettie, one evening preceding the coming birthday of the two girls. "You might give way just this once."

"Why, Nettie, dear, it would be perfectly prepos-terous."

"I can't see it so. You are one of us. You have never been in society since you have been in Washington without receiving all the attention you could possibly desire, and this is to be *our* birthday party; your name will appear on the cards with mine and we ought to dress exactly alike."

"Do not urge me any more, Nettie, I would do anything that seemed to me reasonable for you; but to dress myself like the daughter of a man worth millions, known, as I am, to be the daughter of pov-erty, an employe in my patron's family, would be wholly ridiculous, and would subject me to the just sneers of people whose respect I greatly desire."

"Well, you're the oddest girl I ever knew, and I suppose I must let the *contrary* in you have its own way," said Nettie, looking, lovingly at two beautiful dresses just unboxed from Paris. "It vexes my spirit when I have tried so hard to have you feel as my companion and sister in all things, that this one night you should resolutely balk me."

"Nettie, dear, don't scold. The dresses are not alike. The white one is for you now and the delicate pink at the next grand reception. You never like to wear the same dress twice in a season."

"Oh! but Die—"

"There, dear, not another word. Let us kiss and be friends, and remember that I could not be happy wearing a dress that cost more than my father's whole farm and house thrown in." And suiting the action to the word, she folded Nettie in a warm embrace and kissed the pouting lips into good humor.

"What then are you going to wear on our birthday evening? Are you going to strike another attitude of opposition and stay in your room to spite us all?"

"Not I. I shall make my unobtrusive appearance, and share the honor of having been born on the same day with my brilliant friend, Miss Nettie Hancock, in a beautiful white organdie, trimmed neatly with bands of blue satin, and I intend to be the happiest girl in the house."

At this moment Aunt Ruth came waddling in.

"Lord a massy! How it do take my bref to come up dem stairs; but Jessie told me 'bout yer gounds all de way from dat place where all de bonnets and fol-de-rols comes from."

" Well, there they are, aunty."

" What! dem tings!"

" Are they not splendid? Equal to Grandma Pendergrast's? Now, just own it for once, aunty."

Ruth set her arms akimbo and stood silently eyeing the outspread dresses, while her broad face worked itself into wrinkles of ineffable contempt.

"Gor-a-massy, chile! Dem flimsy tings! Dey de best you could get? Dey's not de least 'count side of your grandma Pendergrast's, what she got to be introduced to de President in. I've tuk 'em out many a time when I was a gal, to show 'em to yer ma. Dem's no more 'count dan white lilies 'side of a full blown red piny. Tell ye what, chillen, tings ain't as dey used to was."

" Oh! aunty, tell us about those 'gounds.'"

" Ask missis 'bout 'em, chile."

" No, no, aunty, you tell us," exclaimed Emma.

" Well, dere was one white as de snow on de hill, and splotched all ober with roses and lalocks all made in gold, and when you stood it up in de middle of de floor, it set stiff up like a tin tunnel, 'cause it so stiff you know, and neber wrinkle a mite, and de train would reach to dat bed."

" Oh! Ruth, is that true?"

" True as you're born, gal. Jest as I tell ye; and yer grand'pa brought it from de Injies in his ship and lots more on 'em. De lace round de trail was as wide as my arm is long, and your grand'ma said it cost heaps, nuff to buy niggers for a whole plantation."

"Oh! aunty, you've been dreaming."

"Go 'long wid your dreaming. Don't know how to fix up now days, you don't."

"Don't you call these dresses elegant?"

"Dey'll do, 'cause dey's de best you can git; but you oughter see yer gran'mamy's green one. Dat was purtier yit. Had bunches of red and yaller lilies, big 'round as de soup plates, all ober it, and den de trails and ruff and de ribbons criss crossing, and de big flowers in de gathers! Neher seed the like. Poh! dem flimsy tings nice! Go 'long!"

But despite her admiration for the dresses of old time, Aunt Ruth could not withhold her praise of the pearls and diamonds and wreaths of floral beauty, that lay scattered about the room, and her appreciation of the "flimsy tings," that lay in all the delicate allurement of satin, sheen and point lace, was greatly enhanced by several showy presents to herself. A jolly laugh at the oddities of the "dear old soul," followed her retreating footsteps.

Nettie was happy. She was thinking, thinking of the tender attentions she had received from one she was learning to love, at the last night's reception. Her heart fluttered with the new hope that she too might be loved. The new dresses were, indeed, of "no 'count," in comparison with this hope.

Aggie Frobish, although unmentioned, has been present with the girls during all this conversation. She, too, is very happy, quietly happy in the love of true noble Max Carter. Gordon has not been heard from, and in the three years since his disappearance, the friendship between her and Max has ripened into a love, soul-satisfying, strong and pure.

Max and George are expected to meet in New York, and come together to attend the festivities of the birthday.

There was an immense deal of curiosity over an item in George's letter, the last mailed before setting sail for home. He had written to Nettie: "I have never loved but once and I have never told my love; but if the woman of my choice be heart whole on my return, you will soon know her."

Who could the maiden be? Guessing was vain. Die, in the solitude of her room, looked that night in the glass and thought she had aged ten years since yesterday; but she said to the turbulent soul within her, "Be still," and wondered with the rest whom he could have chosen, not for a moment thinking of herself as having won his love in those days of servitude and in her then surroundings. The dream of her life was vanishing.

An extract from the last letter of Max to George may explain somewhat to our readers. He wrote:

It's my humble opinion, my boy, that you had better come home. Diana, the peerless, is as sorely beset at our great capital as was Penelope of old. They write me that she has governors, counts and congressmen kneeling as suppliants for her favor. As yet, all prayers and entreaties are in vain. She remains as unmoved as the marble statue of her illustrious namesake. You have kept your faith bravely; for so doing you have my blessing, in return for which I claim your congratulation. I have won the love of the one who will of all others make me happiest, and shall make her my own when the spring flowers bloom. Come home and be my groomsman.

MAX.

13*

CHAPTER XXIII.

RETROSPECTIVE.

"How are you? my jolly landlord of Oxbow," said a well dressed, heavy whiskered, broad shouldered man, as he walked into the traveler's entrance of the well kept hotel.

"Your servant, sir," replied Mr. Frobish bowing politely. "Be seated. Have dinner, sir?"

"What have you to drink, first?" and the stranger cast his eye about. "What the d—l! you haven't turned Granny Ghost Seer and turned out your bar?"

"I have put out my bar, sir, certainly. But I try to supply my table well and take the best possible care of my guests. Have a room, sir?"

"Any other tavern in this little d—d place where a fellow can wet his whistle?"

"I believe, sir, our village furnishes ample accommodation in the line you describe."

"Which way to the best?"

"Well, I incline to think that my spring can furnish the 'sparkling and bright' equal to any you will find in the place, and my wife is said to make excellent tea, coffee and chocolate. We can supply you in fifteen minutes with either, with an excellent steak and as nicely turned a muffin as your heart can desire. Will you try it, sir? No other tavern in the place.'

"No place where a fellow can get a smasher?"

"Not a place, I am happy to say, sir," answered John Frobish, rubbing his hands gleefully.

"Well, I'm deuced hungry. Bring on your breakfast, and mind, old chap, if you don't fill the bill according to promise I won't pay a d—d red cent."

As Mr. Frobish disappeared, the stranger continued:

"Well, well! this is a to-do for a fellow like me. What in the name of the dragon, could have pulled the wool over that old curmudgeon's eyes after this fashion? Keeping hotel without a bar! Well— that beats me. Let me see. It is ten years since Thompson, Wilford and I put up here, and a roistering time we had of it. They were grand companions; never had better. Umph! Why can't men take the pleasures of life in moderation? Both gone, both gone. One made quick work of fortune, education and character, and the other would have followed, only he took a shorter road and blew his own brains out—but damme! it gives me the blues and will spoil my digestion to think of it, and I wont."

"Breakfast, sir," said the waiter. "This way."

"Quick work!" ejaculated the stranger. "Yes I

remember as 'twere yesterday passing 'this way,' through this very door, the morning after that jolly spree at the Judge's. Poor Wilford! that was the first time I ever saw him sprung. The Judge kept good wines, though. And that daughter of his!— what was her name?—O—O—Olivia, yes, that was it. She was a high case."

"Sit here, sir. What will you have? Broiled chicken, beef steak, ham and eggs, mutton chop?"

"Broiled chicken and those 'well turned muffins.'"

"All right, sir."

"And that brag coffee, which I've never found out of the cities."

"Hope to please you there, sir."

"Landlord!"

"Aye, aye, sir."

"Have you time for a chat?"

"Certainly, sir."

"Then order your own breakfast and sit down here. You don't remember me?"

"If I mistake not I have the honor of addressing the Hon. Horace Grey."

"That's my name. Do you remember the visit of Thompson, Wilford and myself here, ten years ago?"

"Distinctly, Mr. Grey. A larking company you were."

"Well, yes. Umph!—ahem! Can't you remember some of the good of us and forget the bad?"

" You know, Mr. Grey, in those days I furnished the element that made 'the bad.' Of course I remember that first."

" What has become of that heiress, up at the 'Lodge,' that Jack Wilford fell so in love with?"

" About four years since she married an old army officer, Col. Vandyke, who took her off to England, drank and gambled away her fortune, and died in a drunken brawl in a house of ill-repute. She came back two years ago with one sickly boy and is living, as broken hearted a woman as you'll find, at the 'Lodge.' Won't live long. Vandyke nearly killed her before he killed himself."

" Is that so?" mused the questioner, laying down his fork with a luscious bit of steak on the point, untasted. " So old Vandyke is dead and died of rum and what was worse."

" It is supposed that his measure of iniquity was very full. He has left one suffering victim."

" You know the Wilford affair?"

" Never heard it."

" Well, I'll tell you. He fell in love with the heiress, or her money ; followed her to Baltimore ; got up an intrigue, and persuaded her to run away with him. The Principal got wind of it, and telegraphed to the Judge, who followed them railroad speed, and pounced upon them in Philadelphia just in time to prevent the marriage. A lucky thing he did. Jack had run to the bad about as fast as possible after he got agoing. He was a good fellow, was

Jack, in the start. If he had only had less money and less love of fun. Eh, landlord, this love of fun?"

Grey spilled his coffee. There was evidently some sickening reminiscence moving him.

"Splendid coffee, landlord, splendid! There was a fine spirited young fellow, Bishop—I think, was his name, boarding here with his wife and child. Sung a capital song and had his joke with the best. I liked him; but I thought he was making too free with the bottle."

"Yes. He went down gradually, run through all his property, then drank up his wife's earnings, grieved her soul out of her and worked her into a consumption. She died and we have always supposed he drowned himself. Mrs. Hancock and Mrs. Rand took the children."

"Oh! those young sprigs, Hancock and Rand, bid fair to go it at two-forty pace."

"We suppose Rand did. Young Hancock turned a short corner about three years since. He is in Europe now."

"And that old parson?"

"Rev. Mr. Duncan. About the time I tore out my bar, and our people decided that 'moderation' in the matter of drink was rather a sliding scale that sent our best to the bottom, he had a 'higher call,' and left us. We've had a live man in his place the last two years. We learned that Mr. Duncan finally lost his place because his 'moderation' became immoderate, and his parishioners decided that a staggering minister was not to their taste."

"Rather a bad record."

"What became of Wilford and Thompson?"

"Gone, sir, gone. Wilford drank himself to death, and Thompson shot himself after a most disgraceful affair in New York. Neither of them thirty years old."

"God bless me!" exclaimed the startled landlord. "What a terrible thing whisky is. I didn't see it so once."

"Landlord," said Grey, laying down knife and fork again. "This licensed liquor drinking is bad business."

"That's my impression, sir."

"We sit here and lay our friends down in drunkard's graves with as little compunction as your cooks have in wringing the necks of your chickens, say 'Poor fellow,' and turn and take a drink of whisky ourselves and hand it to our companions, as if men we e born to be destroyed."

"I've done my best, you see, Mr. Grey, to lay a stumbling block in the way. I don't take it, nor offer it to others."

"And how do you get along? They say a tavern can't be kept without a bar."

"All a mistake, sir. I have laid up more money during the last two years than in any other two since I have run this ranch."

"If your wife sets such a table as this, you'll succeed, I tell you, friend. There is more bad morality grows out of bad cooking than is dreamed of in our philosophy."

"Glad the meal is to your taste, sir," answered the landlord, oppressed with the drift of the conversation.

"Landlord," spoke out Grey again, as if a new thought had struck him. "I drank my first glass in this house and *I shall die a drunkard*," and he brought his clenched hand down upon the table till the glasses rung.

"My God! sir, I hope not."

"I live surrounded by temptations. I have lost all power of resistance. I can't stop myself, and all around me are miserable wretches, sinking, sinking, sinking. Miserable wives like Mrs. Bishop, miserable children to be made beggars—and no man to save, no man to save."

Mr. Grey rose from the table and walked abruptly away, and Mr. Frobish lifted his heart to God in earnest gratitude, that even so late in life he had learned the wrong he was doing and turned into the right path.

Alas! poor Grey. Cut to the quick, looking behind him at the gibbering skeletons of the past that seemed mocking his weakness, warning him of his doom; looking around him at temptations; within at vitiated appetites that tore him like ravening wolves; and before him at the gulf of perdition into which he was surely walking, involving wife, children and parents in his ruin—he yet went forth from that good breakfast, from all its moralizing, its peaceful healing influences, to search, if possibly he might not somewhere find a glass of stimulant to appease the burning thirst, to stay the horrible craving that was drawing his soul to its frightful destiny.

His search was in vain. Though the great distillery had poured out its flood of destruction for two score years, its channels were dry now. There was not in Oxbow a place where intoxicating material could be bought at retail. So surely had Max, Mrs. Frobish and others followed up and eradicated the evil.

Only sober drivers came and went in Oxbow. The lovers of "the ardent" among the working men, moved away to escape the scorching opprobrium of the community, and families that longed for peace and sobriety had filled their places.

The beautiful hills and vales seemed to glow in a truer and purer light; here had been metempsychosis, a change in the soul of things, and as evil communications corrupt good manners, even so did good communications spread out their force and fascinations, drawing within their influence those who might have been led by other and opposing forces to utter depravity.

CHAPTER XXIV.

DISCUSSIONS.

" No wine at our birthday party !"

" No wine at our birthday party, my dear Nettie."

" Oh, Die ! how full of crotchets you are. What will be thought of us ? Why, I have never attended a reception, since I have been at the Capital, where wine was excluded."

"And have you ever in any one instance indulged yourself with a glass ?"

" No, of course not ; but then—"

" Then, of course, we will not offer to others what we will not touch ourselves."

" That's an entirely different thing. All the gentlemen expect wine."

" I think not, Nettie. Does Secretary ——— indulge ?"

" Oh, well ! he's an old man."

" A very well preserved old man, darling. Then there is Mr. G———. Twenty years in this famous centre of wisdom and folly, and has never touched or tasted the unclean thing."

" But his son does."

" Yes, and sorely grieves those that love him most, by yielding to the allurement offered in houses and homes where better things might be hoped for."

" But we shall be called so unfashionable."

" Ah! it is Mrs. Grundy, then, you fear."

"Yes, if you please, Mrs. Grundy; I don't like to be the town talk."

" Well," said Die with a light laugh, "I should rather like to be held up to scorn, if need be, for doing exactly right. And I dou't like to yield my point for fear of observation and do exactly what I think is wrong. What do you say, Aggie ?"

Aggie was already dropping tears through downcast eyelids, as the memory of other days stirred her heart strings, but her answer was prompt and decided :

" In my own or my father's house no wine will ever be offered to our guests."

" Two against one. I'll wait till brother Wash comes."

" And Max," said Die.

" And be defeated four to one," exclaimed Aggie.

" Think of the disgraceful scene at Sec. A's reception only a month ago," added Die.

"Oh, I thank you; such drunken rowdies will not be among our guests."

" They were all Members of Congress; and are you and I willing to lend our influence to lead other and younger men into the very temptations that overcome these servants of the people —this congre-

gated wisdom of California, New Jersey, Illinois and
New York? Senator Hancock's house should have
no such reproach, my dear Nettie."

"Father says you must have your own way; so I
will yield. But I know it will be talked about,"
said Nettie, more moved than she was willing to
own.

"May we never meet a worse cause of notoriety,
my friend," said Die, taking the two flushed cheeks
between her cool hands and pressing a kindly kiss
upon the quivering lips.

"Amen! and amen," ejaculated Aggie with up-
raised hands.

Oh! it is hard, dear reader, for the poor, the lowly
and toiling in life's narrow spheres, to stand firm on
the bulwarks of morality and discretion; hard to
turn aside the shaft of reproach that hurts their
humble lives; but it requires a nobly sustained hero-
ism to meet the keen arrows of jealousy; the fierce
rivalries that sting and wound the sensitive and destroy the good impulses of the weak, in the great
battle of fashionable city life.

It is a fearful thing to hold a position of power
through wealth or influence, in society, if one's
moral status is not based upon enduring principles
of right and justice; if the heart is not imbued with
the purest and holiest Christian trust in God and
love to man. No wonder Nettie faltered in such a
maelstrom of dissipation and folly as Washington.
Even the Judge had some misgivings as to the pro-

priety of excluding from his tables what was offered in almost every house; and when he had said " Let it be as Die says," he had thrown from his own shoulders, in part, the weight of responsibility that burdened him. He knew well that the peerless beauty who made brilliant his receptions was already known as peerless also in her integrity. So the wine was dropped from the bill of fare.

The days sped on, each bearing its own burden of preparation and expectation. Each one bringing nearer and nearer the wished for, longed for day.

George's last letters gave hope that he would reach home three or four days before the birthday festival.

The papers were read with palpitating hearts, and every ring at the door bell started anticipations of telegrams. Notes from Max nearly every day told of disappointed hopes. " No ship arrived," was the message they bore to the waiting household, and the anxiety of suspense was at its height as the family met at the breakfast table on the morning of the party.

" I think we shall have to hold our levee without them, my girls," said the Judge, assuming a gayety by no means felt. " It will only be for a day or so; a squall at sea, or the breaking of a rudder or loss of a paddle wheel, has caused detention. They will be here to-morrow."

> " So laugh while you may,
> And be happy and gay,
> And never a trouble borrow."

"Oh! papa, it will be too bad!"

"Why, yes; I suppose it will. But if they're not here, what will you do? We'll have it all over again when they do come, and the last shall be better than the first."

"They will be here," said Die decidedly.

"So dey will, honey," said aunt Ruth, who had just brought in hot cakes, claiming an old servant's privilege of appearing once at every breakfast time to say "How de" to all the household.

"How do you know, Ruth?" demanded Nettie.

"How I know? Umph! Feels him in my bones. How I know! how I know? You tink dey's coming; you see. Ole Ruth don't fool nobody."

A suppressed smile went round the table, and in spite of the channel through which the hope had passed, there was renewed cheer and expectation.

Ruth saw the effect her words had produced, and after a nod to each, as she handed her cakes, she slipped away to her work, gratified with the good deed done and the pleasant recognition from the assembled family, each member of which she loved as her own life.

"I shall be so disappointed if they don't come," said Mrs. Hancock.

"And I too," said Emma.

"Plenty of beaux without them for to-night," suggested the Judge mischievously, "and to-morrow you can have them all to yourselves."

"I do wish I knew who the 'lady love' that Wash is always hinting at is. It's a shame he does not tell us right out. Isn't it, papa?" asked Nettie.

"No, I think he is in the right of it. Every man

> 'Should still keep something to himsel'
> He scarcely tells to ony.'

And if Wash has been cherishing a love for years that he is still doubtful about, I think he has been wise."

"I do wonder if it's Prof. Hendrie's accomplished daughter, that studies Greek, and sits on the house-top all night with her father counting the stars, and boasts of her utter inability to hem her own hand-kerchief, or make a gruel for her sick mother," queried Emma, with a contemptuous toss of her curls.

"Not a bit of it," said Nettie indignantly. "He has a little bit of common sense, I hope; and I have heard him say many a time that he liked smart women to talk with, fashionable women to flirt with; but when he chose a *wife*, she must know how to get up good dinners and arrange bouquets."

"Shocking," exclaimed Emma. "Suppose Prof. Hendrie were called upon to mend his own boots or manage the planting of a mess of potatoes in his own garden; do you think he could do it?"

"Of course not; but he makes learning a busi-ness."

"And why may not his daughter?" asked the Judge.

"That don't seem to be 'woman's sphere,' you know. And it's my impression," said Mrs. Hancock with dignity, "that George's wife, when he chooses one, will be entirely out of her 'sphere' getting his dinners or arranging his bouquets."

The remembrance of a certain tragic attempt at arranging a bouquet for Master George, flashed through the mind of Die and crimsoned her neck and brow, and her heart beat almost audibly.

"Ruth can cook capital dinners; but Ruth can't say her alphabet," said Nettie, renewing the subject, "and I don't think it makes a pin's difference whether a woman knows how to read or not, in the making of good breakfast rolls or the broiling of a steak, do you, Die?"

Thus appealed to, Die felt herself impelled to answer lest her agitation should become apparent.

"I presume very good dinners have been, and may be again, cooked by very ignorant people; and I have known egregious blunders committed in that much abused and neglected department, the kitchen, for lack of knowledge. For instance, I found even Ruth putting a double dose of soda in her biscuits yesterday because the cream of tartar was all out. Finding them of an unwarrantable golden brown, she sent for me to tell her what was the matter. Said the two 'white trucks' were so much alike, she thought they'd do."

A hearty laugh round the table answered the recital of Ruth's mistake, and Die, forcing herself to speak, had gathered the self-possession she so seldom lost. She added when the laugh was done, "I don't wish to be understood as supposing that a woman ignorant of books cannot get good dinners, or that a good education derived from books need, in the slightest degree, prevent any woman from becoming an expert in that time honored and most desirable accomplishment."

"But anybody can learn to cook in a week."

"Beg your pardon, Nettie dear, all women can't be cooks or housekeepers, any more than all women can dress tastefully and become agreeable parlor companions and ornaments. My impression is that a good cook is all the better for a good education—and a thoroughly educated woman is all the wiser for being a thoroughly disciplined cook and house-keeper, if possible. Every woman should make the very most of herself, and be able to act her part well in whatever circumstances of life she may be placed."

"That's my opinion, Die," said the Judge, with emphasis. "I think it would be an immense folly to take you out of my office and put you into the kitchen; and yet I should feel much more sure of a good dinner if found in an emergency, with you on hand, than if my bodily requirements were in the hands of my darling Nettie."

"And what would become of your office, in my hands, papa mine?" asked Nettie with evident pique.

"It would fare worse than my dinner, I imagine."

"So it seems I am a useless member of the body

14

politic; and as that is the case, I will take myself away to the regions where I can expend at least my censures or approbations, on the delicacies and beauties that are to make the attractions of our parlors this evening."

The whole party rose from the table, having had their thoughts led away from the anxiety of the hour by their discursive chat.

Die retreated to her room, where, turning the key, she covered her face with her hands and burst into tears.

Seldom the strong hearted girl gave way to such expressions of feeling. Almost daily, thoughts were uttered in her presence that would have stung a soul less firmly poised than hers; but she heeded not. What then had so flushed her cheeks and thrown her whole being into such intense emotion at this time?

Only one moment she allowed herself to be overpowered, only one moment bent in womanly weakness before an all conquering feeling. Dashing away her tears, she aroused herself.

"What right have I to yield to this emotion? I know I belong to another class and caste from these, yet is it not as useful and honorable? If they cannot be brought together, shall I weep and suffer? What subtle power fills and thrills me when his name is mentioned? Shall I never conquer this worse than useless sentiment? Why indeed should I conquer it? For nearly four years, through all my efforts, trials, failures and successes, I have striven to stay the growth of this over-mastering love; yet it has grown and strengthened with every hour; am I to blame? What part or lot have I had in this matter? Every week his letters have brought me fresh proofs of his worth, and almost every hour the accents of love have told his praises. I cannot enter the parlor or breakfast room, but his clear honest eyes look through my heart and read my secret, from the canvass that makes him omnipresent. To-night he will be here, and I shall hear his voice, see him as he is, feel his breath perchance upon my cheek, and be thrilled anew with the magnetism that four years since permeated my whole being without my consent.

"O, soul of mine! be calm and still. Love on if you needs must; but meet bravely your fate and be prepared to rejoice in the joy of another. Learn to suffer, and grow strong through suffering; reap the compensation of well doing and unselfishness and be content therewith.

"Oh! how thankful I am that no human soul knows by what a sweet and secret power I have been helped in my desire to be worthy of the highest, and how soul satisfying is the result, even though I cannot grasp and hold fast the source of my inspiration.

"Shall I blush over this absorbing influence? I might as well be ashamed that my eyes are brown or my face attractive; since both facts exist without my volition or consent. For the ten thousandth time let me promise that *I will be true to myself.*"

A gentle rap at the door startled Die from her painful self communings. Dashing a draft of cold water over her swollen face and eyes to remove the traces of her late emotion, she found Aggie waiting for a word to soothe sad feelings that had been stirred by a careless expression of Nettie's, in which Gordon's name had been mentioned with severe reproach; but the sight of Die turned her thoughts from herself, and she exclaimed:

"Diana, you weeping! on this the gala day of your good life? I did not know that your calm eye could weep or your brave heart feel a pulse throb of pain. Tell me, what is it?"

"It is nothing, Aggie, that should cast a shade of sadness for you."

"But you seem so happy here, and they all love you so; and you are so grand and beautiful in all you do and say. Tell me, do, Die, what has given you pain?"

"Aggie, don't you know that even a rosebud can cast a shadow. It may be all as you say; but there are father and mother, brothers and sister, far away, whom I love but cannot have here. Their lives are not as my life; their feelings not our feelings. The two households cannot affiliate, and standing between the two, I sometimes suffer the chilling shadow of the mountain top upon which the sun shines so brigthly. There! that is confession enough, but what dims your eyes, dear Aggie?"

"Die, I've a secret for you."

"I am ready to give it a close warm place of welcome in my sanctuary."

"I am going to marry Max." Die folded the little trembling bird in her arms and kissed her cheek, only saying, "O, Aggie, I am so glad, for he is good and worthy of being loved."

"I have not forgotten Gordon. Oh, no—but I hold him in deep pity as one that was born to weakness; one reared in indulgence. The underlying currents of his life were pure; his boyish instincts were true. I loved him as a child; but there was always in my soul a reservation, a something that was not satisfied, of which I was not then aware."

"And now you have found the fulness of content."

"You say rightly. I do not believe, even if Gordon had not fallen by intoxication, that I would ever have been happy in his love, and yet it was hard to give him up."

"Hard to have an idol broken, even though you knew it was of clay and imperfect. Love is a strange mystery," said Die.

"Very hard to turn myself away from the bright childish vision, and hard—oh, so hard to know of his thoughtless madness."

"And this new love?"

You know how long I was sick."

"Yes, I have heard how terribly the shock paralyzed you."

"Max was the only one, except my parents, that knew my secret. He knew and could tell me about

Gordon. He came often and read to me and comforted me. For a year I did not think of love, and we grew to know and appreciate each other, to think and feel and act together, and day by day we seemed to be more essential one to the other till the time came at last when without speaking, we looked into each other's eyes and read our destiny. Then he opened his arms and I laid my head upon his manly breast, and we were one and indivisible. Were we silly?"

" On the contrary, I think the truest love delights in silence. It is like the nugget of pure gold. Ore that has to be put into the brasier's furnace to separate it from the dross, is not so valuable."

"So you do not condemn me!"

" I! no, darling, I am so glad."

" Do you really think they will come to-night?"

" Die, Aggie, Emma, where are you all? Here's the telegram. They'll be here on the eight o'clock train," shouted Nettie from below.

" Oh! let us be joyful, joyful, joyful,
Oh! let us be joyful—they're coming home at last."

And trilling her voice like a spring robin she danced away, followed by the two girls who had had a life experience that had left an impress upon their maturer feelings which Nettie had never known.

CHAPTER XXV.

THE BIRTHDAY PARTY.

My dear Father and Mother—If you will look back through the long aisles of time for nineteen years, you will find that this is my birthday ; and this day, by one of those coincidences so common in this great world of ours, is also the natal day of dear Nettie Hancock. To-day also, George, the only son of this influential and lordly house, has promised to appear among his kindred after his long journey in foreign lands, and to celebrate these triple circumstances, a great party is to come off to-night at the Hancock residence.

Can you imagine, my dear ones, cards of invitation floating like snow flakes over the capital of the nation, summoning the *elite* of the world—President, Cabinet Ministers, Senators, Representatives, Foreign Embassadors, Lords, Dukes, Counts, and (begging your honest pardons,) court fools in abundance —to the birthday party of Miss Nettie G. Hancock and Miss Diana Dinmont. Nothing would do but our names should go side by side, and that we should share alike the honors of the evening.

In your last, written on the anniversary of my last year's " freedom gift," as you please to call it, you bade me look back to that clear starlight night when I sat by you on that log in the fence corner, and not to be proud. Father, I do look back. Was not that night the time when, under the shining stars of heaven, we both resolved to turn our eyes toward the " palace beautiful," and to lay down our burdens and walk out of the 'slough of despond ?"

I look back, but I see only a better and a clearer light illuminating the pathway from then to now; and I lift my heart in thankfulness to the source of all goodness and love, that we have been kept as in the hollow of His hand to this hour.

Shall I dare tell you? I have painted that picture. The grand sweep of hills shimmering in the moonlight; the winding Alleghany; the humble home at Rocky Glen; the sorrowful maiden sitting upon the log by the side of the broken fence in her old brown hood and shawl; the sleeping man; and the weary mother coming to the stile; I have painted it all and it hangs in my room to remind me daily of you all, and of all the past. Of the mighty force you, my beloved ones, have brought to bear upon your own lives and fortunes, enabling us to lift ourselves out of it all. No eyes but mine read that picture. All call it "beautiful." To me it teaches 'Faith, Hope and Charity,' and patience and humility. I shall not grow proud for I have passed life's proudest moment, and that was when I was able to pay your debt to the Judge and have you free.

Oh! father do you know what installments you pay me when you write of your happiness; of your fine crops; of Lulu's growth and improvement; of Tom's usefulness and self reliance; Egbert's wonderful developments; and Edward's faithful good ways? Believe me when I tell you that such letters to me are more than all the empty *eclat* of my fashionable life a thousand fold.

I sit here in my chamber—it is my last hour before the assembling of the brilliant throng. The mirror before me reflects a beautiful girl, on whom the hand of time has only stamped the impress of nineteen summers. She is like both father and mother, yet very unlike; a combination of the two. She is not expensively dressed, yet she will be called "elegant" ere the morrow. A fine white organdie trimmed lightly with folds of blue, a broach and bracelets of pearls, a present from Judge Hancock, white kid gloves and a pretty fan will complete her attire. Do you recognize your barefoot child of seven years ago begging her bread? Do not start that I call myself beautiful. I know that I am, and I know, too, that I prize tenfold more than beauty the gift of the steady hand with which I write these words, the power which was given me to learn the alphabet, and to direct my steps upward to all that I am. Yet I do not despise the gift of beauty. It is well in its way.

George and Max Carter are coming. I hear the carriage wheels, the cries of joy below. Good night, father and mother. Amid all this show and gayety my heart turns ever, like the flower of the Lupine, to the west and to you. DIANA.

Die sealed her letter, and with trembling emotion prepared herself to appear by the side of Nettie and George, to receive the congratulations of the evening. To her sensitive condition the house seemed to thrill with the joy which had entered with the welcomed son. She was ready, but she hesitated. " Surely they will come for me. Ah! I hear Nettie's trilling laugh. Now, nerves of mine, be brave and strong, and bear me truly through this trying hour."

" Oh! Die ;" exclaimed Nettte, " where are you ? It is time we were in our places. Wash waits for you to come. You are beautiful; oh! how beautiful !"

" And so is my dear Nettie. If we satisfy each other that is enough; is it not ? Are George and Max well ?

" Splendid! Don't you fall in love with my **darl**ing brother. It will be just like you."

" Hush ? Nettie, don't frighten me."

" Frighten Die Dinmont!" said Nettie in tones of lugubrious mockery, as they descended to the library where the father and son awaited them, ready to escort them to the drawing room.

George stood facing the door talking to his father.
A bright transparent cloud, shaded with the very
blue of the sky, floated towards him. With out-
stretched hands he sprang to meet the answering
offered hands. But, as if a power unseen controlled
him, he opened wide his arms and folded to his
breast the airy vision, and pressed an ardent kiss
upon the brow, as the eyes were uplifted to meet his
own.

At that instant the side door opened and Mrs.
Hancock, Emma, Aggie and Max made their appearance ready for the evening, and in the confusion
the embrace which George had given Die escaped
observation.

"Come, it is late and our guests are coming," said
the Judge, offering an arm to each of the two belles
of the evening. George gave his attention to his
mother and Emma, Max to Aggie, and so marshaled,
they entered the brilliant drawing room to receive
the congratulations of hundreds of the most exalted
of the nation.

Shall we leave them to bow acknowledgments to
the "airy nothings" that fell upon their ears as
group after group was announced, gave out their
greeting and passed on? Yes, for our stiff homely
pen knows not the art of such portrayals.

There is no stupidity more stupid than such stereotyped occasions where the actors themselves go
through their parts, like players at a rehearsal, each
one doing his best; because of the reward that is to

be received; each with some personal interest to advance; each wishing it over, each at heart berating society for its tyrannical exactions, and half resolving never to be so caught, jammed, jostled, worried and excited again.

There may be novices, amused by gorgeous glitter, that go through their role with pleasurable excitement; but they are few, and a half dozen repetitions will wear away the novelty, and leave the whole resting as a dull, unmeaning drudgery upon every sensitive and sensible heart and brain.

* * * * * * * *

There was a strange gathering at Senator Hancock's that festival night.

Strange rumors were abroad, and the Senate chamber and Representative's Hall had witnessed angry and fearful discussion during the winter. The words "Secession," "Division of North and South," "Traitorism," "Tyranny," "Constitutional Liberty," "Disaffection," and "vested rights," etc., were current terms in all earnest conversations among men Doubt, dissatisfaction, threatenings, ridicule and insult, crimination and recrimination were the order of the day.

Still parties were held, and receptions given, and old and young seemed, for the hour, to forget the ominous aspect of the political horizon of the nation.

Jefferson Davis might have been seen on that eventful evening, promenading in lively chat with

the wives and daughters of influential men, who
had been drawn to the Capital by the approaching
crisis, and whose political status was yet doubtful;
while his elegant and insinuating lady made herself
more than usually agreeable to those that stood ready
to be drawn into the toils of her designing husband.

Military officers gathered in groups and talked
earnestly in low and broken sentences. Members
of Congress appeared ill at ease. A fearful storm
seemed about to sweep over the devoted city and
country, and the flashings of the lightning and the
low growling thunder were seen and heard upon
every side.

The great rebellion was about to be inaugurated,
and even for one evening, amid the joy and gladness
of a birthday festival, the machinations could not
be laid aside; or the covert endeavors to win the
pledges of the young and thoughtless to the side of
rebellion.

Failing to find the usual stimulus necessary to
keep up a vigorous excitement, the older men retired
early. Davis, after sounding both Max and George
with insinuating jests and party allusions, bowed
himself and wife away to follow out his diabolical
purpose in other homes, and among those likely to
receive more cordially his overtures.

George found little time amid the throng of com
ing and departing guests, to nearly every one of
whom he was a stranger and must needs be introduced, to pay any attention to Die, nor was she at

leisure to think of the new comers after the first salutation. More than her proportion of homage and admiration fell upon her, unsought and uncared for. George watched the tide as it swayed to and fro, and heard with beating heart the expressions concerning Die that fell about him, from those who had no suspicion of his interest in the protege of his father and sister.

" She's a beauty, by George," exclaimed one.

" If she were only an heiress!" spoke his companion.

" What, then?"

" I think I could win and wear the jewel—if it were worth a half million."

" *If?*" said the first speaker with a doubtful shrug.

" If me no if," answered the other theatrically.

" And what if I, with my half a million, should try? Do you suppose I should succeed?" asked the first speaker.

" Never saw a poor girl yet that less than that would not buy."

" Your epaulettes as Colonel under the new organization might win. Hey! Ewert?"

" Hush!" answered Ewert, looking round in alarm, and both young men moved away, leaving George with burning brow to be the unintentional listener to another group of whispering gossips.

" One gets so mixed up in Washington society. Northern people have not a particle of discrimination. Just to think of that *hired girl* being introduced here among the first families of the nation! It is disgusting," and the bedizened head gave a contemptuous toss.

"Why, Mrs. Gilman, they report that our Governor has bowed his stiff neck at the shrine of her beauty and been refused."

"Shocking! I wonder you dare repeat such a scandal."

George led his partner to the refreshment room. Even there the whispered criticisms did not cease. He was indignant, and resolved as soon as possible to find Die.

The evening was wearing late. Departures had thinned the crowd. Die disengaged herself from the throng around her, and threw herself wearily into a seat in the recess of a window to rest. She had been playing a brilliant role, into which she had been able to throw no feeling, except a desire to make even the throng of butterfly admirers that circled about her, happy; but she had played well.

CHAPTER XXVI.

THE DISCLOSURE.

"Oh! Die, here you are, hid behind the curtain," exclaimed Nettie, as she approached, radiant with happiness, leaning upon her beloved brother's arm. "I have hardly seen you this evening."

"No, in such a crowd unless one is very careful, one loses one's friends," answered Die with a tone of sadness.

"I should say, one finds them," responded Nettie. "I declare I am tired to death shaking hands and being congratulated by everybody I ever knew."

"Truly a sad case, Nettie dear. Come sit with me a moment and rest yourself."

"Isn't it too bad? George won't tell me who the lady is that he has loved with such idolatry all his life, and I am dying to hear."

"Surely to save his sister's life he might divulge his secret."

"'Tired to death and dying,' Nettie dear? Don't you think that you can survive till morning?" asked her brother.

"Oh? George, you're just as great a tease as ever.

How closely Max and Aggie cling together. 'Was it not dreadful, Wash, about Gordon?"

" It was a fearful tragedy."

" There! I called you Wash and I don't mean to. Don't you like George best?"

" I do decidedly. Have never fairly forgiven father for bestowing upon me so grandiloquent a name."

" Oh! what's in a name! 'A rose by any other name would smell as sweet.' This beautiful half blown bud you have for instance."

" In the Orient, men tell their loves by flowers."

" Oh! ho! Why not in this way proclaim your long undeclared passion!"

" I will, little sister. The lady is with us this evening, and if my guardian spirit is propitious, I shall find opportunity to present my bud."

" It's Aggie, Die, our darling Aggie," exclaimed Nettie.

" Not so fast, my impetuous sister. If I read the signs aright, I shall not dare offer my favor in that direction. See how Max bends his tall head to the *petite* beauty. Ah, ha! I read his secret well."

" Who in the world then? George, do give me a hint."

" What! yield on the first eve of my arrival, my treasured secret of years' keeping? Lay bare the love that has swayed my destiny, and held me bound fast in its toils; that has kept me good when temptation lured; that has whispered 'beware' when the gay and thoughtless and sometimes the very wicked said, ' come,' with strange enticements?"

" You tempted ! *You*, my immaculate brother ! I did not dream that even the shadow of a shade of wickedness could dim the brightness of your untarnished life."

" Sorry to scatter your illusion, deary, but there was a time when your humble servant stood on the brink of a precipice as frightful as that over which poor Gordon hurled himself, and but for my friend Max and the unnameable one, I should have gone with him."

"Oh, George, it is not so ?"

"Nettie, I speak the words of truth and soberness to-night. Once, on such a night as this, one whose eyes sparkled brightly and whom I was beginning to look upon with fluttering heart beats, pressed the wine to my lips, and I drank and forgot my manhood, and talked with thick and clumsy tongue, and spoke impudent words to a good friend. Once, twice, thrice, I was guilty."

" And then ?" exclaimed Die breathlessly, her face blanched and every feature quivering with excitement.

" And then, in a midnight walk (my spirit was restless and I could not sleep) I saw a young girl sitting upon a log in a fence corner beside a man, heavy with the stupor of strong drink, watching him as he lay helpless among the leaves."

" Oh ! brother that is romance."

Before George could answer, the Professor came
for Nettie, and led her away to join in the last dance
for the evening.

"Will you join the dancers?" asked George, offering his arm to Die.

"Excuse me, not to-night," she answered in a suppressed voice.

"Will you walk with me?"

She took his arm.

"I was restless and could not sleep," he said,
bending to her ear. "So I arose in the night and
walked toward Oxbow. As I passed the 'Glen' I
met a man staggering under his load of self-indulgence. I followed him, knowing he must soon lie
down or fall, and that he would need care. I saw a
daughter meet a father; I heard her words of filial
love; I stood in my place and watched with her;
and I prayed as I had never prayed before, and beneath God's stars vowed to be a man, and in all
future time abstain from all things that could intoxicate. I have kept that vow. One month after I
made another vow to my friend Max to hold as a
secret, known only to my own soul, my love, my
almost adoration, for the pure, sweet girl with
whom I had held my strange night watch, until such
a time as I might speak without fear of incurring
injury either to her or to myself. I have kept that
vow too. The time has come for a revelation.
Diana, dearest of all earth's treasures to me, am I
understood, and will you accept and wear my rose?"

Trembling with emotion, almost sinking beneath the change of thought and feeling which had been wrought in the last ten minutes, she lifted her eyes to his in confidence and trust, took the flower in her left hand, and while she raised it to her lips placed her right hand in his. No words were spoken; but in their hearts, audible to the inward perception of each, were sounding the words, "united forever more, forever more."

There was no opportunity for further demonstrations; no kiss or embrace. Diana fastened the flower upon her bosom with the pearl broach, quietly remarking:

"It is meet that the precious gifts of the father and son should be united. I love them both. Come, we must take our places again and receive the adieux of our departing guests."

With another pressure of the hand, laid so confidingly in his own, the proud heir of the great Hancock estate led his companion to the center of the drawing room. Nettie, glowing with her dance, was already there.

One by one the throng departed, leaving behind the lovers happy in each other, satisfied with the present and hopeful for all the future.

Shall we leave them here and now, dear readers?

Reader—No; all this is too sudden, too unexpected. It is not according to our experience that a whole household should be so blest.

Author—And why not? Is it at all improbable

that two beautiful, accomplished and good daughters of a very rich man, high in position, honorable in all his thoughts and actions, should find, in the great Capital of a great Nation, two men that were attracted by their youth, good looks and social position, to offer them marriage and to win their love? Is it strange that Max and Aggie, the tender and quiet little Aggie, should love and be happy? Is it wonderful that the long waiting, faithful, trusting love of George and Diana, should have found expression in a rose bud?

Reader—But we were expecting a startling denouement; waiting for a scene.

Author—What kind of a scene? One in which the calm, self-poised Diana Dinmont and the self-controlled George Hancock were to be the actors? Truly, you were waiting for impossibilities. I have been trying through my whole tale to show you how great and noble natures could live without scenes; and could recognize something subtle and all pervading within themselves, invisibly drawing from all surroundings a power to harmonize and purify, at the same time throwing around them a golden aura in return to lighten and brighten, and entice upward toward the Good, the True, and the Beautiful?

The throng was gone; the last slippered foot had glided over the brilliant carpet spread from the door to the carriage steps; the last rumbling sound of wheels had died away upon the streets, and the weary inmates of the home kissed each other their "good nights," and turned their several ways with hearts throbbing with high hopes for the morrow.

Diana sought the solitude of her room, and standing again before her mirror, she tried to realize her happiness. Every fibre of her frame was permeated with the soul-satisfying truth that she was beloved and could love in return. Again she traced their love to its beginning, and now she dared fully to acknowledge to herself that it had been the inner light of her life; the inspiration that had revealed the possibilities of her own soul, the strength of her own nature. Again she recalled the steps upward during all the long years. Steps not taken without pain, struggle and self-denial; steps that strained every nerve in the going, and yet the strain had brought everywhere its compensation.

She questioned herself closely as to what lever she had used the most successfully for her own uplifting. Always, a love of truth, unselfishness, and an unwavering belief in the right of every human soul to do its best and grandest work

By looking closely into the needs of her own life she had learned to realize the needs of the humblest human soul born in the "Image of God," and she knew, too, from actual experience, the exacting demands of that strange, incongruous mass, called society.

Society! how little it had aided her, and how very little it had hindered her; only enough to make her feet more firm in her upward journey. Out of the depths of her own spirit had come the propelling force that had made her what she was. Not a question arose in her own mind as to her fitness to wear on her bosom the rose that represented the long tried love of George. He was her superior in wealth! She his superior in innate power to secure to herself all that wealth could procure to satisfy the wants of her nature.

He was better educated in the theories of science; but she was far beyond him in that practical knowledge which fits one at all points for the uses of life. She would not have exchanged her knowledge for his. His standard of culture would undoubtedly, by the mass of the world, be pronounced higher than hers; but hers was a broader and more Catholic. Not for an instant did her past early life appear to her as a degrading thing, to be blushed for or kept hid; and as she stood there before her mirror, glowing in her young beauty, her whole being pulsating in the happy consciousness of a newly recognized love, her highest bliss next to that love, was her own recognition of the fact that through self-accepted struggles she had won fitness for her present position. She was very hapyy, and kneeling with clasped hands by her bedside, she thanked God with an overflowing heart for all the sources of that happiness.

CHAPTER XXVII.

OXBOW RENOVATED.

The unaccountable disappearance of Gordon was communicated to his parents by Max in the kindest manner possible, after a due lapse of time. At first the mother heart found excuses and reasons for it all, and seemed to bear up bravely, then came anxieties and restlessness, and as weeks wore into months the feeling that shocked at first became intensely painful.

Max often received letters from George and never failed to be accosted daily by the anxious father with the question, " What news?"

Mr. Rand wandered about like one half crazed. His grey hairs grew whiter and the furrows of care and grief wore deeper channels on his once smooth self-satisfied brow. He did not ask for Gordon nor speak his name; his tongue would have refused his thoughts utterance had he attempted it.

A pressing necessity, an imperative driving business would have been to him an immense relief; anxiety and suspense were eating out the very foundations of his life. Alas! wealth that seemed so desirable, grew into a haunting shadow that cursed his existence.

The poor mother tried to solace her aching heart in the care of her new found babes. She taught them to speak the name of mother, and to hang about her neck, and rest upon her knees with loving confidence. The mirth and music made by them rendered life bearable, yet with every passing hour she found it needful to repeat to herself her lesson of faithfulness and trust. Much as her soul was tried, the mother's hope did not die. " He will come again," she would say to herself a thousand times a day. Not a mail was brought in that her heart did not flutter, and her eyes look out their intense longing for a letter from over the sea that should tell her " the lost was found, the dead was alive again."

Oh! weary suffering soul, " who shall deliver you from the body of this death?"

As the autumn days were wearing away and the soughing wind of the year's decay moaned gloomily about the old house on the hill; as the glowing leaves lay strewn at her feet beneath the trees where he had played; as the vines withered that he had helped to twine and the flowers fell that he used to love, the old home grew too lonely. Every spot and nook seemed permeated by his spirit. Not a chair or sofa in the whole house but gave out to her his image; the carpets upon the floor; the bits of statuary in the corners; the vases upon the mantles; the hat rack in the hall; the ballusters upon which

his hands had rested as he bounded from stair to
stair; his vacant place at the table; everywhere,
everywhere, he had left his impression; everything
echoed his cheery voice and gave back his rollicking boyish laugh; "and where was he?"

The suspense became unendurable agony. The
mother grew into a statue of marble, endowed with
life and motion—doing mechanically her duty with
unflagging fidelity and determined purpose.

There was at the bottom of this woman's heart a
doubt and fear that her son, who had once appeared
before her a stupid inebriate, might have again fallen; have plunged headlong into some powerful
abyss of sin and shame in which he might be still
wallowing in untold hideousness. Yet she spoke not
her thought. While she could bear it and live, how
could she? How can a mother train her lips to
speak ill of her child?

Max saw her fading day by day. He felt that he
ought, perhaps, to unvail to her eyes the frightful
figure that was hidden beneath all this uncertainty;
to prepare her for the worst; to guard her against
what might come. Yet how could he do so terrible
a thing? Should he tell her all? and take away all
the beauty and glow that her love and pride had
thrown around her lost darling? or should he hold
that blighting power within his own hands; and if
Gordon was indeed lost forever, let her live on in
blissful ignorance of his weakness and folly? He
resolved to say one thing to her: That her son did

15

indulge in the inebriating cup; that he might have met his fate in some midnight revel; that he might, through his agonising consciousness of his own instability, have resolved to secrete himself for a time from all friendly recognition, to struggle alone with his relentless enemy. He bade her hope and be brave to meet the worst. The relation of Aggie to her son was minutely detailed, with a design of adding a new interest to her broken life; giving one more chord of love to vibrate in the unstrung harp.

Aggie became to her almost as a daughter, and soothed with her sweet quiet ways many an hour of watching and waiting. Oh! wretched longing mother! Oh! stricken maiden! The loved one was not, and the love that went out and found no resting place, came back with weary pinions to lay the one green twig of sympathy upon their hearts; they loved each other.

Hettie Bishop was very lonely at the "Lodge" without her little brother and sister, and went often to the hill to spend days with them. She was a sweet good child; but they could not reconcile her to the idea of a home in Washington, far away from the grave of her mother, or those who had been interwoven with all the thoughts and feeling of the past.

Mrs. Rand asked that she might be added to her household, and Mrs. Hancock, not loth to lay down this much of her assumed burden, assented and the child was made much happier in a new home.

Mrs. Rand seemed more calm after her talk with Max; but still she hoped on. At every step on the porch, every ring at the door bell, every rustle at night in the yard, every bark of old Dell, her pulse bounded and something whispered "He's coming."

But he came not. "Hope deferred maketh the heart sick." The doctor said heart disease would be the result of all this, and advised change of climate, scene and interests. He was wise and knew well that

> "All houses in which men have lived, or died,
> Are haunted houses. Through the open doors
> The harmless phantoms on their errands glide
> With feet that make no sound upon the floors."

So as the winter winds began. to whistle fiercely about the casements and sway the low branches of the vines against the walls, to shout down the chimneys and whisper wierdly through the keyholes, Mr. and Mrs. Rand, their children and old servant, went away into a new home built by the miser uncle, more grand and capacious, that had been waiting twenty years for the presence of woman; for the softening and harmonizing loves and plays of children; for the holy influences of husband and wife, to make its stately splendors attractive.

The new did not blot out the old; it only overlaid it with new figures, rendering the past more shadowy and dim. Bending all their energies to the present needs, the grieved father and mother grew more engrossed therewith, and at last gained a measure of happiness in the new loves, that twined innocently about their lives, drawing out the best that was with-n them.

*　　*　　*　　*　　*　　*　　*　　*

When Judge Hancock was about to leave the "Lodge" to take up his new duties in the Senate chamber, he had a long talk with Max, who used every possible argument to induce his patron to annihilate the distillery.

"Would it be right to do that?" asked the Judge, "there are many interests invested in the works. Will it be just?"

"I believe, sir," answered Max respectfully, "that if you were to close up the concern to-morrow and support each family until they could find other employments, you would be the gainer in ten years, and these same families immeasurably better off, provided they do not throw themselves again into the vortex of dissipation."

"I do not quite comprehend your mode of reasoning," replied the Judge in a tone of incredulity.

"It is this: A distillery always draws about it a class of inhabitants whose proclivities are in unison with the work, and they are not apt to be of the best class."

"Does that necessarily follow?" was the abrupt question of the proprietor of Oxbow.

"I think so, sir—ask yourself. Would you be willing to arrange a home for your family under the shadow of a distillery?"

"No! a hundred times, no," answered the Judge excitedly.

"There is not a good school in the village Your agent indulges to excess; your distiller is a habitual drinker and abuses his family; Owen, your outside manager, is no longer fit for his place, and his boys are rowdies, his wife a broken down woman; Nolly, your head carpenter, often staggers over his work: old McKay, who has been a teetotaler for forty years, is the only sober teamster in your employ."

"I think you are mistaken, Mr. Carter," said the Judge, flushed and uneasy, "they do as I do myself, drink in moderation sometimes; but do you do right to say there is not a sober man among them!"

"Judge Hancock, I believe I speak the words of strict truth when I say you have not a man now in your employ, directly connected with your distillery, that does not disguise himself with strong drink at times, and that is not surely growing worse."

"I have tried for many years to manufacture only for mechanical purposes," replied the Judge.

"And have you succeeded?"

"It seems not from your statement."

"I said I believed you would be the gainer in ten years. Your numerous tenants, indeed the whole population of the country, now devote their energies to raising corn and barley, being sure of a market. Every hour your lands are becoming impoverished, and your wealth of soil floats away in the form of alcohol. Take away this temptation, encourage stock raising on the lands, turn your extensive buildings and water power into other channels of trade and commerce. The town will enlarge, your property increase in value, and the people in wealth, morality and happiness."

"You may be right, Mr. Carter."

"I know that I am right in one thing—that ardent spirits or alcohol cannot be used as a beverage, without impoverishing and ultimately demoralizing the whole community in which its manufacture is carried on."

"Is there any other business that presents itself to your mind that might take the place of this, without too suddenly checking the currents of industry?"

"Yes; Chapman & Bros. were here last week prospecting, and one of them remarked that it was the best place in the State for a cotton factory, and one of the finest localities for the re-establishment of 'Horton's' great paper mill, which you know was burned three weeks ago."

"Did they?" Self interest was coming to the aid of right.

"But they both declared they would not set up any kind of a business in the neighborhood of a, distillery."

"Wind it up, wind it up," said the Judge. "I should have done it long ago, but for the idea of breaking down so many people who seemed to depend on it for support."

"God bless you, sir," exclaimed Max cheerily, "now I can work with a will."

He extended his hand and his employer shook it heartily.

"You said there were no good schools."

"None that do honor to the place."

"Maxwell Carter, I have felt for a long time that a man who held the destinies of as many people in his hand as I, should do more to elevate and improve them and less to degrade, than I have done. But I have had no time to think or act. Select the most eligible site on my lands, use my funds, set all these idlers to work, build for the town of Oxbow a seminary for boys and girls. Let there be in it a public library room, a lecture hall, school rooms and whatever else your thought may suggest. When it is completed I will deed it and the ground upon which it stands to the town of Oxbow forever more, with a hope it may make some slight restitution for the wrong done in the past."

Another hearty hand shaking followed, and the gratified Max promised to use his utmost endeavors to carry out the will of his patron.

The old distillery was transformed in a few months to a thriving cotton factory and a paper mill, demanding new enterprises, which came speedily at the call.

An iron foundry sprung from the debris of the old hog pens, and a machine shop, a rolling mill, and a nail factory followed in quick succession, each and all requiring operatives. The operatives demanding new homes developed saw mills, planing mills, sash and blind factories and all their adjuncts, and Oxbow trebled itself in three years and the prophecy of Max was more than fulfilled.

Rocky Glen, with its beautiful sweep of hills, was chosen for the site of the Judge's glorious charity. Its whole base devoted to gardens and lawns, its clear bounding water turned into cascades, and its little pond into a large reservoir, in the centre of which fountains played fantastic tricks from the mouths of the mimic monsters of the deep, made of the ore that had so long slept beneath the hills.

Churches sprang into being, elegant dwellings crowded out of sight the squalid hovels that had once sheltered the habitual dram drinker and his suffering household.

The farmers had a market ready and sure for all the products of the varied departments of agriculture, and the people, through all the elements of life, found themselves taking steps upward.

George looked with astonishment on his return at the magical transformation. Expressing to his father his unbounded admiration at the result of the abandonment of the distillery, he was electrified by his answer:

"To your beautiful Diana we are indebted for all this. But for her quiet, persistent and firm example, teaching me hourly how great and noble and self sacrificing a soul can be, I should never have realized the power that I held in my hand for the weal or woe of my fellow men. Her learning to read, her teaching her whole family while earning her bread by daily toil; the development of Heckel Dinmont into a good citizen, husband and father, through her hourly influence, compelled me to think of the evil I was doing. Thinking led to action. Max helped my wavering morality by convincing me that I could do more for the people without that distillery than with it. You see the work that is begun. I scarcely know which is the greater of the two."

"And I," answered the son, bowing with reverence and filial love, " scarce can tell which has been the greatest of the three. The subtle magnetism of a brave, humble, true life that moved you to this grand work; the broad humanitarianism that impelled you to listen to the voice of the charmer, or the wonderful executive ability and unswerving integrity of Max that has completed and rounded out the whole, making it all so grandly beautiful."

Talking with Max a few days after, and breathing out his admiration, the young architect of Oxbow disclaimed all honor.

"I have done nothing. It is easy to work out problems on other people's capital. A very little thing to move mountains if you have faith, in the shape of gold and silver."

"And a good brain to organize and plan."

"George, my boy, you are the same George to me as in the days when I taught you lessons of old

I have learned the truest lesson of my life since I came to Oxbow."

"And what may that be?"

"That the good of one is the good of all; and that we cannot infringe, in the slightest degree, upon the interest of the humblest citizen of the community, without bringing a reaction upon ourselves."

"And you have squared your life accordingly?"

"No, I am only trying."

"And do you ever fail?"

"I find that all successes are but partial failures, and that every effort that takes me higher only shows me the more clearly how much there is above to be struggled for; how immeasurably the distance beyond that is still to be reached."

"And shall we never reach the goal?"

"Never, while there is one human soul above us to stimulate us to further attainment, or one below to be lifted into a purer atmosphere."

"Then we must struggle on until our barge is stranded upon the breakers that an all-wise God has laid below the waves of life's great ocean. Is there to be no rest?"

> "Labor is rest; if we labor aright,
> Struggle by day brings the sweet sleep at night."

and it shall be even so unto the end."

The two friends parted, the one to return to the "Lodge" to which the family had come but a day previous, the other to carry forward some enterprise that was to advance the prosperity of the stirring little town

CHAPTER XXVIII.

CLOSING INCIDENTS.

The first inaugural of President Lincoln followed the birthday party within a week, with the usual festivities. Washington was in wild commotion. The rumbling of discontent shook the nation from centre to circumference. "Rumors of war" filled the atmosphere to suffocation. Danger and doubt pervaded every household. The butterfly revelers grew alarmed and gathered in flocks like summer birds, and took their flight to safer and more prosperous regions.

The Count urged his marriage, as he wished to return to his native land. George had not yet visited his old home on the Alleghany. The Judge, from hard work and fearful mental anxiety over the threatened secession, was too ill to attend to his labor in the Senate, and begged a release of a few days to rest and recruit for the trial ahead; and now the whole party were at home.

It was on the morning following their arrival that the conversation detailed in the closing of the last chapter, was held. Preparations were made for an unostentatious wedding, as the Count so desired and the quiet Emma much preferred.

Every morning brought accumulated evidence of the impending rebellion. Max and George held long, earnest conversations by themselves, which resulted in resolves to devote themselves to their country with heart and soul, if there was need.

Count Armour offered his services in the cause of freedom, and owned himself a malcontent in his own government, ready and willing to throw his energies into the conflict, as did his illustrious countryman, Marquis de La Fayette, into the revolutionary struggles of our fathers.

George lay lounging upon the sofa a few mornings before the wedding. His brow was troubled and his lips compressed with some deep and firm resolution. Diana sat beside him, busy with her embroidery. He took her hand in his.

"Darling, it is hard that you will not consent to my earnest pleading and become my wife at once. If you loved me as I love you—"

"Be patient, my friend," answered she, laying her fingers upon his lips. "We have loved each other only as ideals in all these past years; let us learn to love each other as realities, as actual human beings. One year, even two or three, are none too long to convince two human souls that they are fitted for the marriage relation that ought to blend two lives into one."

"Ah! but how can I wait? These are golden hours."

" And are we not enjoying them goldenly? You are only twenty-three and I but nineteen. We are not of marriageable age, my love," was her playful answer to his complaint, and she stooped and kissed his troubled brow.

" Die, do you know how wonderful you are?" asked the lover, looking up into her face with a look of intense admiration.

" Wonderful; no! Wherein am I wonderful? In the fact that I have won the love of George Washington, the son of John, the illustrious?"

" Hush, Die; you shame me. You are wonderful in the work you have done; in the education you have gained; in the strength you have acquired. No other woman I know on earth has done so much."

" In what, my worshipful knight, has your lady love excelled all others? Has not Nettie a far better education than I?"

" Aye, in some things; but she has had all the aids that wealth and time and teachers would give. You have built your own castle; you have labored for your bread."

" I have worked no harder," answered Die, assuming a serious tone and manner, " than thousands upon thousands of girls who labor with unceasing toil, in thousands of rich men's kitchens throughout our country. If some gentle hearted Nettie would only teach them the alphabet and call them sister; some noble, generous patron, like your father, give

an approving word; if work were made pleasant by
a sense of grateful love, and a feeling that sustained
them and prompted them to higher attainments, they
might do as I have done; aye! and more.   Nettie
is far my superior in technicalities."

"Why should she not be, my darling?   What has
she had to do but learn?"

"*What has she had to do but learn?*   What has she
not had to do, to fill her place according to the
exactions of the so-called 'social sphere,' in which
her life revolves?"

"To dress, to sleep and eat.   What else?'

"Aye, to dress, to sleep and eat.   Is that all your
manly eyes can see?   I was compelled to rise with
the sun in order to answer to the demands of *my
sphere*, and my morning labor was performed while
Nettie slept, because Mrs. Grundy and her satellites
made it imperative that she should give two or three
hours after I was in bed at night, to the convention-
alities of society."

"What advantage did you gain there?"

"I gained both health and strength and steady
habits.   At night, if I was faithful, my work was
done and my evenings were my own for study or
thought.   I had no demands on my toilette at any
time that a few moments could not satisfy; no hours
were spent in receiving or returning fashionable
calls; no days were given to getting up new
arrangements for parties or balls; no time was spent
for sick headaches or neuralgias; no weeks of turmoil

in preparing for examinations and school exercises, tableaux or private theatricals; no months were given to watering places. I tell you, my friend, as to the hours spent in actual uninterrupted study, I question if the advantage has not been upon my side. Pardon me for saying it, but I think your sisters have given more hours to dressing for dinner, to reading love stories in *Godey*, the *Ledger*, and other papers of that ilk, and the novels of the day, than they or I have given to the real business of education."

" Then you think that every girl might improve her condition if she would but try."

" I only know for myself, that wherever I found a will there was a way; and I honestly believe that my condition of life has been more promotive of improvement than that of your sisters, less wearing to my soul and body."

" You have no longing then for a life of fashionable ease? No desire to be the bright particular star of some upper sphere, raying out your splendors among the envious first circles?"

" There! I said we did not know each other well enough to marry. If you had known me you would never have asked that question. ' A life of fashionable ease,' forsooth! To be the slave of whim, to bend to the taste of the uncultured, to be ruled by the tyranny of etiquette, in fine to sacrifice self on the altar of the almighty dollar, for the benefit of merchants, mantua makers and milliners. Oh!

George; I would rather be 'scrub and nuss gal' than what the world calls a fashionable woman."

"Oh! you're a jewel, Die."

"Nonsense! I am simply Die Dinmont, and have tried to do my best. All things have worked together to help me. Why, pray, should there not be self-made women as well as self-made men? Abraham Lincoln, for instance, and your noble friend, Max?"

"Oh! they are men."

"Indeed! And are men supposed to be more capable of self-elevation, of using the highest and noblest faculties which God has given them, than women?"

"Such is the stereotyped belief."

"Then we, my gallant knight, will destroy the plates and start a new impression. But George, this is not what we should talk about. Tell me what clouds your brow this morning?"

"My father has just received letters from Washington; private dispatches demanding his return as soon as possible. His friends think war inevitable; the north wholly unprepared for the conflict; indeed foolishly indulging an idea that the south is not in earnest."

"He is thrice armed who hath his quarrel just," answered Die. "But, George?"

"My darling—"

"What will you do in case your country calls you?"

"Give myself, my fortune, all that I have and am, for Union, Liberty and Right."

"God bless you for those noble words. A war *will* come, my friend, and the hearts of the brave will be tried."

A ring of the dinner bell startled them. They rose; he folded her in his arms a moment, whispering,

"I am all thine, and my country's."

"And I am thine as thou art mine," was her response, and together they joined the household; happy in each other, but troubled and sad over the impending fate of the nation.

The wedding ceremonies were fixed for the morning of the fifteenth of April. Hardly were they completed when a telegram was placed in the Judge's hands, announcing the bombardment of Sumter and demanding his immediate presence at the Capital. The wedding party proceeded, as had been intended, to New York. Die insisted upon returning with the Judge to alleviate his cares and toils. It was in vain George remonstrated and begged of Die to remain at the Lodge. At Harrisburg they heard of the call of Abraham Lincoln for seventy-five thousand volunteers. Max and George left the party and presented themselves at once to the Governor of their State, answering to the call.

The Count and his bride and Nettie bade them a tearful farewell.

"I will be with you anon," said Count Armour. "Give me time. Liberty has friends in France." "*Vive la Liberte,*" were his last words as he waved his adieux from the car window.

Buoyant with loyalty and enthusiasm, yet pale with emotion, George and Die parted, each to a high and holy duty, little thinking of the fearful conflict that was to divide their lives for years to come.

         *   *   *   *   *   *   *   *

On the evening of the 19th of April, two ladies entered the improvised hospital, where the wounded and dying of the noble Massachusetts braves had been laid, the first martyrs of the rebellion, the victims of the Baltimore massacre. Strangers to each other, entering at different doors, yet bound upon the same errand of mercy, Clara Barton and Diana Dinmont stood face to face, offering themselves as sisters of mercy, to nurse, to soothe and comfort. Their services were gladly accepted, and then and there each took up her mission of love and bore it onward unflinchingly and faithfully, until peace once more waved her white pinions over the beloved land of their birth.

Clara became to the soldiers of the Union army the "Angel of the Battlefield." Diana lived in the hearts of her country's defenders as "The Light of the Hospitals." In the bloody war of the rebellion no truer or braver heroes acted their part than those two noble women.

Senator Hancock gave fortune and strength of heart and brain to the cause of the loyal North, and after three years of the most severe and unremitting labor, he passed away from among men. Truly it might be said :

" He wrapped the drapery of his couch about him,
And laid down to pleasant dreams,"

He was well at eve. In the morn, he was at rest. The gentle, faithful wife soon followed him.

Count Armour remained but six months in his own country ; gathered recruits for liberty and returned ; offered his services to the United States Government, was accepted, and laid down his life at the battle of Fredericksburg.

Emma grew brave and strong under the pressure of emergencies, and in active work for the Sanitary Commission, soothed the sorrow of her early widow- hood.

Max fought side by side with George, and passed through the fearful conflict unscathed. Long before the surrender of Lee, he wore the shoulder strap of a hero, and no man thus honored, claimed more of the love and gratitude of the rank and file than General Carter.

Mr. and Mrs. Frobish were the truest friends of the Union, and the great tavern at Oxbow was turned into a " Home for the Soldiers," where the returning weary one, discharged, or upon furlough, found rest, quiet, comfort and motherly care from the landlady of the olden time. The jolly host of the Oxbow still cheered, with his hearty good will and merry laugh and jest, the sinking spirits of the weak and wounded.

Aggie gave her hand to Max in the early stages of the war, and cheered many a lingering month of

duty while they waited for the tardy commands of
" Onward to Richmond ;" but a new care and love
was laid on her heart, and yielding to the demand,
she returned to her childhood's home to divide the
energies of her earnest young life between her little
Max and her country's defenders.

Mr. and Mrs. Rand, hearing of the disinterested
benevolence of the landlord and his wife, in giving
up their home for government uses, and moved by
their long cherished love of Aggie, sent her a title
deed to the house on the hill and all its surroundings. Into this they moved when the cares and toil
of the " Home for the Soldiers" no longer needed
them, and its duties devolved upon other and
younger hands.

On the 19th of April, 1865, Diana Dinmont became
the happy wife of the happy husband, Major General
George W. Hancock. The wedding tour was a trip
to Kansas. The meeting between the loving parents
and their brave, dutiful child may be imagined, but
can hardly be described.

Heckel Dinmont, when he took his homestead
claim from the government of the United States,
thought he had placed himself almost beyond the
pale of civilization ; bnt he awoke one morning to
find his pretty farm located exactly in the way of a
railroad, and precisely on the site needed for a
station, at the end of the bridge that must span the
river at that point. It was useless to resist circumstances, or rebel against the logic of events. Tom

laid out his fields into town lots which sold rapidly, and straightway a flourishing village sprang into existence, to which the superintendent of the road affixed the name of Dinmont, in honor of its generous and gentlemanly proprietor.

Heckel was a rich man without his own consent or concurrence; but he took it as a necessary evil and got along with it pretty much as other men do. He entered the ranks as a private soldier, was shot and crippled at the battle of Lexington, and discharged from service, having by his wound partially lost the use of one leg. Tom worked bravely in the engineer department through the weary four years, keeping an unblemished record of honesty, sobriety and honor.

Heckel Dinmont, after he left the army, met one very great misfortune against which he battled with all his manly force. It was of no avail. His neighbors decreed he should represent them in their State Legislature. He took his place, resolved to do his best, and it is said his best was *very good*.

"Who would have dreamed, Mary dear," he said, as he bade her farewell, for his post of honor, "that the A, B, C's, would have amounted to all this? We have surely taken ' Steps Upward.' "

CHAPTER XXIX.

MYSTERIES EXPLAINED.

While Miss Clara Barton was making her earnest search for "the missing men of the Union Army," during the autumn of 1865, she found among her letters, a coarse envelope enclosing a smaller one, dircted to "Mr. Maxwell Carter, care of G. W. Hancock, Oxbow, Pa." On a soiled slip of paper inside the envelope, were a few words, written in very awkward penmanship and sadly misspelled, stating that "in the autumn of '64 an officer was wounded in the skirmish near Brazos, Texas; that the writer, an emancipated slave and his servant, took him to the quarters of a colored woman, who nursed him till he died. That he wrote the enclosed letter and made him promise to send it on safely, at the close of the war, if he could; that he had taught him to read and write, and he only wanted to say that Col. Gilbert Bishop was the best man he ever knew." The following is a copy of the letter received by Max:

My best Friend :—With a deep desire to leave for my children a little better record of their father than they can have at present, and also to put an end to an uncertainty and suspense always more painful than the facts, I write this, hoping (almost against hope) that it may sometime reach you and other friends   I must write briefly, as I am dying of a gun-shot wound through my lungs, received from a guerrilla, while leading my regiment to the defense of Brazos.   I cannot live, but my servant is faithful and has followed me from the commencement of the war ; I can trust him.

The first hour of consciousness that came to me after leaving Oxbow, that long to be remembered night, found me on a heavily laden steamer, that was transporting Oxbow whisky to the Indian stations at the head waters of the Missouri.   The boat hands told me they found me hid in the coal hole and nearly dead. They did not land the boat between Oxbow and St. Louis.   A good hearted fireman nursed and cared for me.   I left the steamer at Wyandot, joined a party of mining speculators, went with them to Boulder City, and plunged into the mines ; resolved, if sobriety and industry could retrieve the past, no effort on my part should be wanting.   Remorse for the past gave me strength for the future ; how could I leave my children with only orphanage and a heritage of shame ?

While in the mines, I was one day surprised by meeting Gordon Rand, as a fellow laborer ; trying, like myself, to forget the past. Dissipation had done for him a fatal work.   He died three months after I found him, of consumption.   On his death bed he told me of his deserting you.   The brother and sister, who were his associates on the vessel, left it with him, and in a state of inebriate insensibility he married the girl.   They took ship for California.   The vessel was burned at sea, and most of the passengers went down with the wreck.   Being a good swimmer, he, with a half dozen others, saved themselves and were picked up by a passing ship.   Trying to reform and still overborne by temptation, he had wandered out to the mines.   Still the brilliant boon companion, always welcome where there was genius or talent, he was constantly led into the deep degradation of drunkenness.   Now, he was dying ! Oh ! if his mother could but bless him, and forgive him for that one only vice, he would end his life with joy. Aggie he had wronged ; but he had left her to a better fate than a life with him could ever have realized. No language of mine can give you any idea of his penitence ; and would to God I could embody his anathemas against intemperance and those whose life work it is to make and sell the terrible poison. His last words were a blessing for his mother.

I laid up money and purchased claims, worked hard, and never drank a drop after I left Oxbow. My claims will be found well authenticated at Boulder City. I joined the army in May, '61 ; have been promoted to the rank of Colonel, and hope I have done some good. God bless you all ! I am dying.

GILBERT BISHOP.

Mrs. Rand was not overcome by the letter. She was only too thankful that the end of her darling was not worse; that he died loving her and was penitent.

"My injudicious indulgence ruined my son," she said to her husband; "I will try to atone as best I may, by teaching the children of Gilbert Bishop self-denial and self-control."

Lightning Source UK Ltd.
Milton Keynes UK
UKHW011611160119
335572UK00012B/1205/P